BASEBALL GIRL
A Novel

STEPHANIE VERNI

Book jacket designed by Stephanie Verni
Author photograph taken by Jennifer Bumgarner

ISBN-13: 978-0692370841
ISBN-10: 0692370846

Mimosa Publishing

FOR

All my friends I met through baseball:
I love you all dearly.

My Parents—Doug & Leni Parrillo &
My In-Laws—Mark and Jo Verni:
Thanks for your constant love and support.

And especially for my two wonderful children, Matt & Ellie—
You would not be here today if your father and I
did not meet while working in baseball.

As always, for Anthony, with love.

For those who got to play catch with their dads,
With hearts full of love that are full and glad.

To dads who are with us both near and far,
Or perhaps watching baseball from the stars.

~ Stephanie Verni ~

BASEBALL GIRL

PROLOGUE

My father was forty-four years old when we saw our last game together in person. He was weak and pale, and yet there we were at the ballpark. Despite his rapidly declining condition, he somehow managed to wear a sheepish grin as I wheeled him up the handicapped ramp and he saw the field, the white lights. There was mist in the air. I was afraid something might happen to him that night, and that I'd have to explain to my mother that God waved him home during a baseball game. My father would have joked, saying it was divine providence, that God knew—and seemed to respect—his affinity for the game; he would kneel to what he believed was a great cathedral—its patterned grass in the outfield, bleached white bases, and perfectly rounded pitcher's mound. He often told me, especially when I was very young, that he could hear the angels sing every time he entered a ballpark.

It was tradition that the two of us would attend every home game on Sundays. Right after church, we'd sprint home, change out of our dress clothes, jump into shorts, jerseys, and sneakers, and zoom off in the car. Like children excited to see the circus for the first time, both my father and I felt its uniqueness, knowing that every time we went to the ballpark, it would be a new game, a different memory, and an experience we would share forever. The car radio dial was always set to the pregame show as we both listened to player interviews and anxiously awaited the announcement of that day's starting lineup.

My mother rarely ventured to the ballpark with us. She didn't care for the game too much, which I never understood. Not liking America's pastime was a sin to me, and she never understood why I preferred to wear a numbered jersey as opposed to a tutu. She was appalled at times by my father's insistence that his little girl must learn and like the game. Sometimes I'd hear them arguing after I went to bed at night, my mother imploring him to allow me to do other things in my spare time, like sing in the choir, join the gymnastics team, or dance ballet.

I didn't particularly love gymnastics or ballet. My singing voice was not one that warranted an audience. I was much more in tune to watching the pros turn double plays and hit game-winning RBIs. I was vested in the team because my father was vested in the team. I was enthralled with baseball because my father was enthralled with baseball. I loved the game because my father loved the game. If people ever try to tell you that you can't learn to love something, they're wrong. I learned to love baseball—every fair and foul ball, every interminable rain delay, and every hot dog with mustard I could buy. I loved the way the sun would set behind the arched, brick walls, the way the grounds crew unfurled the tarp in inclement weather, and the way the music vibrated my seat when the team tied the game in the ninth inning.

Love. Pure and simple.

It's difficult to describe love sometimes, and even more difficult to put into words a love you have for someone or something, either while you have it, or later, when it's gone.

My father passed away on a Sunday. On that eerie late morning, as I woke to a sense of gloom and understood the inevitable was about to happen, I turned on the radio and sat with my dad as we listened to the pregame show. Yet, on that day, not even baseball could lessen the pain that would consume me as I watched that demon Leukemia suck every ounce of energy out of his still young, but tired body.

I was eighteen that afternoon in early May when he passed and was just completing my first year of college. My sister, four years older than I, had come home for the weekend, leaving her infant and husband behind to be with my mom, dad, and me. All three of my father's girls were in the room—my mother held one hand on one side of him, and my sister and I were on the other side—as he peacefully left this world, just as the rookie Clarkson hit a lead-off homer to start the game.

After he passed, I never stopped going to those Sunday games that year. I was determined to continue with the tradition, even if it meant I had to go by myself. I wasn't a groupie, a collector, or an autograph seeker; in fact, at that time, I cared little about the pomp and circumstance that revolved around the sport of baseball and the players. That's not what it was about for me.

For me, baseball was about my father. About sharing the day with him. About getting to know him little by little during our chats at the ballpark when he'd tell me stories about his own father and his father's father. I gained precious insight into my family and our traditions by spending time with him, and I wouldn't trade one minute of those cherished moments to sing in a choir, join the gymnastics team, or perform ballet for a visiting queen.

I'd never trade it. Not for one—not one—minute.

But what I didn't expect were the lessons the great game of baseball would teach me, and how it would affect me for all my years to come.

THE FIRST OPENING DAY

I went to my first ballgame when I was seven. I remember being greeted by musicians dressed in red and white and playing what I learned was called ragtime music. My father held my hand and explained why there were so many happy people buying popcorn and peanuts and hurrying to their seats.

My father closed his office that day and took me out of school. My sister had no interest at all in going, but I did. There was never any competition between my sister and me. She preferred to stay home with my mother, and I wanted to go—begged to go—and finally, after many pleas, I got my way.

In the days leading up to that game, I sat in my elementary school class and dreamed about being there. I wore my jersey over and over again to school that week until I was finally made fun of for being a tomboy. One kid asked me if it was the only shirt I owned.

On Opening Day, I got up early, dressed, ate breakfast, and waited for my dad to come down the stairs.

"Ready?" he said with a smile on his face.

I talked his ear off on the entire ride to the ballpark. I couldn't contain myself when I saw the red, white, and blue bunting dressing the stadium and watched crowds of people bustling as they entered the gates.

The team took the field. My dad and I cheered. We clapped and screamed and watched a home run soar over the outfield wall.

Opening Day 1980.

The Blackbirds won, 7-5.

There's a picture in a frame on my mom's dresser of my dad and me that was taken on the front lawn after we returned home from the game, a little sunburned and tired, but ecstatic because we were a part of all the excitement that took place at the ballpark that day.

In the photograph, my right hand holds a Blackbirds pennant, and my face wears a grin that runs from ear to ear.

The left hand firmly grips my dad's right hand.

ONE

"It may only be my second pro season, but I'm living out a fantasy I've had since I was a kid. I've wanted to play ball my whole life. It's a dream come true to step out onto this field, and I'll do everything I can to make this dream last."
~ Joe Clarkson, Blackbirds Outfielder

Francesca Milli was jolted out of bed by the loudly ringing radio alarm clock next to her bed as she groped, half awake, to turn it off. She placed her two feet on the floor, smiled broadly to herself, and stretched. It was Saturday morning—a morning typically reserved for recuperating from the previous night's antics, sleeping in, and being utterly lazy. However, on that day, she had a job interview.

A sophomore at Bay City University, she spent much of her time the same way most college students spend their days: going to classes, studying, doing research in the library, and partying. She had no intention of applying for an internship this early in her collegiate career at the university—that was until she abruptly changed her mind. After clandestinely eavesdropping weeks earlier on a conversation between two communication majors, she got the idea to work in her field as they did. One girl secured a job working for a local advertising firm, while the other had her fingers crossed for a stint writing copy at a television news station. If they can do it so can I, she thought.

Not long afterward, with this notion fresh in her mind, a curious coincidence happened. On one ordinary Tuesday during the semester, on the way to her mailbox, she walked through the university union and checked the employment and internship positions board. She stopped in her tracks when she saw the posting. She quickly took out a pen and paper and wrote down the information she saw in bold print on an index card: Public Relations Assistant Needed—Bay City Blackbirds. As she read the list of qualifications necessary to be an applicant, she began to feel somewhat confident that she possessed a majority of the necessary skills, so she wrote down the job description word for word, and sprinted back to her college dorm and began to write her application. Crafting a resume was an entirely different dilemma; her experience was limited and hardly compelling. She baby sat for a neighbor two summers in a row, spent her senior year working at a women's shoe store, and served as the late morning salad bar girl at English's Chicken House. It took some creative manipulation and embellishment, but when it was completed, she clearly conveyed that she was a hard worker, joined clubs and organizations in both high school and in college, and wasn't afraid to try something new. As well, writing had always come naturally to her as a student, so her cover letter ended up sounding better than she expected. When she was sure everything was error free and ready to send off, she signed her letter, taking care that her cursive signature looked confident, included her resume, labeled the envelope, and put a stamp on it. Moments later, she was skipping to the mailbox just down the hill from West Hall, her hand shaking as she grabbed the handle and opened the door to the mailbox. She was hopeful, unusually giddy at the thought of the possibility of this extraordinary job coming through, but she didn't want to jinx it. The chance to combine baseball with her academic course of study was certainly a long shot, but it was worth a try. She chastised herself for being overly optimistic and then played the devil's advocate, telling herself she was not allowed to think about it for the next several days.

However, she didn't have to wait that long because the unimaginable happened. She received a call only days later from the public relations office, and by Saturday morning, she was on her way to Blackbirds Park to be interviewed for what she considered to be a dream job: working in professional baseball.

She took a hot shower, the kind that could melt the skin off your body, dried her hair and then clipped it up, applied blush and mascara, and made herself a bagel with cream cheese. Her roommate had gone home for the weekend, so she had the place to herself. She was wearing the simple black dress with low pumps that her mother insisted was a "go to" staple for any wardrobe, grabbed her winter coat and gloves, and sped off in her friend's yellow Mustang, the wheels screeching against the cold asphalt, as she navigated her way to the ballpark.

It was a frigid and gloomy February day. The heavy clouds hung low, swallowing the tops of the ballpark into its wintery grasp. There were remnants of frost still on the car's windows when she arrived. As she walked through the glass, corporate-looking doors, the ballpark looked dreary in the dead of winter, devoid of its vibrant, lush state that it typically exuded in the summer. The black sign with red lettering above the door read Bay City Blackbirds, the logo prominently fixed to it on the left side; she let out a sigh of relief not only that she had arrived, but also because she had arrived early. She was typically punctual, but this made her even more satisfied with how her morning began.

The receptionist greeted her warmly, and Francesca refrained from pinching her own cheeks as she stood in the lobby of Blackbirds Park.

"May I help you?" she said with a smile.

"Yes, I have an interview with Isabelle Drake," she said.

She asked Francesca to wait a moment while she buzzed Ms.

Drake's office, and Francesca took the first deep breath she could remember taking that morning. Her hands were slightly trembling, and
she couldn't exactly identify whether it was jittery, nervous excitement,
or a quiet, restless concern that she might blow this incredible opportunity altogether.

While she waited, the receptionist ushered Francesca to a small,
poorly lit kitchen off the reception area. It was dark, devoid of windows;
instead, a long, full mirror adorned the far wall above the counters. They
were clearly underneath the ballpark, and black tables with chairs were
set around the room. An employee of the club came in to refill his coffee cup, and Francesca and the receptionist waited patiently.

She offered Francesca coffee from a machine with half a pot
remaining. She poured her a cup, and Francesca added her creamer and
sugar. They left the room, and turned, making their way back to the lobby, where Francesca calmed and subdued herself as she examined the
plethora of memorabilia that decorated the reception area: team photographs, trophies, and banners were displayed around the walls and
encased in a glass bookshelf. Years of nostalgia were crammed into one
intimate greeting space, a small sampling of the team's best moments.
For all the times she spent in her seats rooting for the Blackbirds, she
had never stepped foot into these offices. She was always among the
fans, in the stands, with a view of the field. Her father would have loved
this.

"Hi, Francesca? I'm Isabelle Drake," a polished woman in her
late twenties said as she stretched out her hand and exhibited a very
firm handshake. She hadn't expected the woman to be so young, and
Francesca mimicked the grip, being careful not to squeeze too tightly.

"Hello," she said. "It's nice to meet you Ms. Drake."

"Oh, no. Not Ms. Drake! Are you trying to make me feel old or something? In this business, we are on a first-name basis. Please, call me Isabelle."

Francesca smiled.

She escorted her out of the lobby, and through a set of white double doors as they walked down a long, narrow hallway with green carpet, the walls plastered with baseball photography and framed *Sports Illustrated* covers that featured some of the Blackbirds greats.

When the pair entered Isabelle's office, Francesca sat in the chair situated across from Isabelle's unkempt desk, where papers were piled high all over the top of it, allowing only a small space for her to work. There were two items on the wall—a corkboard filled with directions, maps, and a large-sized calendar with red circles indicating special dates, and a plaque recognizing Isabelle for her exceptional work in community relations. Again, Francesca knew they were underneath the ballpark, although she couldn't pinpoint if they were on the first base or third base side. Additionally, the diminutive size of the office left Francesca feeling slightly claustrophobic.

"Sorry for the mess," Isabelle said, sitting behind the desk and looking across to Francesca, surveying the pile of letters and notes. She cleared her throat. "Actually, I'm not that sorry. If I were, I would have made the time to clean up this disaster before you got here. I'm really more sorry that I have to squeeze you in here for the interview."

"No problem," Francesca said, filling up her senses with every element of the Blackbirds offices.

"So, Francesca, tell me a little bit about yourself and why you're here today interviewing for this job."

Francesca began to talk, telling Isabelle of her affinity for baseball, and that she understood the game. She told her of her father's love for it and of their traditions, and that she'd been rooting for the Blackbirds ever since she was a little kid. She explained her course of study at college, and that she was a communication major, a second-semester sophomore who wanted to gain valuable work experience in her field. And finally, she admitted to being a student of the game.

When Isabelle began to discuss the responsibilities of the position, Francesca could feel herself growing more fascinated, her excitement for the job growing exponentially, as Isabelle further described the game duties and working with the media. As she listened to the details, the requirements, and the vast experience she would gain by having a job such as that one, in addition to working for her favorite team, Francesca sat up straighter and talked with more sophistication than even she realized she had in her.

"Do you know how to score the games?" Isabelle asked.

"Yes," she said. "My father and I always scored the games. We used your game program's instructions, and my dad taught me how to score the Blackbirds way."

Francesca may have won Isabelle over with that one particular answer.

Isabelle continued, dissecting the particulars of the job—that it required an eighty-one home game commitment, plus additional office hours during the week; that missing a home game was not acceptable; that front office employees were prohibited from dating a player; that as a member of the public relations community for the ballclub, all employees were expected to conduct themselves in a completely professional manner. When Isabelle was through enumerating the specifics, Francesca sat silently in awe with a smile plastered across her face.

They were all fair, respectable requests and stipulations, and none caused Francesca any pause. In fact, they only made her want the job more. She wanted to work there so badly she could taste it.

When the pair shook hands at the end of the meeting, Isabelle walked Francesca back out to the lobby and said goodbye. Francesca thanked Isabelle for her time, and said, genuinely, "I hope to hear from you soon."

Before she left the offices and headed back to campus, Francesca stopped to take one final look around. Just then, as she looked outside and beyond the double glass doors, she noticed that snow had started to fall. She stood for a moment and breathed in, observing the surreal nature of her surroundings. She was like a kid in a candy store. And then she saw it there in the corner behind a glass cabinet: the championship trophy from 1980. There it was, right before her eyes.

She supposed she could have speculated that she wouldn't be considered as a strong candidate for a job with the Blackbirds, or that she would never be in that lobby looking at the sentimental banners and photographs on the walls as a part of her daily routine, but to the contrary, she didn't have that thought at all.

Instead, she imagined receiving a favorable call from Isabelle, like a minor leaguer being called up to the big leagues. That at nineteen, and with three months left of her sophomore year in college, she would secure a job with a big league ballclub, and in some way, fulfill her father's dream of being connected to baseball.

Yes, she could have been wrong about it.

But, luckily, she wasn't.

Two

"This game of baseball isn't easy, but what helps make it easy is a solid understanding of the fundamentals of the game.
Once you've got them down, things start to happen."
~ Freddie "The Fly" Montrose, Blackbirds Bench Coach

"So, what exactly will you be doing?" Francesca's mother asked her as they sat down to enjoy a meal together at Celine's, one of their favorite Bay City restaurants with a view of the harbor and the skyline. Nestled on the east coast, Bay City was originally an industrial town that had turned corporate over the years, with pockets of hip neighborhoods, local restaurants, and boutique shopping. The harbor was glistening in the moonlight, splashing gently on the boat docks that were just off to the right. Her mother arranged to take her out to celebrate her new opportunity, though she was unsure as to how exactly Francesca was going to manage college life and a job.

The French café was about twenty minutes from campus, and it quickly became one of their favorite spots for dinner. Spending time together on Friday nights had become one of their new routines after her father passed. The restaurant was small and intimate with twinkle lights and candles above the tall, white fireplace amidst the French decor. Her mother was peering over her readers as she pursed her lips, studying the menu as if it were the first time she'd seen it. She was trying her best to be supportive of her daughter's new line of work.

Francesca watched her sip tea with her pinky out, her fingers painted red, as she gingerly held the cup with her hands. Her ladylike demeanor was so delicate, and Francesca observed her mannerisms while she attempted to answer each question with enthusiasm, trying to educate her mother about what she would do as employee of the ballclub.

"I'll be working in the public relations office, scoring the games, running and distributing the press notes, helping out with the media— that sort of stuff," she said.

"And you're sure this won't interfere with your studies, right?"

"No," she said. "I'm going to have to work a lot, but I'll be able to manage both."

"You know how your father felt about getting good grades."

"Aren't you the one who cares more about good grades? I'm confused," Francesca said. They both knew her father was way more lenient than her mother ever was. Her mother glared at her, trying her best not to smile.

"Yes," her mother said. "I don't want this education to fall apart at the seams."

"It won't," Francesca said. "Look, my college education has already helped me get a job with a professional baseball team. And my favorite one, at that."

"Yes, I know," her mother said. "That's what I'm afraid of."

Francesca knew deep down inside that her mother was all bark and no bite. She couldn't say no to her, and the talk of her academics was so silly. Hadn't she always earned good grades? Had she ever let her parents down before? She pressed on.

"So?" she asked.

"So, what?" her mother replied.

"Am I going to be able to take my car to campus? I need to be able to get to work."

Francesca knew there would be more questions. There always were with her mother. She couldn't help herself, though; her mother was a worrier—overprotective and loving to a fault.

"Do you really need one?"

"Yes," Francesca said emphatically. "What? Would you rather I take the city bus back to campus at midnight after games?" Francesca knew this particular point would help her secure the car.

"No," her mother said. "I suppose not. Are you going to take good care of it?"

"What do you think? Of course I will."

"And you have a place to park it that's safe?" she asked.

"Yes. In the garage next to the dorms."

It wasn't a difficult argument to win. Her mother let her have the car, and they spent the rest of the time chatting about classes and her mom's new job. She had stayed at home and done volunteer work for many years, but since her father's death, she felt she needed an income. Her mother was young: a widow at the age of forty-four, now only forty-five, and an attractive woman who was meticulously put together from her manicured nails down to her highlighted bob. Francesca worried that her mother was lonely rattling around in that house by herself, but at least her job as an administrative assistant for a realty company seemed to be keeping her busy. She recently mentioned that she might like to become licensed.

Francesca offered to move home after her father's death—to keep her mother company since campus was only thirty minutes from their house, but her mother insisted that Francesca enjoy college life and living in the dorms. They talked daily, but it didn't stop Francesca from worrying about her mom.

"So, do you have to wear a baseball uniform or something like that?" her mother asked as she took a sip of her French onion soup.

"Let me put it to you this way—what I have to wear isn't very attractive."

In the morning, she wasted no time. She showered, dressed, had a bite to eat, and for the last time, borrowed her friend's Mustang to get to her training session.

Five students were hired to do the job, and all five reported to Isabelle Drake.

After checking in with the reception ladies, the group waited in the lobby until Isabelle came through the door and greeted them excitedly. She put them all at ease, and then walked them back through the double white doors and down another hallway to a small room where the training would take place.

Each of them received a welcome packet that outlined the game duties and office duties, and the group received an overview that touched on aspects such as parking, proper attire, working with the media, and general office rules. Afterward, they were escorted to another room and briefed on employment materials from human resources.

While they were waiting in the hallway, they had a few minutes to mingle and get to know one another. They were all from colleges and universities in the area. Three of the five were communication majors; the other two were business majors.

"I'm so excited. Are you?" a girl named Mona, with short, red hair and freckles across her nose, asked Francesca. "I can't wait to work with the media. I'm studying public relations and just wrote my first press release. Did you see the one in our packet? I hope I did it right."

Francesca nodded and smiled at her. She was one of the peppiest people she had ever met. Mona's mention of the press release made Francesca feel a little guilty about her dismal attempt at writing one in her journalism class. She had received a "C" on the assignment, which was a low grade for her, but the kind instructor was going to give the students a second crack at it for an improved grade. Francesca made a note to look over some of the samples that Isabelle provided in the welcome kit.

Dan, a broad, strapping guy who resembled Clark Kent with his dark-framed glasses and slicked-back, black hair, was also a sophomore, and he sat down next to Francesca.

"So, I hear you know a lot about the game," he said.

"Really? Who said?"

"Isabelle."

"Really?"

"She said you already know how to score the Blackbirds way."

"Yes," she said. "My dad taught me."

"I wish my dad liked baseball, but he's more of a football man," Dan said. "You're lucky your dad has an interest and you have someone to go to games with."

"Oh…yes," she said. "Lucky."

When they were leaving the human resources office, Isabelle stopped to give a few last minute pointers about where to park and how to enter the ballpark on game days. The training session had been informative, if not a bit overwhelming. Francesca was unsure as to whether or not she would be able to maneuver her way through the ballpark with all its nooks and crannies, special seating areas, and party rooms without anyone else guiding her. They'd all taken a tour earlier and were introduced to all these behind-the-scenes areas—places she never knew existed until today—and her enthusiasm was heightened. It made her yearn for Opening Day to arrive.

"Oh my gosh!" Mona said. "Isn't that Zeke Watson?"

Mona's eyes lit up like a Christmas tree, and she could barely contain herself as a man strolled toward them.

"It is," Francesca said.

Zeke Watson was walking down the hall toward them, his unmistakable stride the dead giveaway. He was wearing jeans and a button-down with a leather jacket, his sunglasses propped on the top of his head. It was late February, but a blindingly sunny day, as two inches of iced-over snow covered the ground and reflected the natural light.

Francesca found herself studying him. He was about six-foot-two with a receding hairline, and looked much more slender than she remembered him looking on the field in his baseball uniform. He retired about six years ago, and was recently inducted into the Blackbirds Hall of Fame.

"How you all doing?" he said when he reached them.

"Wonderful," Mona said.

"Great!" Dan said.

"Are you all the new hires Isabelle was telling me about?"

"Yes, we are," Mona said.

"Well, welcome. I think the Blackbirds are going to have a great season now that you're all here to straighten things out."

He smiled, and then swiftly moved past them and into the office, where the woman from human resources was waiting to meet with him.

Francesca's roommate, Samantha—Sam for short—was sitting on the bed thumbing through the latest edition of *Vogue* when she walked through the door.

"Well?" Sam said. "How'd it go?"

"Great," Francesca said.

"What's that in your hands?" she asked.

"My uniform. And it's God-awful ugly."

Francesca started to pull it together so she could show Sam the full effect of the most dreadful uniform ever known to man, knowing Sam would be its toughest critic. As a marketing major, Sam's professional goal was to find some type of employment in the fashion world. She spent hours combing through her issues of *Vogue*, tabbing pages she liked, and watching shows on television centered around celebrity fashion. Her sandy brown hair was silky and straight, and her big, blue eyes sometimes looked a grey/green depending on the light in the room. Sam's eclectic wardrobe was extensive, and because she was only a couple of inches taller than Francesca, they were always sharing clothes, and Francesca readily admitted that she got the better end of that deal. Any money Sam made from her part-time job at The Limited either went directly to clothes or memorabilia, and Francesca liked her from the first moment they met when they were paired up as roommates.

Francesca dramatically held up each piece of clothing for Sam to scrutinize and bemoan: an Izod looking shirt with the Blackbirds logo on it, manly looking tennis shorts, and to top it off, a white pair of sneakers. Francesca hated white sneakers with a passion. They reminded her of nurses' shoes, and she despised the looks of them, too. On colder days, she would be permitted to wear tan khakis—with the white tennis shoes. She felt anything but pretty in her frumpy uniform. She may have loved the sport of baseball and treasured her jerseys from her younger days, but the uniform she was being asked to wear was just plain ugly—and unflattering. On most days, Francesca wore jeans with feminine tops and cute shoes or boots. And she only ever wore tennis shoes when they were absolutely necessary, like when she actually played tennis.

"Ugh. The Blackbirds need to take some pointers from this magazine," Sam said, pointing to the one she still held in her hand. "No ugly or unflattering clothes in here."

"Oh, well. Can't have it all, I guess," Francesca said, trying to find a bright spot among the elements of a pathetically, drab uniform.

"If a player doesn't ask you out, just blame it on the clothes they make you wear," Sam said.

"No worries there. It's against policy to date a ballplayer—and no flirting at all with the married ones."

"Right. And I'm not allowed to leave my dorm room," she said.

"I'm serious. It was spelled out loud and clear."

Sam made some kind of sound of disbelief and waved her hands in the air.

"Come on," she said. "Let's go to your mother's to pick up your car."

"Okay," Francesca said.

"You know I'm only doing this for your mother's pot roast, right?"

It took three additional Saturday training sessions for the team of public relations assistants to be properly prepared for Opening Day. Isabelle was a tireless tutor and teacher; she offered her crew everything she could, scheduling sessions that would sometimes run from ten in the morning until six in the evening. From organizing the press credentials to helping coordinate press packets and player appearances, Francesca and her counterparts were expected to be diligent workers and ready for anything.

By the end of March, Francesca started to feel comfortable with her new employer and with the people she was meeting. Her favorite employment perk came in the form of two complimentary tickets to every Blackbirds home game. She was the hot shot among all her friends and classmates. They were clamoring to come to the ballpark, and she started to jot the growing requests for game tickets down in her planner when they started to overwhelm her. It was funny how people crawled out of the woodwork when you had access to something they wanted for free.

Francesca's mother agreed to attend the team's home opener. Francesca's sister, Cissy, along with her husband Cam, were going to visit, taking the four-hour ride south with Emma, her young niece. Cissy and Emma would stay at her mother's house and watch the game on television, while Cam and her mother would attend in person.

How often she wished it could have been her father sitting there with her mother. He wouldn't believe her good fortune. He would have treasured getting a behind-the-scenes tour and seeing the place from an insider's vantage point. She could almost envision what his face would have looked like—that devilish twinkle brightening up his eyes as the corners of his mouth turned up revealing pure delight. He would have relished the thought of her working in baseball.

Francesca tormented herself with these types of thoughts regularly; she became an expert at making herself crazy with grief, wishing he were with her now, sharing her experiences, and watching her grow from the new adventures in her life.

Three

"Spring training is a time to get ready. It's the time to practice and work out some of the kinks and get rid of bad habits. It's great and all, but there's nothing better than seeing the ballpark dressed for Opening Day, knowing it's time for a new season of baseball to begin."
~ *Zeke Watson, Blackbirds Hall of Famer*

Trumpets sounded and horns played. Dixie bands strolled outside the ballpark. The sun was shining high in the sky, offering fans some warmth on a sixty-two degree day. People came out to see baseball. To welcome the Blackbirds back for another season.

Red, white, and blue bunting hung from the upper deck. The grass was green—greener than Francesca ever remembered it being—coiffed to perfection. The scent that hung in the air could not be mistaken for any other smell in the world. It was an amalgamation of popcorn, cotton candy, hot dogs, beer, and fresh air.

All of the public relations assistants were frantic as they darted around managing their designated shifts that rotated with each home game. If you were scheduled for shift one on Monday, on Tuesday you were scheduled for shift two, and so on. That way, there was no griping or wishing for a different shift. You just knew when it was your turn to do that shift's specific game-day tasks.

Francesca was a greeter on Opening Day, which meant she assisted the entertainment director who was on a head set down on the field; it was her job to help ferry folks who needed to be on the field for pre-game ceremonies from the waiting area to their spots on the warning track behind home plate. She shook a lot of hands and smiled, though the smiling part came quite naturally. Francesca pinched herself to make sure it was real.

She was there, standing on the field.

At Blackbirds Park.

At one point, she looked in the direction of the seats she shared with her father to see who was seated in them now. She couldn't tell.

At the home plate entrance, Francesca's first responsibility was to escort the mayor to the field, and his job was to throw out the ceremonial first pitch. Mayor Callahan was dressed in a fitted suit with a red tie, looking very sharp, and holding onto his right arm was his wife, wearing red pumps and a black dress with red trim. They had coordinated their looks and worn Blackbirds colors. There was an entourage of press and security around them, and Francesca moved the group from the entrance to the field and onto the warning track.

Guiding the esteemed entourage of people would be enough to make anyone feel nervous, but Francesca handled the situation well. She spoke when spoken to and smiled pleasantly. Only when she had to get the mayor onto the field did she become anxious because he was a conversationalist and posed for photos with anyone who asked.

"I need to get you into position to throw the first pitch, Mr. Mayor," Francesca said.

"Thanks for keeping us on track, young lady," he said.

Once she got him situated and he threw the first pitch, her nerves started to settle down.

As she moved the mayor back to the warning track for the National Anthem, Joe Clarkson jogged by on his way to the outfield. Number 6. You couldn't miss him. He was tall and broad, with tan skin from the Florida sunshine and the spring training games, a bit of his wavy, chestnut hair scooting out of the back of his cap. She read in the press notes earlier that he was suffering from tendonitis, which seemed surprising for a 22-year-old who wasn't a pitcher. She assumed he'd been getting taped up, because his elbow was wrapped. His head was down, but his eyes looked up at her. A little smile crossed his lips, and he nodded as he slowly trotted toward the outfield.

As the National Anthem began to play, Francesca was standing just slightly behind the mayor who had tossed a rather good pitch into catcher Buck Thomas' glove. More surprising than that was the applause he received despite his somewhat disappointing approval rating of late. He shook hands with Buck Thomas just at the right moment for the local television stations and newspaper photographers to get the shot. Francesca was certain the mayor's appearance at the ballpark would make the news and expected to see it on the front page in tomorrow's paper.

She escorted the mayor from the field up to the luxury suite where he would watch the game with other dignitaries and corporate executives. So this was how the other half enjoyed the games, she thought. Not too shabby. The suites were adorned in Blackbirds colors of black and red and white. Gorgeous photography hung on the walls, and there were tables placed strategically in the middle of the room where people could gather and talk.

After she made sure the mayor was set and bid him farewell, the mayor thanked her, and she felt pleased with the job she'd done, and headed back to the offices. It was the top of the second inning by the time Francesca returned to the communication area to continue with part two of the day's job: answering mail. She sat and filled requests for schedules, stickers, and even player autograph cards, while she kept a keen eye on the game as it was broadcast over the in-house television. Occasionally, Francesca could hear the bellowing chants of the crowd from above; the office where she was situated was underneath the stands, and it rattled the ceiling when fans pounded their feet.

"What is that request for?" Dan asked her, as he sat across from her at the table handling his own pile of letter requests.

"I can't even read it," Francesca said, giggling, placing her hand over her mouth as her eyes opened wide. "It's hysterical."

"Here, give it to me," he said.

She handed him the letter, still chuckling a little. His eyes grew wide.

"Are you kidding me? That's bizarre. Disgusting. You handle that one."

"Who would write this?" she asked, grossed out. It would later become the first of many odd requests that she would encounter in this line of work.

"Some weirdo," he said, smiling and trying not to laugh.

Francesca couldn't imagine who would write to a player and ask him for a personal piece of equipment, or as the writer of the letter stated himself, "even a jock strap would do."

At the end of the day, the group gathered in front of Isabelle's office. She congratulated the assistants on a successful Opening Day, and asked each person to share a story of what they would remember most from it.

"I was so glad I got to escort the anthem singer out to the field," Mona said.

Dan thought for a moment. "I enjoyed running the press notes. I liked being in the press box with the reporters and seeing how they write their stories."

Francesca couldn't wait for her turn at running the press notes. For the first four innings, Dan was essentially with the media, handing out press notes, assisting in the press box, and scoring the game for the first three innings. Afterward, he met Francesca at the office to respond to fan letters.

The other two assistants enjoyed working in the control room with the scoreboard.

"What about you, Francesca?" Isabelle asked.

"I'd like to say it was escorting the mayor, but I don't think I'll ever forget reading a letter from a fan who asked one of our players for his jock strap."

They all laughed and begged for more details, but no one laughed as hard as Isabelle. Overtired, it seemed her lack of sleep had caught up to her, and she laughed until she cried.

After that initial, overwhelming day came to a close and the evening turned to dusk, Francesca gathered her things and exited the ballpark. Her car was parked next to the player lot in the "game day" employee area.

"Hey," a voice said, chasing after her, "you dropped your tag."

Her credential—the laminated tag that must be worn at all times around her neck to gain access around the ballpark—had inadvertently slipped from her hand as she swung it from its cord the way a lifeguard twirls a whistle. She hadn't noticed or heard it fall. She turned around. It was Joe Clarkson, and he was jogging in her direction, handing over the lost identification he picked up from the concrete.

"Thank you," she said.

"You're welcome," he said, smiling at her.

"That could have been a disaster. Losing my credential on game day number one. I appreciate it."

"No problem," he said, looking at her. "Didn't I see you earlier today?"

"Yes," she said. "I believe you passed Mayor Callahan and me on your way to the outfield. Good game, by the way."

"Thanks," he said. "I'm Joe."

"I know," she said, suddenly feeling stupid, and as if she were a groupie, which she was not. Francesca knew him as a fan—and her father had predicted Clarkson's solid rookie season, but never lived to ever see him swing the bat in the big leagues. "I'm Francesca."

"I know," he said.

She looked at him quizzically. "How did you know my name?" she asked.

"Just read it on your credential."

"Ah, right," she said, feeling her cheeks become warm, and looking away from him. "Thanks again."

She was digging in her purse, searching for her keys. It suddenly occurred to her that she wanted to get out of there as quickly as she could. She wanted to speed off in her cheesy Buick Skylark, leaving a cloud of dust behind her, erasing all evidence that this humiliating interaction ever took place.

"No problem," he said. "See you." He stuck his hand up for a salute-style wave.

But before she could open her car door he called to her again.

"Hey, Francesca." She turned. "Nice uniform, by the way."

Four

"You know what a pitcher can sense? Fear. He knows when you're
intimidated in the batter's box. He knows if you're shaking in your shoes.
He'll fire a fastball under your chin to let you know who is in control."
~ Kevin Desmond, Blackbirds Manager

There was a storage room full of Blackbirds memorabilia in the ballpark that was located in the most inconvenient place. It was situated on the upper deck, and the only way to access it was to walk across metal subway-looking grates in order to reach the door. The grate was see-through, and what was straight below was the lower level. An acrophobic—one who suffered from a fear of heights—would not want to stand on it or cross it. And since Francesca wasn't necessarily fond of heights, but at the same time had a job to do, her solution was not to look down.

Dan and Francesca made a trip up the ramps with their cart on a mission to stock up on player cards and team photos for the abundance of fan mail they needed to answer. The ballpark gates had not yet opened. They were trying to get the task accomplished before batting practice and pre-game started.

"Can you imagine getting stuck up here in this storage room? There's no air. It would only be a matter of time before you would die, spooked by the ghosts who live in this room," Dan said. He was trying to scare Francesca because the door could lock if they didn't prop it open. The handle on the inside didn't work, so the door had to remain ajar.

Normally, Francesca would not have let his chatter bother her. Dan was a fan of horror films and watched all sorts of violent thrillers. She, on the other hand, couldn't be bothered with the genre, but that night, Dan was deliberately trying to scare her, recounting stories about the ghosts of the ballpark. However, Francesca sensed he might have been just as spooked by it all as she was. Being in the room was eerie enough without his anecdotes filling the silence.

"You know what they say, right?" Dan said. "Rumor has it that Emerson's bones are buried beneath the ballpark. Perfect place for hauntings."

"Yeah, right," she said.

Joe Emerson was the darling of the ballclub the day the ballpark opened back in the late 1940s, but was tragically killed in a boating accident that October. Some say he could have been the best player the Blackbirds had ever seen—comparisons to Babe Ruth had often been uttered whenever Emerson's name came up. Rumors ran rampant that his recovered body had been buried under home plate because he loved the ballpark so much.

Dan and Francesca propped open the door with a large, wooden wedge that was kept inside the storage room to do its job—to keep the door from closing.

As both of them were keen on not staying in that room for too long, they hurriedly filled the cart with everything they needed. As they were about to turn the cart around, the door to the storage room slammed shut with a loud "thud." The two of them looked at each other, and Francesca felt a chill run up her spine when she heard Dan scream. Like a girl.

"How the hell will we ever get out of here? What if no one finds us?"

Francesca ran to the door, tried to open it, did her best to pry it open, and when she realized that she couldn't do it, she started to frantically pound on it.

"Let us out! Help! We're locked in here! Let us out!" she yelled.

Dan remained stoic. After his initial scream, he may have gone into shock.

Then, there were three bangs on the door. They jumped back.

The door slowly opened, and Mona was standing in front of them cackling a wickedly, devilish laugh. "Oh my gosh! You two should have seen your faces!"

"I'm going to kill you!" Dan shouted, lunging toward her.

"What the hell, Mona? You trying to scare the shit out of us?" Francesca asked.

"Oh, go easy," she said, wedge in hand. "I'm just having a little fun with you two. We need more of the anniversary posters. Isabelle said to come and tell you guys to grab some."

"You grab them," Francesca said, walking past her, pulling the cart.

Ridiculous Mona and her practical jokes. What Mona failed to realize, however, was that one practical joke deserved another.

After that, Dan and Francesca swore to sick the ghost of Emerson on her and craft their revenge. But like all well laid plans, they needed to be developed over time.

It was August. The season was winding down. Francesca made it through and even managed to earn solid grades, despite her hectic schedule, with very little hassle. As a matter of fact, she learned how to budget her time, delving into projects and assignments much earlier than she normally would have in the past in order to complete them without crunching at the last minute. Her mother was pleased.

Her dedication and incredible drive also set her apart from the other assistants, and Francesca soon became Isabelle's right hand girl; she was chosen to work in the office twenty hours a week, in addition to her game duties. When the semester ended, she moved home for the summer to live with her mother, though they seemed to be passing ships in the night. Her mother worked days, and Francesca worked all of the Blackbirds home games, which meant working mostly nights and weekend games. However, they managed to squeeze in some time together.

One night, Francesca came home a little early on a Friday evening. She was on the first shift, and left the ballpark at about ten o'clock. When she arrived home, she noticed the lights were not on in the house, an unusual occurrence for her mother, a woman who hated the dark and always had to have night lights on in strategic places around the house. As she turned the key to the door, she heard muffled sounds coming from upstairs. Her mother's car was in the driveway, so she assumed she was home.

She walked up the flight of stairs in their Cape Cod style home, each stair creaking ever so slightly from years of use. The door was ajar, and the only light in the room was that from the full moon, shining in through the large picture window. Her mother was sitting, her back to the headboard on the bed in her underwear, wearing one of her father's old, soft t-shirts that still smelled of him. She hadn't cleared out his drawers. She couldn't bring herself to do it, though she managed to give away his suits, slacks, and dress shirts from the closet to Goodwill.

"Are you okay?" Francesca asked, hearing her mother sniffle, wiping her nose to conceal just how hard she probably was sobbing.

"I don't know, Fran—," she tried to say. "I don't know."

Francesca walked over to her, kicked her dirty white sneakers to the floor, and sat next to her mother on the bed. She put her arm around her.

"We're going to be okay, Mom," Francesca said, hearing herself say the words out loud, but questioning them at the same time.

"Are we? I mean, how does someone go on after something like this? What's it all about, anyway?"

In that quick switch of role reversal, her mother needed life's questions answered. At twenty, what did Francesca know? She lost her father and had never dealt with the death of a relative before. At times, it felt like he was just away on a trip, and that at any moment, he'd walk through the door. Francesca would occasionally peek in his home office, hoping to catch a glimpse of him there, as if he had the powers to trick death and bring himself back to life. But like her mother, she wasn't sure what it was all about, either. How could you love someone like that and then have your heart broken by a loss? The finality of death could be so oppressive, like being smothered by a heavy blanket that only had one, tiny hole from which to breathe, offering just enough air to allow survival.

The two sat in silence, the moonlight streaming in through the window, a strange sense of comfort filling a room full of things that belonged to a dead man, along with two people who were having trouble accepting his absence.

"What's going on?"

It was early, and Cissy was on the phone while her young daughter screamed her lungs out in the background. Francesca's mother had gone to work; the realty company was having an open house and she needed to help out.

"Why didn't Mom call me back last night?" Cissy asked.

"It was a bad night," Francesca said as she buttered her toast, the phone propped between her ear and her shoulder. "Mom's still grieving. It was awful. She was wearing his shirt."

Cissy sighed. She missed her father, too, but she wasn't at home enough for the last few months to witness his demise. His mind was still completely in tact, but his once strong body had enough, and gave in to something more powerful.

"I should come for a visit," she said.

"That might help," Francesca said. "But wait a couple of weeks until I'm back at school. She'll need some company then."

"Rabbits," Cissy said.

"Rabbits?"

"Yes! Rabbits! That's what she needs. Let's get her some rabbits."

Francesca pulled the phone away from her head, and looked at it, as if she misheard Cissy's words through the wires.

"I'm not understanding," Francesca said.

"Mom always wanted rabbits—bunnies—whatever. Do you remember that story of her with Grandma and Grandpa? How she thought she was getting rabbits for Christmas that year, but all she got were books and toys. You know that story…it was her worst Christmas ever. Maybe she just needs a diversion besides her work. Something to come home to."

"And you would choose a rabbit for her over a dog? A dog she can walk and talk to and pet and play with? A dog that she can cuddle up with at night and will sleep at the foot of her bed? You would choose a rabbit over man's best friend?"

"You're forgetting something, Francesca."

"What?"

"Bunnies don't bark or shit on your floor."

It was Mona's birthday, and Francesca and Dan were eager to help her celebrate. They were on the phone late into the night, talking about her birthday cake and celebration, and it would not be without an effort to get back at her for the storage room incident.

Francesca had to run an errand, and stopped off at a local hardware store. After that, she made her way to the grocery store and bought two cans of cake icing.

After the afternoon game that Sunday, all of the assistants, along with Isabelle, gathered in the conference room to sing "Happy Birthday" to Mona. She was thrilled to hear everyone recognize her birthday, and helium balloons hung above a couple of chairs.

"Cut the cake!" Francesca said, looking at Dan.

She grabbed the large cake knife, and couldn't seem to make a dent past the icing. She tried again, and again, and couldn't figure out what was wrong.

"Use some muscle," Dan suggested.

Still, she could not do it. And then she saw it. There was large, round sponge—the kind used to wash a car—underneath the icing. She started laughing.

"Very funny, guys. Very funny."

Everyone was laughing, and within a couple of minutes, Isabelle re-entered the room with the cake from the bakery that Francesca and Dan hid in the back of the refrigerator in the kitchen earlier that day.

Five

"Every player has a moment he remembers.
Whether it's a hit or a catch or pitch—you remember because the fans
remember and they never let you forget it."
~ *Zeke Watson, Blackbirds Hall of Famer*

The unexpected drive to the pennant that year created a magnetic frenzy. The Blackbirds hit their stride, winning game after game and filling the stands. At one point, the team won seven straight; it was something to behold. Everywhere you went, Bay City was cloaked in red and black and white. Banners hung in city windows, signs for the Blackbirds were painted on buildings, and the media interviewed player after player for segments each evening on the news. "Flying to the pennant," "Join our flock as we soar into postseason," and "Birds of a Feather Flock Together" bumper stickers were seen all over town as the public relations campaign for the team raged on. The city was energized, and the Blackbirds made headline after headline and were all anyone could talk about that September.

At times, if the sun set in just the right place and its rays hit the building at precisely the right time, you could have sworn Blackbirds Park was smiling.

Francesca moved back into her dorm room that fall semester, and reunited with Sam again. Sam waltzed through the door from an outing with her friend, Patty. They had asked Francesca to join them for the day, but she decided to sleep in because of her late night the previous evening, as she worked and endured an extra-inning game that ended after midnight.

"Where did you get that Blackbirds pennant?" Francesca asked Sam.

"Got it at the flea market downtown," she said. It was retro looking, and a little bent at the point. But Sam loved used goods of all kinds. She was an experienced and successful thrift store, yard sale, and antiques store shopper. In fact, half of her wardrobe consisted of vintage clothing she collected from various stores that she'd then alter and tailor.

She kicked off her shoes and straddled the pillow at the head of her bed, using push-pins to hang the pennant way up high on the wall. When she was done, the crease was barely visible. They all examined it.

"Nice," Francesca said.

"There's more too."

"What else have you got there?" Francesca asked.

"Look."

She unrolled a poster of Joe Clarkson who was having a phenomenal second professional season with the club. Because of his good looks, he was a heartthrob. In the photograph, he wore his baseball pants and a generic shirt, and was leaning on his bat in larger than life form. His chiseled body and twinkling eyes were front and center. The tagline at the bottom read: "Joe Clarkson works hard at his job, and expects you to do the same. Stay in school." It was a public service announcement in poster form for the city's education board.

Sam reached up and tore down her Pink Floyd poster and grabbed the tape. Right then she stuck Joe Clarkson on her wall, above her bed, the pennant just above it.

"Where'd you get that one?" Francesca asked.

"Same flea market," she said. "There was a table with a lot of Blackbirds memorabilia on it."

She stepped back and surveyed her artful display.

"So, do you think I'll ever get to meet him?"

"Who?" Francesca asked.

"Joe Clarkson."

"You like him?"

"Come on, Francesca! He's a hell of a good looking guy!"

Sam had a one-track mind, and it typically wasn't on her studies. She was a big flirt and was not shy about sharing her feelings with anyone who would listen. It was no surprise that she was enamored with Joe Clarkson. Half of the city was. But in truth, it was hard to name a guy she didn't have a crush on.

"Since when do you even care about baseball?"

"Since my roommate works for the team and might meet this hot guy," she said.

Francesca didn't have time to elaborate on this conversation, and never told Sam the story of the lost credential and Joe Clarkson from earlier in the season. She didn't have time for old tales because she needed to get to the ballpark. There was another game, and she was scheduled for the last shift, so she needed to arrive by four o'clock.

"Don't you get sick of wearing that uniform?" Sam asked as she watched Francesca dress.

"Only every day," she said.

As fate would have it, there was a horrible accident on the highway, and there was the potential for Francesca to be late for her shift. Isabelle hated lateness. The assistants were always expected to be on time. Punctuality was a key to success in the organization. To that end,

Francesca was impeccable, and had never been late. Her blood pressure started to rise as her car sat—idle—in traffic, and she began to panic.

She turned on the radio, desperate for the traffic report. It was worse than she expected; the ramp to the highway had been closed. They were clearing the accident. "It should reopen momentarily," the radio report stated.

She watched other cars peel off at the next exit ramp. At one point, she recognized the detour route, because she used it once when she came home from a night out with her colleagues. She tried to re-member how to go…up the road to the second light…make left…con-tinue on the Boulevard to the ballpark. She had to take a risk. She didn't want to be late.

When the blue Honda took the next exit, she followed, putting full faith in its driver. The car had a Blackbirds sticker on it, so she was betting that it was heading to the ballpark as well, and that she could follow its lead. When the car turned down a road she was unfamiliar with, she took a gamble, and continued following it.

Minutes later, they were heading toward a traffic light that led to the ramp to the ballpark. Relief! She looked at her watch. She had a couple of minutes to get there without spoiling the integrity of her punctuality thus far. Perhaps she wouldn't be late after all.

After Francesca parked the car in the lot, she began to sprint as fast as she could to the offices. Running with vigor and determination, she entered the glass doors and made it to the lobby.

"Crap!" the guy said aloud when she inadvertently knocked his arm and caused the assortment of newspapers and typewritten papers he was holding to fly all over the hallway. She wasn't looking where she was going—too busy and too worried. She hadn't noticed him in her flight to be on time.

She turned back.

It was a mess.

"I'm so sorry!" Francesca said, apologizing profusely. "I didn't mean to bump your arm."

She immediately dropped to her hands and knees and began gathering up the papers, moving around the floor so no one would step on them in the hallway, keeping her head down, focused on collecting them as quickly as she could.

She made brief eye contact with him, embarrassed to look at him for too long, and placed all of the disheveled and disorganized papers into his arms. His press credential got in the way, and he moved it aside as he straightened out the stack. He thanked her, and hurried along, obviously in a rush to get where he needed to go as well.

When she walked through the door to the offices, Dan was waiting for her.

"There you are! I was getting worried. We have a new duty tonight. We're supposed to be in the control room in five minutes."

"I know, I know," she said. "Accident."

"No. It's not an accident, we were scheduled to be in the control room together," he said excitedly.

"No, silly. An accident. I was stuck in an accident."

"Are you okay?

"No…I wasn't in the accident…I got caught in…never mind. Let's go," she said.

"Oh," he said. "Well, put your stuff down and let's get moving! You're supposed to teach me how run the audio board for the game. I've never done it before."

"Relax," she said. "I'm here. I know what to do."

What Francesca liked best about her job—besides being linked to a professional ballclub whose name was the in the newspaper every day—was that she was able to gain a little bit of experience in a lot of different areas. The variety of tasks she had to perform kept the job entertaining; it was never boring. Countless projects, endless media requests, donation requests and fan letters to answer, and good, old-fashioned, grassroots public relations skills were some of the duties she performed regularly. Working in the control room was also a bonus. She filled in twice for the audio person, who was essentially the deejay for the ballpark. She loved that when she played the music for the fans she could see the faces of happy folks dancing and cheering in their seats, the direct result of her work that day. There was also a strategy to it, and it required the audio person to select the right songs for the appropriate moment. For pitching changes, songs such as "Na Na Hey Hey Kiss Him Goodbye" and "Hit The Road, Jack" were among Francesca's favorites to play because the crowd would undoubtedly chime in and sing. For close games, she cranked up the likes of "We Will Rock You" or "Centerfield." She noticed Dan's hand shaking as she instructed him to play the cart or push the button to make it go live out in the seating bowl; she smiled at him sweetly and told him it was okay, and then he did what she said, and he seemed please with himself.

This calm, confident demeanor, along with her genuine love for the game was what set Francesca apart from the other four assistants. She believed her work was an investment in the team. At least that's the way she saw it.

That night—the night after she taught Dan how to use the audio board—she ran into Isabelle in the press box lounge. They were both getting a soft drink after the Blackbirds won a close game, 6-5. It was a nail biter, and they talked about it.

"You know, Francesca, we're looking for someone to work in

the office part-time to full-time hours in the off-season. Do you think it could work for you? You wouldn't have to work crazy hours while you're taking your classes, but you could put in the time on your winter break and on weekends if that would work. I'd rather hire someone from within rather than go looking outside for help," she said.

Francesca looked at her in disbelief and smiled the broadest smile.

"Of course! I'd love to do it. You know I would!"

"Great," she said. "We'll talk about the specifics later. Right now, we both need to get out of here and get some sleep, because we'll only be back here in a matter of hours."

They walked to the offices together, and Francesca and Isabelle grabbed their respective purses. Francesca overheard Isabelle listen to her phone messages, huff, and then said aloud, to no one in particular, "Is there no end to the madness?"

"You walking out?" Francesca asked, peeking her head through Isabelle's doorway.

"No, unfortunately, I have to handle something before I go. I'll see you in the morning."

"Okay. Goodnight," she called to her.

As Francesca approached the glass doors to exit the offices, she could see there were still fans milling in the parking lot, the die-hards, waiting for the remaining players to come out. How did the players ever get used to the invasion of privacy?

She stopped at the doors, digging around her purse in search of her car keys before she walked out in the dark. As she started to open the door, she heard someone call her name.

"Pssst—Francesca! Come here."

It was a man's voice, but she couldn't place it right away. She turned around and saw Joe Clarkson standing there in the shadows behind the championship trophy case.

"You startled me!" she said when she moved closer.

"I'm sorry. It's just…I have a big favor to ask you."

"What is it?"

"I don't feel like being harassed by all those fans out there. I just don't have it in me tonight. Do you think you could go get my car and drive it around to the service entrance gate? I'll wait for you there and just jump in. I can even drop you at your car if you'd like."

"Is your car a stick shift? Because I have no idea how to drive a stick," she said.

"You're in luck then. Automatic."

"Actually, I believe that means you're in luck, and I can drive it."

She opened up her hand so he could drop the keys into it.

"Thanks," he said sounding grateful.

"You know right before I walked out those doors, I was wondering how you guys do it night after night. It must get a little tiring at times."

"You have no idea. You know which one is mine, right?"

"Yes," she said. "The black Beamer."

"You got it."

He made a ton of money and lived in the sports limelight, but Francesca didn't envy him for having to live each day in the spotlight. The hometown fans loved their players, and they would wait around for hours just for a glimpse, a photo, or an autograph.

As she walked to his car, Francesca smirked to herself knowing Sam would kill to hear this story. She didn't mean to keep some of her baseball stories to herself, but sometimes keeping information from Sam, a person who tended to talk too much, particularly during inopportune moments, was probably the best thing to do. She loved Sam, but sometimes just keeping quiet was the smartest thing to do. Plus, Sam might hound and harass her about him. Francesca had to work with Joe Clarkson a lot, whether she was taking fans to meet him during pre-game or assisting with an autograph session, and he was always extremely friendly and cordial. Plus, the fact that they were only two years apart in age perpetuated their camaraderie.

This wasn't the first time they had a conversation; there were many that had taken place over the course of the year. Sometimes Mona would say, "How come when I have to escort Joe Clarkson, he hardly says a word, but when Francesca works with him, he never shuts up?" This made Francesca laugh. Maybe it came easily between them because she never fawned all over him like Mona and Dan did. Maybe it was easy because she could talk about baseball like a normal person, and not like a silly, awestruck girl looking to reel in a player for marriage. She didn't know why it was easy. It just was.

She climbed into the black, impeccably kept car that still smelled brand new, and she supposed the fans that were waiting were bewildered by the girl who was getting in Joe Clarkson's car in an unfeminine, outdated uniform.

She locked the doors, and turned the ignition. She thought she escaped them, but it was just wishful thinking.

The fans were determined. Instead of leaving Clarkson's car alone, they assumed she would drive the vehicle directly to Joe Clarkson, and their intuition was not incorrect. They started running along the side of the car, banging on the windows and hood, chanting, "We want Joe Clarkson!"

Admittedly, Francesca panicked a bit. It was an unnerving feeling, and solidified her instinct that she had no desire to ever become famous. All it took was her standing in the grocery checkout line to determine that fame could ruin your life. Magazine covers speculated about the lives of the rich and famous. Who needed that? It only disrupted the normalcy of one's life. She watched as Princess Diana became the tabloid's favorite, constantly stalked and hunted, and wondered if the media realized that she was a person with feelings who had a right to some privacy.

She had to think quickly in this situation, though. She couldn't just drive right to the service entrance even though it wasn't far from the player lot because the fans would catch on to the ploy. So, she decided to do what anyone who watched a lot of cop dramas would do.

At that moment, Joe Clarkson's expensive sports car went for a little spin down the street to trick his followers, the driver of the vehicle smiling a little mischievous smile as she gave the horn a quick "toot" as she revved the engine.

"What took you so long?" he asked when Francesca pulled up next to the service entrance, and he emerged from behind the shadows of one of the brick columns.

"I had to outsmart your fans. I just drove down the block for a minute. But here I am with your lovely, noisy little car, all safe and sound. Hop in," she said, as she opened the driver's side door and made her way out of it.

"I'll drive you to your car," he said.

"No, thanks," Francesca said. "Too risky. You take yourself home and get rested for tomorrow. Big game, you know."

"Really?" he said, with a smile. "Thank you. Are you sure I can't drive you?"

"What? And risk being seen and mobbed after my brilliant ruse? Nope, I'm good," Francesca said.

He gave her a wave and a look of appreciation, and took off, without hassle.

Francesca made her way to her own crappy car and hoped it would start.

It did, and she took off into the night, thinking maybe, just maybe, she would tell Sam about this one. She was her best friend, after all.

Zeke Watson's Grand Slam

I was ten and healing from a very bad case of strep throat. My dad had tickets to a Sunday afternoon game in September. It was a relatively warm day, hovering around seventy-two degrees, though the sun was not out, making it feel a little chillier. My mother was concerned about my sickness and didn't want me to go to the game, worried that I hadn't fully recovered, though all signs indicated that I had.

Zeke Watson was struggling at the plate. His batting average had gone from .325 earlier in the season to .278. The press berated his hitting, speculating about his future.

My father was a firm believer in Watson; he loved his stance at the plate and his tenacious work ethic. He kept telling me that Watson had it in him, that one day he'd be a Bay City legend.

The Blackbirds were down by three. Watson came up in the bottom of the ninth inning with two outs and the bases loaded. The pitch was delivered, an inside curve ball. Watson got his bat on it. Out it flew, over the outfield fence.

The stands erupted. My father and I jumped up and down, high-fiving each other like two silly idiots. It was a spectacular ending.

My father showed me how to record a game-winning grand slam that day on the scorecard in the program.

"Let it be a lesson to you, Frankie," he said. "That ballplayer just showed us all that anything is possible. Even when you're down and out, it's not over if you give it all you've got. Things can turn around. Remember that, okay?"

I looked at my dad and gave him a hug.

I would remember it. Always.

Six

"I never dreamed we'd make it this far. That doesn't mean I didn't believe we had the talent and the drive, but they surprised the hell out of me. This team's got more heart than I expected. I'm proud of them. Proud of all of them."
~ Kevin Desmond, Blackbirds Manager

Earth, Wind, and Fire may have been one of Francesca's father's favorite groups with a hit in the late 1970s called "September," but the Blackbirds were a hit with the fans this September.

There were parties and non-stop, flattering articles about the team.

There were banners and balloons.

There were happy players and ecstatic fans.

There were tired, but thrilled, front office personnel, smiling as seat after seat was sold, the team setting club attendance records night after night.

It was September, when everything mattered, and nothing could be taken for granted.

Francesca was working more hours than she had all year. Getting ready for a potential playoff spot was intense. The entire front office worked late into the night; she would often return to her dorm well after two in the morning, exhausted, but giddy, because of all the celebrations.

Her academics were suffering a little, but she did her very best to stay on top of all of it. It was difficult not to get sucked into the drama that was the Blackbirds that year. The team was all over the news, and Joe Clarkson was hitting better than he had all season. It was safe to say that since the All-Star Break, Clarkson's bat was on fire. There was clearly something different about his stance. Francesca's father would have been able to sum it up succinctly and discern the altered mechanics of it, though Francesca was pleased with herself because she could plainly see that his right elbow was raised a tad higher than it had been. It seemed to make the biggest difference in his swing.

It all came down to Sunday afternoon's game, the last game of the season. Because the Blackbirds lost on Saturday night, Sunday's outcome mattered. If the team won, they were going to the playoffs. If they lost, it was all over for them. On September 30, they would know for certain if the Blackbirds would be continuing on to postseason play.

At some point during the afternoon, Francesca conducted a reality check. As she stood in the Blackbirds dugout, waiting to assist with the pregame ceremonies, she took a moment to cherish the past season. She took a mental photograph of the ballpark that day—there was an aura to it. It wasn't decorated for postseason play yet, but the air held a sense of magic. The whole year felt magical. The regular season was about to end, and she was a part of it. She worked for the ballclub, and she had to slap herself sometimes because it felt like she was living a fairy tale.

She took a deep breath in and gazed toward the heavens and the blue skies. She could feel her father with her. She could sense his eyes upon the field. She desperately wanted to believe he knew she was there.

She must have looked ridiculous standing there, allowing emotions to envelope her because she dabbed a tear from the corner of her eye and swallowed the lump that caught her by surprise in her throat. What was she doing, crying on the job? This is ridiculous, she thought.

"Hey, you okay, Frankie?" Joe Clarkson said as he approached her, glove in hand, ready to take the field for batting practice.

She nodded.

No one had ever called her by that name but her father.

There were two outs with no men on base in the bottom of the ninth inning; the Blackbirds were at bat. Francesca was sitting among the reporters counting pitches, and waiting to run the post-game press notes. The crowd of reporters in the press box sat elbow to elbow as writers typed frantically as they covered the last game of the season.

Francesca was trying desperately not to bite her nails.

The public address announcer spoke: "Now batting, number 6, Joe Clarkson."

Her heart sank a little.

Down by one run, Clarkson walked to the plate. He knew he needed to get on base or hit a homer to tie the game. This was it. The season could end here. Her heart was racing.

The first pitch came in; he swung and missed. Strike one.

The second pitch, low and outside. Ball one.

The third pitch, high and outside. Ball two.

The fourth pitch, right down the plate. Strike two, looking.

The fifth pitch, Clarkson swung. He hit it far, out to the outfield. The fans stood. They were all thinking it was going to go over the centerfield wall, but just then, the centerfielder, Jose Herrera, had other plans. He made the leap of his life, arm outstretched, reaching over the outfield wall until everyone lost sight of it. The fans held their breath. When he came down from his leap, he pointed to his glove excitedly, and there was a ball in it. Clarkson was out. That game and the Blackbirds' season were over. Herrera's catch was named the play of the game, and the clip ran over and over that night on the ESPN highlights reel.

Press box duty required workers to be quiet. Clapping, screaming, yelling, or cheering were not permitted. When the game ended, there was nothing but dead silence.

All hopes for postseason play were dashed that late September day.

Poor Joe, Francesca thought. Poor Joe. And then Francesca thought that maybe Joe Clarkson would want her to retrieve his car for him again. She guessed that perhaps he would not want to face the fans after that last out.

The front office employees all tried to pick up their spirits and celebrate the season that was, but it was difficult not to feel an enormous amount of disappointment for what could have been: a playoff spot, or a shot at a championship.

On Monday evening, George Gibbs, the team president, hosted a crab feast in the picnic area at the ballpark. The entire front office was invited, including part-time personnel. Gibbs offered kind remarks about the season and praised the team and its employees for sticking it out and giving the city what it deserved: an exciting season. Champagne was poured for everyone, and Gibbs made a toast, ending it with, "No worries. We'll get 'em next year!"

There were dozens and dozens of seasoned, fresh crabs strewn over tables, with corn-on-the cob, hot dogs, hamburgers, sausage and peppers, and beverages provided by the team. There was music playing over the ballpark's loud speakers.

Francesca was sitting at the table with Isabelle, Dan, Mona, and some other folks from the public relations office, as they relaxed and enjoyed an afternoon off with their peers.

"I don't know about you all, but now I can actually get some work done," Isabelle said, laughing. "My desk is even messier than usual. I've got some catch-up work to do this week."

"I have an exam tomorrow in my history class," Mona said. "I'm not even sure what years it covers."

They laughed. Mona's situation was not unique. They had all fallen behind over the last two weeks with their schoolwork because preparations for post-season had begun. Now it was over, and they could focus on other aspects of their lives.

Francesca found herself looking around, but there was no sign of Joe Clarkson in the crowd of players who had agreed to come to this end-of-year celebration, some with families in tow. She wondered if he had decided to go home to Texas.

Zeke Watson walked over and sat down next to Isabelle. Rumors had been swirling that he might become the club's hitting coach next year.

"Mind if I join the Dream Team over here," he said, smiling. He participated in a tremendous amount of community events because he was a year-round resident of Bay City. Francesca assumed he that he must love it, especially since he was one of the most beloved players to ever wear a Blackbirds jersey. And he was constantly attending baseball card shows.

"Not at all," Isabelle said. "Of course, we'd be honored if you sat with us. Maybe you could tell us a few stories to get us out of this funk."

"Ah, no need to be in a funk," he said. "And my stories aren't worth a damn. It was a good season. The team played well. They'll be contenders again soon. They've got it in them."

He took one of the hammers and turned his crab over. He looked puzzled.

"So, is someone going to tell me how to eat these things?" he asked.

"You're joking!" Isabelle remarked, her face looking as astonished as her voice sounded. "You've lived here for years and have never picked a crab? Shame, shame, Zeke!"

"No," he said. "I've never picked a crab. I've only ever eaten crab cakes."

"Well, just watch Francesca over there. She can crack a mean crab."

Francesca smiled. She was going to teach Zeke Watson how to crack a crab. She spun her mallet and looked at Zeke.

"Are you ready?" she asked.

"Ready as I'll ever be, I guess," he said. "There's just something unappetizing about eating something when its eyes are still staring at you."

"Reserve your comments until after you have been educated," Isabelle joked.

"That's right," Francesca said. "I'm a master crab-picker. You only need two tools: a mallet and a knife. Now get ready to dive in."

Watson had been her father's favorite player. Francesca couldn't help but to smile thinking her father would be amused if he could see her now.

Hours later, with a full belly, and disgusted by the amount of food she ate, Francesca decided to take herself home. She attempted to wash the crab smell off of her fingers, but all expert crab pickers know that what gets rid of the smell is a lemon. She checked her face in the mirror, saw the bags under her eyes, and tried to fluff up her hair. It was probably useless.

She was walking down the hallway, heading to the parking lot, when she heard him say, "Hey, Frankie."

She turned.

"Hi, Joe," she said.

There was an uncomfortable moment that passed; she didn't know whether to congratulate him or say she was sorry about the final game. She decided not to say either. Instead, she looked at the massive pile of stuff he had in his hands, along with the stuffed duffle bag that was hoisted over his shoulders.

"Clearing out your locker?"

"Yes. I needed to hide. Making the last out in a big game sucks."

She nodded.

"See? It even has you speechless."

"No, it doesn't have me speechless. It's just that you can't really look at it that way. Every out counts. The ones in the first inning matter just…"

"I know, I know…just as much as the freakin' ones in the later innings. I get that. It doesn't make me feel better. I couldn't face the looks of pity at the crab feast. I let a lot of people down."

"No, you didn't! It's a team sport. And anyway, no one feels that way. It was a great season. We all had so much fun."

She opened the door for him so he could exit with his handful of belongings, a satchel of clothes, a couple of bats, and something she couldn't quite decipher. She thought about asking what it was, but reconsidered.

"Thanks, Frankie. Thanks for trying to make me feel better."

"Sure. Just don't run into Zeke Watson on your way out. I don't think I made him feel better. I made him pick crabs for the first time, and he has cuts from the claws all over his fingers. Do you know how that hurts when the spicy seasoning gets in there?"

"You look good in normal clothes," he said.

He smiled. Then, Joe Clarkson turned and was gone.

Francesca would never forget that first season she worked for the Blackbirds. She had purchased a journal to document her year, writing in it often and savoring the details. It was an escape for her to crawl into bed with her pen and her recollections and record the day's events. The moments were like snapshots once they were over, and she didn't want them to fade too quickly. Lost in thought, she wrote.

She wrote about how chills ran up and down her spine when she heard the echoes of a player taking swings during batting practice when she took her walk to the press box. There was an eeriness that lurked in the shadows of that quiet ballpark, much altered when the ball met the bat. Silence, then, crack!

That sound. That glorious sound was music to her ears. Rhythmic, hypnotic. The lulling sound of a crowd, either intently watching or vehemently cheering, was among her favorites. She remembered sitting in the stands, when spring arrived, during batting practice with her father, as they watched the early games when it was chilly and blustery, just to hear that sound. Because after a cold and bleak winter, there was rejuvenation: baseball had returned. It was spring. Everything was new. A new season. New roster. Clean uniforms and perfect fields. And perfectly crafted bats that were ready for action.

Now, however, it was the end of the season. It was October. A deafening stillness filled the ballpark, and Francesca knew winter was coming, and winter meant no baseball for several months.

She stood and looked around at the view from the lower level, and hoped she would be working for the team again next season, but she wasn't sure of the protocol. Did the team invite you back for another year, or did they hire a whole new group of rookies? She would wait to see what Isabelle said, but because she was asked to work during the off-season, she held on to the hopeful notion that she would return. The field was still gorgeous. Verdant and scrupulously manicured, it was an impressive stage as the Blackbirds gave it all they could, despite that they fell short in the end.

She flung her bag over her shoulder and bid the season, the players, the team, and the front office personnel farewell.

No matter what the outcome, no matter where she landed or what she would do in her life from that point forward, she would cherish that Blackbirds rookie season forever. It was her dream job, and an unexpected one at that.

Just before she left, she spotted them. She found the two seats that had been the seats she shared with her father, and she sat.

She sat for a good, long while, until the lights were ready to be turned off and it was time to say one last good night.

SEVEN

"If I had to choose between opening presents on Christmas morning and baseball, I'd pick baseball. It lasts for almost nine months, and you never have to return an ugly sweater."
~ Freddie "The Fly" Montrose, Blackbirds Bench Coach

It was the second Christmas without her father, and the family was doing its very best to get through the holidays without falling into a morbid slump. They were still in such shock last Christmas, still bearing the weight of his loss. Francesca could barely recall the holiday, except for hearing her mother cry at night. Staying upbeat and positive throughout it was a challenge for her. There were times when she felt her father's loss more severely than others.

Her grandparents—her mother's mom and dad—had flown in from Florida, where they lived year-round, and were staying with them for Christmas week. They were an excellent distraction that year, especially for her mother. Both her mother and her grandmother enjoyed baking, so they indulged and created the most elaborate batch of Christmas cookies ever imagined. They were so intricate, they looked as if they came from Roma's Bakery down the street. Some were recipes they collected from Martha Stewart, others were family favorites, and still others were out of the latest edition of *Better Homes & Gardens*.

"So, I see you have amassed quite an assortment here," Francesca said, observing the mound that was growing ever larger on the counter. "Who do you expect will eat all these cookies?"

"More than that," Cissy said, taking a bite of a fresh one from the oven, "who uses the word 'amassed' in everyday conversation?"

Francesca heard her grandmother chuckle. She found her sister hysterical, while Francesca, on the other hand, simply found her annoying. It wasn't her fault that Cissy had the vocabulary of a twelve-year-old and never opened a book in her life; she never read beyond the Star Tracks pages of *People* magazine. She barely made it through college, and even refused to show Francesca her grades when they came in the mail one winter semester.

"These cookies are for neighbors and anyone you'd like to give cookies to at work, as well as for us," her mother said. "Please, take some to work with you this afternoon, Francesca." Francesca had agreed to help answer the phones at the Blackbirds since so many people were out of the office for the holidays.

"So how's that job going, by the way?" her grandmother asked.

"Very well," Francesca said. "They've asked me back for next season, so I'm thrilled."

"Your grandfather and I will have to come up for a game next season," she said.

"I'd be happy to get you tickets. It's part of my compensation plan."

"Wonderful, dear," her grandmother said.

Emma crawled into the room. She was wearing the most adorable little Santa-like outfit. It was velvet with white trim, and her rotund belly filled it out perfectly. She even had rosy cheeks from running errands with Cam, who dropped her with Cissy, and headed upstairs to wrap up the last minute gifts he apparently bought on his shopping spree. They were gone for hours.

"What do you think Cam got me for Christmas?" Cissy asked,

directing the question at Francesca.

"Do you really think he'd tell me? And if he did, do you really think I'd tell you?"

Cissy slapped Francesca's arm and rolled her eyes as she walked away, chasing Emma before she began to climb the stairs. Francesca's mother desperately needed to childproof the house now that Emma was mobile. There were too many little stairs and turns that the curious little toddler could get into during her explorations. Francesca decided to baby-proof during winter break so neither her mother nor her dopey sister would have to worry about it.

Emma crawled right over to Francesca and tugged at her jeans. Who could resist her adorable, chubby face, and her beautiful blue eyes with long, dark eyelashes? She was a stunning baby.

"Are you sure you don't want to cash this kid in? I swear, she could be the next Gerber baby!" Francesca said, as she reached for Emma and picked her up.

She started to pull on her hair, as Francesca's was well past her shoulders, and Cissy wore hers short, in sort of a sassy pixie cut. Her sister had always been fashion conscious and stylish. She had a fantastic figure—small waist, big breasts, and the whitest teeth on the planet. When she smiled, her whole face lit up. Emma looked like Cissy as a baby, minus the twinkling baby blues. Those were Emma's gift from Cam.

"No. No modeling for my baby. After I saw that episode of 'Jerry Springer,' I swore I'd never prostitute my baby for money. Never."

Their grandmother's mouth grew wide, and she giggled again, turned to Francesca, and said quietly: "Tell me she didn't just say she watches 'Jerry Springer.'"

"Man, am I glad you're here," Isabelle shouted to Francesca

from her office door as she saw her walk past when she arrived. "Come here when you get a chance."

Francesca hung her coat in the closet, tossed her purse on the workstation, and peeked in through the door. Isabelle was all dressed up. She was wearing a black dress, tall boots, and a sophisticated red scarf around her neck. She never saw her look so stylish. Her hair had been curled, and it softened her normal look. She had very sharp features and typically wore her hair straight down in a shoulder-length bob.

"You look nice," Francesca said to her. Isabelle may have blushed.

"Thanks," she said. "I'm meeting my boyfriend's family for the first time tonight at a dinner. Are you sure it's okay?"

"Gorgeous," she said.

"Thanks. I don't know why, but I'm unusually nervous."

Francesca was a little shocked that she was letting her guard down like that. She wasn't one to ever talk about personal issues in the office. At least not with her.

"Any chance you can attend a banquet on January 17? It's the annual Celebrate Sports banquet, and I'm trying to fill our four tables. We're one of the sponsors of it."

"Sure," she said, flattered and knowing immediately that she had no plans on January 17. In fact, she was pretty sure she had no plans in January at all, or February for that matter.

"Great. Thank you. I'm giving you two tickets, so bring someone with you."

"Isabelle, I think I'm the one who should be thanking you. Sounds exciting!"

Isabelle did her best not to laugh. "Here's my best piece of advice: Don't nod off at the table, and do your best to smile."

Francesca laughed. Could it be that Isabelle still didn't understand Francesca's genuine enthusiasm for the sport and her job? Attending the banquet would be a huge thrill for her, not a sacrifice of her time.

"I brought you these," Francesca said, handing over a very fancy tin of cookies with a big red bow on top. "Thanks for everything this past year."

"You're welcome," she said. "You earned it. You were our best, but don't tell anyone else I said that."

"My lips are sealed."

"Well, I hope not for too long. You need to help me eat a few of these things."

First, Francesca heard the stairs creak, followed by the awful high-pitched squeak of the front door, early on Christmas morning. Besides those isolated sounds, the house felt still. Awkward. She wondered how they would all muster up the strength not to cry this year. There were so many traditions they had to let go of because they were Dad's traditions.

They no longer went to the nearby farm and cut down a tree; instead, they bought one from the firehouse. They no longer organized the neighborhood Caroling Crawl, which went up and down several nearby streets singing Christmas carols, and then everyone ended up at their house for a night of drinking, singing, and silliness. It was probably her dad's favorite night of the year. He actually had a beautiful singing voice, and her mother could play the piano well enough to bang out Christmas favorites, her father leading the way. It was one of those parties that typically lasted until three in the morning, and a night that was talked about by all the neighbors for the rest of the year. Her father could let loose at that party, something he wasn't always good at doing.

However, when he was diagnosed with the illness, he attempted to enjoy every last minute he had, and at the Caroling Crawl the year before he died, Francesca's father had the time of his life.

They no longer went to Christmas Eve mass. When Francesca asked her mother to attend, she said she couldn't, and Francesca let it go at that.

So when she heard the squeak, it startled her. Usually, it was her dad who snuck down the stairs—from the time when Cissy and she were little until they were adults—to light the tree, put on the Christmas music, and make the hot chocolate. Francesca wondered who was awake and downstairs. Sometimes the thought hit her—as if it had not been real until that exact moment in time.

Her father was dead.

The reality of it was sometimes too much for her to handle.

She climbed out of her bed and slid into her slippers. She was wearing flannel bottoms and a long sleeve tee, so she grabbed a sweatshirt to warm her until the fire got going in the family room.

She tiptoed down the stairs, and saw the back of a man, rolling up newspaper, tossing logs on the fire, and striking a match.

"Good morning, Cam," Francesca said. "What are you doing?"

"Hey, Francesca," he said. "Just trying to carry on some of the traditions."

She could smell the chocolate, and knew he'd been up to something in the kitchen.

She walked over to Cam and hugged him. A tear fell from her eyes onto Cam's flannel shirt.

"Thank you," she said.

Cissy was a lucky woman to have found a man like Cam. He loved her sister more than any person should love another human being. He would do anything for her, and after they started dating, he quickly became a member of the family. Her dad had loved him, too. Cam was even-tempered and kind. He was probably one of the most thoughtful guys she knew. And Emma was the light of his life. Francesca was happy for them.

And at that very moment, she was happy for herself, as well.

"Wait, Mom. There's one more present to open," she heard Cissy say.

Wrapping paper was balled up in clumps and scattered all over the carpeting, Bing Crosby crooned in the background, and for the most part, they did their best not to get too weepy during all the celebrations that morning. Cam had poured hot chocolates with marshmallows, and Emma fulfilled her job as being the cutest in the room. She helped keep their minds off of things. Emma was far too young to understand the giving of presents or the reasons for the tree and the music, but she beamed with excitement nonetheless. She was right at home with all the commotion. Francesca's grandfather must have taken a hundred pictures of her as she tore paper off of packages while she sat on Cam's lap. In fact, she had more fun with the wrapping paper than with the gifts inside them. Her little giggle was infectious, and made Francesca laugh every time she heard her cackle.

Her sister left the room, but returned with a rather large and tall box, wrapped on all four sides with a big bow on the front—not the top—of it. Francesca had no idea what it was.

"This is from Francesca and me," Cissy said, handing it to her mother, as she gave Francesca a wink. For a moment she was confused; they hadn't talked about getting her mother a present from the two of them. She had spent money on a cashmere sweater and locket for her mother's charm bracelet.

Cissy placed the package down in front of her mother. Their grandmother's eyes opened wide.

"Oh my God!" her mother exclaimed, reaching into the box.

Then Francesca knew. Her sister had done it. From the both of them.

Her mother picked one up, and held it near her face, the baby bunny wiggling its nose and looking at her, its ears droopy and its whiskers long. They had given her rabbits.

Francesca looked at her grandmother, who was crying.

"We should have given those to you when you were ten and had asked for them on your Christmas list," her grandmother said, her voice cracking.

Even her grandfather was getting emotional. The three of them hugged, her mother holding the bunnies next to her face, smiling, and Francesca snapped a photo she would treasure for the rest of her life.

That night, after they ate their meal and played with Emma; after they watched the rabbits hop across the kitchen floor and giggled like schoolchildren; after they snuggled up to watch *Scrooge, The Musical* with Albert Finney; and after they ate way too many of the picturesque cookies, Francesca went upstairs to her room to get ready for bed. As she washed her face, she looked at herself in the mirror. So much had happened over the last year and a half, she was reeling from it all. The job, college, worrying about her mother, balancing her responsibilities—all of it. It was overwhelming at times, and her father would have known how to keep her balanced, but she just kept marching on through life. She thought of him constantly. She didn't know how her mother pulled it together today—or any day for that matter—but she did know her sister was right. Those bunnies, along with Emma, were a much-needed distraction and brought so much joy to them all.

She patted her face with the towel, peeking over it and into the mirror, and into her own eyes. She saw herself there, and for a moment, she thought she saw her father gazing back. How many times had she been told she looked just like him? Their facial structures were similar—they both had pointed chins and almond eyes, their hair dark and shiny. How many times had she heard her father and she were so much alike? Their temperaments, their likes, their ability to be motivated, their love of reading. So many things in common, and so many things Francesca could no longer share with someone she enjoyed talking to regularly.

When does mourning end, she wondered? How long would it take to not miss someone as much?

Frozen and still, Francesca quietly slunk her body down to the floor, and balled herself up, wrapping her arms around her knees, her forehead on top of them, tears sliding down her legs. She cried. She cried like she hadn't cried since the day he passed away.

But she did it as quietly as she could so her mother wouldn't hear her.

MINOR LEAGUES

My father enjoyed having a game of catch. I acknowledged I was the son he never had. And I never minded that. Of course, he had to throw with his left hand, as he'd lost the use of his right hand in a debilitating accident during his first year of marriage to my mother. At that time, he played in the minor leagues.

It was the off-season, and he was renovating the house they bought together—their first home—when his hand became lodged under heavy machinery. His brother did everything he could to try to dislodge his hand. By the time he was rushed to the hospital, the damage had been done, and his hand could not be salvaged. The official diagnosis was median nerve palsy, or the paralysis of the thenar muscles. My father was never able to properly hold a ball again, and it severely altered his ability to accurately throw a ball because his thumb did not work the way it should. The muscles and tendons had been damaged for good.

He was subsequently released from the team, and my father's dream of playing baseball died that day.

But his spirit didn't die.

A man in his condition who had received that kind of news could have given up entirely on his future. He could have turned to alcohol, sunk into depression, or given up on any hope of a happy life.

Apparently, there was an underlying sadness for a bit, but he managed to carry on. He had no choice. My sister was on her way, and he needed to provide for his family. Instead of wallowing for an inordinate amount of time, he turned his misfortune into a bit of fortune. He took classes at the local college and became the apprentice to an insurance man who was about to retire and sell his business. My father persevered.

He was a contributor to his community, participated in town events, and everyone knew of his undying affinity for the Blackbirds. His life had been a rich one, despite that his was cut much too short.

I never knew anyone like my father. At his memorial service, others said the same.

Our relationship was always full of love, which is why it hurt so much to say goodbye.

There are some things that will break a heart, consistently, for an unspecified and unknowable length of time.

Eight

"Honestly, this is quite an honor. I'm touched to the very core. It's surprises like these that make life interesting—and rewarding."
~Zeke Watson, Blackbirds Hall of Famer

It was fortunate that the sports banquet took place while Francesca was on winter break, otherwise Sam would have forced her to take her as her date, even though Joe Clarkson was not scheduled to attend. Fortunate still was the fact that Sam lived on Long Island and just received over twenty inches of snow, which kept her in New York. Sam wouldn't have expected an invitation on account of the treacherous, winter weather. Francesca, always striving to keep things professional, worried that Sam might embarrass her with her boisterous and flirtatious personality.

Therefore, the lucky recipient of the second ticket fell into the hands of Francesca's mother. She saw the tickets sitting on the counter next to Francesca's purse.

"Francesca, there are some tickets here, along with your purse, and I need to clean the counter so I can finish making dinner," she shouted as Francesca concentrated on *Jeopardy*. It was the one show she and her mother made an effort to watch together.

"Who is Dick Clark?" Francesca called from the family room.

"What was the question?" her mother asked.

"Who was the host of American Bandstand?"

"Such an easy one," her mother said, rolling her eyes. "I hope it was for one-hundred."

Francesca got up off the couch and strolled into the kitchen. Commercial break.

"What are those tickets for? A concert?"

"No," Francesca said. "A sports banquet. I know how much you love sports."

"It's not that I don't like sports, I do…I did."

"When?" Francesca asked incredulously.

"When I was younger."

"Before Dad?"

"Yes, and with Dad. But, as you know, it was Dad who had the love affair with baseball."

Her mother paused, and her eyes started to water, but Francesca wasn't concerned. She was peeling an onion.

"And what did you have a love affair with besides Dad?" Francesca asked.

"My girls," her mother said.

Francesca smiled.

"What?" her mother said.

"I don't know, Mom, you're just funny sometimes."

Her mother shook her head. She diced a few tomatoes and threw them onto the salad, their grilled cheese sandwiches already on the griddle, but needing to be flipped. Francesca grabbed the tongs and turned them over. It was their favorite Thursday night girls' meal. Salad and sandwich. And *Jeopardy*.

Francesca set the dishes on the table, placed the napkin and fork down and poured them each a glass of Ginger Ale. Francesca sat down, her mother beside her. From their vantage point, they could see the television.

"So, who are you taking with you to the banquet? A date?"

"Would you like to be my date?" she asked.

Her mother looked surprised at first; she cocked her head and furrowed her brow. She even pursed her lips, something she did when she was thinking deeply about something.

"When is it?" she asked.

"Next Friday."

She took her fork and punched it deeply into her salad, took a bite, and crunched on the lettuce and the crouton. *Jeopardy* had come back on. It was time for the Daily Double.

"Count me in," she mumbled out of the side of her mouth, her mouth full, and her eyes dancing with glee. "Sounds like fun."

They were at a boutique her mother had read about in the newspaper on the outskirts of the city that carried dressy clothes for more formal occasions. The banquet was in a hotel in Bay City near the harbor, and the honorees were required to wear tuxedos or ball gowns. They decided to treat themselves to new cocktail dresses. Moreover, Francesca was pleasantly surprised that her mother had agreed to attend in the first place, with no arm-twisting.

It was a Saturday, and they spent the morning at the boutique, each of them trying on over fifteen dresses, until they each decided on that special one. Her mother's dress was a midnight blue A-line cut, with thicker straps, a tight bodice, and beautiful detail around the bustline. The dress looked terrific on her, and Francesca could see a little sparkle in her eye. She spun around a couple of times, and she caught her mother looking at herself from all angles. Francesca's elegant black crepe ruffle dress came to just above the knee, and had a V-neck and a satin black ribbon belt that could be tied in a bow.

After they made their purchases, they walked down a couple of blocks in the freezing cold, scarves around our necks and faces, the wind whipping, the temperature so cold it hurt your face. Angel's Café sat near the water, and the water was still and glassy; it looked as if parts of it were starting to freeze.

They each ordered a crock of French Onion soup. They sat and talked. Francesca told her about Sam and her odd obsession with Joe Clarkson. She also told her about Isabelle and her boyfriend, and how she was nervous to meet his parents. The discussion then rolled into Francesca telling her about her studies, grades, and professors. Her mother nodded and listened. She offered feedback. She told her a story about how, once when she was in college, she had slept through an exam and completely missed it. She told her how she regretted not finishing college, having left after her junior year, and that even at her age, she still considered going back to finish what she started.

They talked for nearly two hours during that particular lunch—rare, candid moments being exchanged between mother and daughter. As it was all unfolding, Francesca realized something noteworthy that had been happening right before her eyes: she and her mother were becoming friends.

"Sit here," Isabelle said, holding out chairs for both Francesca and her mother. She introduced them to her boyfriend, Rob, and they all sat down at the table with others from the front office. The banquet room was loud, upbeat, pounding music playing in the background. Francesca and her mother had found their way to the hotel without a glitch. They hung their coats on the rack in the lobby, and were escorted by one of the student ambassadors to their table. They were wearing their new dresses, and spent over an hour getting ready for their night at the banquet.

The room looked beautiful for a sports banquet. There were very grand centerpieces on the tables designed accordingly around the theme of baseball. Each table boasted a huge, glass vase, with pennants and baseballs on sticks jutting out of them, with glitter and white lights strewn around the bottom. The head table seated fourteen, as the banquet honored both outstanding student and professional baseball and softball athletes from the state. As Francesca looked over the program, she noticed there were two college athletes selected (one male and one female), six high school athletes, two minor league athletes, two major league athletes, the emcee of the event, and an award for manager of the year. They were all hoping it would be Kevin Desmond.

As people milled, shook hands, and laughed and talked, the energy and excitement folks were feeling about the upcoming season were contagious. Even Francesca's mother began chatting about how well the Blackbirds season went, and how she was excited to see how the team play would play this year.

Just as Francesca's mother finished her sentence, Zeke Watson extended his hand to hers, gave her a quick smile, and said, "Is it okay if I take this seat?"

Francesca's mother became unusually flustered.

"By all means," she said, as she shook his hand.

"Zeke, this is my mother," Francesca said, as their hands were touching.

"Can't be," Zeke said. "This woman is far too young to be your mother."

"I'm afraid it's true," her mother said.

"Well, I hate to tell you this, but your daughter—according to Isabelle, and I've now seen it for myself in person—can crack a mean crab." And then leaning into to Francesca as an aside, he whispered,

"Did I say that right?"

"Yes, you did," Francesca said.

Alan Ford, the event's emcee and the play-by-play announcer for Blackbirds Radio, took his place back at the microphone after Kevin Desmond, the Blackbirds manager finished his speech. After much media speculation, he received the Manager of the Year award for his amazing season with the Blackbirds, and graciously accepted it.

"Congratulations, Kevin," Alan said as the applause winded down. "As most of you know, that is typically our last award of the night. However, we've decided to add one final award to the program, and the best part is, the recipient is not sitting here at the head table, and has no idea he is receiving something this evening. We decided to catch him totally off guard.

"You see, players can play sports, and they can do it well. They can have outstanding careers, set records, and make fans for life. But how does one truly make fans and retain fans well after his career is over? I'll tell you—it's by connecting to the community. It's because one cares about the community enough to get out there, make appearances, start his own foundation, build and rehab fields, and get kids to stay in school, while at the same time, encourage them to play ball.

"Tonight's recipient has done just that. He's created his own foundation, which he runs daily. With his team of six full-time administrators, he keeps very busy. He's in constant contact with the Community Relations department at the Blackbirds, and works in conjunction with the department on projects. He rarely sits still because he's in constant motion—visiting schools and civic groups, getting his hands dirty by rehabbing fields in the inner cities, and even recently, helping to reconstruct a dugout at a local school.

"For all of his tireless efforts, for what he's been committed to doing since he retired seven years ago, tonight, we present the very first award for Outstanding Commitment to the Community to our very own Hall of Famer, Blackbirds former first baseman, Zeke Watson."

Zeke rose from the table, clearly surprised by the acknowledgement of such an award. Every person in the room stood and applauded. He made his way from the table, through the crowd of almost six hundred people, up to the stage, where he shook the hand of Alan Ford, whispered something in his ear, and then smiled at the audience. As the audience's applause began to wane, Zeke looked toward his table and gave Isabelle a thumb's up. Alan Ford spoke again.

"Zeke obviously has no prepared speech as we've completely blind sided him with this honor, but if he'd like to say a few words. Zeke..."

Alan stepped away, and Zeke stepped closer to the microphone.

"Thank you so much for this recognition. Honestly, this is quite an honor. I'm touched to the very core. Surprises like these make life interesting—and rewarding. You know, I've been a part of the Blackbirds organization for years. I came from Milwaukee to the Blackbirds during my third year, and I never looked back. Bay City embraced me, and in turn, I embraced this city. It's my home. I can never imagine living or immersing myself in any other place. The fans are so supportive, they love their team, and they honestly just want to come out to Blackbirds Park to watch some good ball. I'd also be remiss if I didn't acknowledge the fine works of those at my table over there—Isabelle Drake and the entire Blackbirds Community Relations department. Those people work tirelessly to keep fans happy, and the organization wouldn't be the same without them."

Francesca watched Isabelle smile as the audience applauded, and she received an acknowledgement for her all of her department's hard work.

Francesca's mom was beaming almost as much as Isabelle. She

reached over and patted Francesca ever so gently on the leg.

"Thank you so much for the honor, everyone. I'll look forward to seeing you at the ballpark or around Bay City. Enjoy the rest of your night," Zeke said, clearly choked up. The audience stood again, clapped, and Alan thanked everyone once again for attending the banquet.

The house lights became a little brighter, and some people stood up, tired from sitting, stretched, and gathered their belongs. Others made their way over toward Zeke to shake his hand and congratulate him.

Zeke left his jacket on the back of the chair at the table, and Francesca made her way over to him, jacket in hand, to make sure he didn't leave without it. He thanked her and gave her a big hug.

"Congratulations, Zeke," Francesca said.

"This is for all of us," he replied, and gave her a big hug.

On the drive home, Francesca's mother was chatty. She talked about the food and how it wasn't too bad for a large function. They made fun of the "rubber chicken" with the sliced carrots on the side and the heaping pile of mashed potatoes that accompanied it on the plate.

"Why do you call it 'rubber chicken?'" Francesca asked.

"That's what we always call typical banquet food."

"But it didn't really taste like rubber."

"No, darling, it didn't. It wasn't bad."

"But I mean, it wasn't rubbery at all, so why did you call it that?"

"I don't know…it just came to my mind."

"So you didn't have fun?" Francesca teased.

"No! I had a great time. It was a nice night out."

"Even if you don't love baseball?"

Her mother looked at her for a split second from the wheel.

"Yes, even if you don't love baseball. But I think I just might give it another chance."

"You? Give baseball another chance? Who are you and what have you done with my mother?"

"Very funny, Francesca."

"This doesn't have anything to do with Zeke Watson telling you looked pretty tonight, does it?"

"Francesca! What a thing to say!"

"I just mean, didn't it make you feel good to have someone tell you that?"

She was quiet behind the wheel for a few moments, the sound of the wheels of the car on the asphalt road filling the void of the silence.

"It was nice, but remember, he told you that you looked pretty too."

It was true. He had told Francesca she looked nice. And Isabelle. But that was Zeke's way. He was nice to everyone.

"I had a nice time. Thanks for taking me with you, Baseball Girl."

Now it was Francesca's turn to be silent. Those words hadn't been spoken to her since her father was alive. *Come on, Baseball Girl, let's get to the ballpark*, her father would say, as her mother would tell him to stop calling her that. *She's a girl, Archie. She doesn't need to eat, sleep, and drink baseball all the time*, her mother would reply.

Francesca remembered their exchange word for word, as it happened regularly with every game they would attend. And now, things were off-balance. Her mother now had the sole responsibility of parenting. How lost her mother must feel having to do it on her own when she and her father had always been a team. Francesca realized her mother was probably clinging to lost ideals and situations, as she struggled to keep the memory of her husband alive. For Francesca's sake.

At that moment, Francesca understood what she was attempting to do.

And now her mother was using his words.

STRIKE OUT

Little Dave Unger used to come and knock on my door to play ball. He knew I loved baseball as much as he did, and he didn't mind that I was a girl. He'd show me his trading cards and his pennant collection, and sometimes, if he went to the game and got an autograph from a player, he would get one for me too. He was a good friend.

That was until I struck him out during the neighborhood kids' game on July Fourth. All the families in the neighborhood got together at our local park for an elaborate picnic, replete with baseball, hot dogs, apple pie, and illegal fireworks. It had become tradition that there would be a game for kids, with an adult game to follow.

Somehow, I got talked into pitching an inning.

I didn't know why, because I wasn't a stellar pitcher. I was more comfortable playing outfield. I could run pretty fast for a girl, and had better than average agility. I could anticipate where the ball would go, and get there to make the catch. Pitching, on the other hand, was just unnerving. I always believed the toughest job on the field was that of the pitcher. It was constant stress, and it required consistency, something I wasn't typically good at achieving. Throw the ball over the plate, I would tell myself. Focus and pitch. It's not that hard.

But it was. Pitching was hard. It was tough work.

Little Dave Unger came up to the plate. I thought it was ironic that people put "Little" in front of his name, because Dave was anything but little. He was a big kid, the biggest on his team, and definitely one of the largest sixth-graders in school.

Little Dave Unger stepped into the batter's box. I pitched to him.

Strike one. Looking.

I pitched again.

Ball one.

I pitched again.

Strike two. Swinging.

I pitched again.

Strike three. Looking.

Little Dave Unger threw his bat down and marched off into his team's dugout, making the last out of the inning.

He never talked to me after that.

When my father asked why Little Dave didn't come around any-more, I told him I thought it was because I struck him out in the game.

My father told me not to worry, that boys don't like to be shown up by girls, and that it takes a big man not to let it bother him.

"You were just doing your job," my father said to me when I couldn't understand how someone would dismiss me because of something so trivial. "People hold grudges all the time, Frankie. You're right. You had a job to do, and you had to do it the best you could. Don't ever sacrifice your own integrity, talent, or brains to make someone else look better. You just have to be who you are, and if a boy—or anyone—can't deal with that, then he probably isn't the type of person you want in your life anyway."

Nine

"What you're seeing is a little competition among the boys.
They're out there fighting for a spot on the team,
and it's only a 25-man roster. "
~ Freddie "The Fly" Montrose, Blackbirds Bench Coach

Francesca was tapping her pen on the yellow pad as she talked on the telephone with Isabelle. They remained close, even though Isabelle lived in New York and worked for a rival team. Several years ago, she was offered a promotion to move, and she thought it was the best time to do it. Additionally, her boyfriend—who became her husband—had an opportunity to work with a law firm in Manhattan, so they decided to move to The Big Apple to give it a chance. They were enjoying it and didn't have any plans to move back anytime soon.

Isabelle left the Blackbirds just before the team moved into its new home in the heart of downtown Bay City. The new ballpark boasted state-of-the-art amenities with an old-time feel that the city, in conjunction with the team, built for mere millions and millions of dollars. Blackbirds fans were thrilled with their new baseball home. Francesca was responsible for holding two open house dates to get fan feedback on some of the new amenities and seating. The fans were involved, and the turn out was tremendous. Now that they were at their new site, the front office employees no longer had to worry that home plate was haunted by deceased players of the past or that they would become trapped in the upper deck storage room. Everything was new and classic and welcoming. There was a fountain near the entrance; historic old-time touches abounded above archways and on the seats; the outfield was greener than any Francesca had seen before; the scoreboard was sharp and big, and the old-time scoreboard operating machine that resembled an extremely large typewriter with pink ticker tape was gone, replaced instead by flashy electronics that took weeks for the stadium productions team to learn. They were on a high for months as they became accustomed to their state-of-the-art surroundings, and the new park resembled a combination of traditional baseball blended with innovative touches. Blackbirds Park felt like a new home, and Old Blackbirds Park went down in history.

The two women were chatting and comparing notes about their respective jobs over the telephone, Francesca with hers on speaker, her door closed. She valued Isabelle's opinion so greatly, and loved the suggestions she would offer; she was the mentor who taught her everything about working in baseball. "So, how many appearances are your guys making this year?" Francesca asked.

"Somewhere in the neighborhood of two-hundred and fifty," Isabelle responded. "Are you trying to match our numbers?"

"I'm working on it," Francesca said.

"Well, let's hope you have better luck than I had when I was there. If it weren't for Zeke and The Fly, my numbers would have been lousy. Yours seem great, and I'm so glad my protégé has done well for herself and with the department. I'm also glad you've had better luck than I had with Clarkson. He doesn't seem to mind getting out there for you," she said.

"Sure, but he's older now—and I don't let him get away with much."

"Good for you for making one of your star players get out there and work for the community! I'm proud of you," she said. Isabelle and Joe Clarkson didn't always see eye-to-eye.

It was Francesca's sixth season as a full-time employee with the ballclub, and her fourth as the director of community relations. When Isabelle decided to leave four years ago, the club offered her Isabelle's position. She worked hard under her direction as an assistant director for two years and had attempted to make a name for herself. Each day Francesca spent working for the Blackbirds endeared her even more to the club, and she never wanted to leave.

The hours were nonsensical to those who did not work in sports: in season, when the Blackbirds played eighty-one home games, Francesca worked each one of them, often late into the night and through the weekends. When the team played two consecutive weekends, she worked twenty-one days straight. She worked from nine in the morning until seven or eight o'clock at night. She froze doing her community work in the cold April months when the winds whipped in from the water before summer arrived, and then again, when the city became cooler in the fall. On one particular Opening Day, it even snowed.

The commitment to the job didn't leave much room for romance, or even for a date, for that matter. But Francesca did have time to flirt with Joe Clarkson. Innocently flirting with him had been something she engaged in over the last several years. And then, without warning, the winds blew in from a different direction and everything changed.

"I'm only going to do that appearance if you come with me," he said.

"I can't, Joe. I have to be in the office that day."

"I'm only going to do it if you come. That's it."

Francesca was asking him to attend a dinner banquet at one of the newspapers that covered the Blackbirds, but it was being held an hour north of the ballpark, and he didn't want to go alone. He was willing to attend, but he was insisting that Francesca go with him.

"Come on," he said. "You never attend these things with me. You always send the assistants."

"Well," Francesca said, "that's what they get paid to do. Plus, I attend three times as many dinners and functions as you do."

"I know, but I want you to come," he said playfully, but sounding childish. For some reason, Francesca didn't say no.

"Ok," she said, "I'm only doing this because you're so willing to attend, and they've specifically asked for you to be there."

"Right. I'm going and you're going. Shouldn't I get a gold star for that?"

Francesca opened her desk drawer. In part, he was mocking her. He knew she had gold star stickers in there, because she often starred the important dates on the players' guest appearance itineraries. She knew it seemed elementary, and that it was corny, but it got the players to pay attention.

"Come here," Francesca said. Clarkson walked toward her. She placed the gold star sticker on his Nike sweatshirt. "Thank you," she said.

"Meet you here Thursday at four," he said. "I'll drive."

"Dan Sturgis is on line two," Francesca's assistant called to her from her cubicle.

"Hey," she said. "What took you so long to call me back? I was afraid you weren't interested."

"Are you kidding? I was on vacation—just got back. I'm so excited to speak with you."

"Good," Francesca said. "Can we meet for coffee at noon?"

"Sure. Where?"

"Tommy's Bagels. And don't be late."

"See you then," he said.

Francesca was thrilled. It was turning out to be a great day. After she made a few phone calls, scheduled a handful of players for an upcoming instructional clinic, and attended a brief meeting with the team's public relations director, David, she walked the eight blocks to Tommy's Bagels, her favorite spot for a coffee and little lunch. It was a partly cloudy day, but the sun was peeking through now and then, which was helpful because the thermometer read twenty-two degrees. It was frigid, actually. Francesca didn't mind walking in the city and getting some fresh air, even if it meant feeling her lips go numb and crack. That was why she always carried Chapstick.

Dan and Francesca had kept in touch, and when her assistant director decided to leave her post and move to Florida to pursue graduate school, Dan was the first person she called. She wanted to see if he was interested in helping her run the department. He was employed, but he wasn't passionate about it and was still searching for that perfect opportunity.

He was already there when Francesca arrived, and was dressed in a suit. His dark hair was slicked back, and he was wearing glasses with a dark frame. Always cleanly shaven, Francesca could smell his cologne as soon as she approached him, though her senses could not detect exactly what scent he was wearing. She rarely saw Dan in a suit, but she deduced that he probably wanted to be as professionally dressed as possible because he knew she was going to interview him. She already talked to the vice-president and human resources director, and they were in support of hiring Dan, especially since he worked for the ballclub for two full years and many people in the organization already knew him. There was no question he had a leg up on the competition.

Silently, he sat and listened to the duties of the assistant community relations director. He hardly touched his bagel. He was writing on the side, serving as a stringer for community newspapers, and he even occasionally wrote for *The Gazette News*, a large paper on the outskirts of the city. Because Francesca knew he had a side income, though it wasn't much, she figured he might jump at the chance to work for the Blackbirds in a full-time capacity, even though the salary wasn't going to be stellar.

Still he sat. He focused and listened. Dan had been her closest friend—besides Isabelle—at the ballclub. There was no doubt they would work well together.

After Francesca relayed all the details of the job, eating and talking while Dan stared at her, Francesca finally said, "Well? What do you think?"

"I'm afraid to talk. I don't want to curse it."

"Good grief, Dan! Are you still carrying on with your nutty superstitions? You're not going to go on and on about Joe Emerson's ghost, are you?" she teased. "You wouldn't dare curse it. Do you want the job or not? Besides, we're at the new park. The ghosts have mysteriously vanished."

"Look," he said, "I'm in my suit hoping you'll tell me to come to the office right now and get started and fill out human resources paperwork. Yes, I'm in. I couldn't be more appreciative or happy," he said.

He smiled at Francesca, and looked at his bagel. Then, he finally took a bite of it.

On Thursday, Francesca left work a little early to go home and dress for the banquet. She was living in a two-bedroom apartment, the one she shared with Sam for the past several years. Sam decided to follow her boyfriend to Los Angeles to see if they were meant to be. Since he was her third boyfriend in the span of a year, Francesca thought the odds were that Sam would return within six months. However, the six-month mark passed, and she managed to stay with him, despite his inconsistent schedule as a cameraman and filmmaker. Sam found work casting extras for television shows and was loving it. Meanwhile, Francesca was able to manage the rent payments on her own, turned the second bedroom into a cozy office, and was only fifteen minutes from her mother.

Francesca wore a plain black, but elegant cocktail dress to the event—a newspaper banquet and gala benefit for *The Gazette News*. The newspaper had booked one of the swankiest hotels for the event an hour outside of Bay City. Big supporters of the Blackbirds, it was only right that the team sponsored two tables in support of the fundraiser.

She was able to fill the two tables with front office personnel, but Francesca needed a player to join them, which was why she asked Joe to be there. He was one of only four on the current roster who actually lived in town during the off-season, because he had relocated when he signed. She had asked two other ballplayers first prior to asking Joe, but *The Gazette News* wanted Clarkson to be there. The fact that he agreed to attend helped the newspaper sell out the event.

When Francesca and Joe arrived and walked through the door into the great ballroom, people recognized Joe Clarkson right away. They drove up together, listening to his collection of music as they spent the hour in the car together. He was an eclectic guy, and Francesca was amazed at his knowledge of the arts. One of his best friends starred on Broadway—a woman he'd grown up with—and she seemed to have opened his eyes to the plethora of musical tastes from the theatre. He was playing everything from "Phantom of the Opera" to a selection from Miles Davis, and then he surprised her with some classic Rolling Stones. Her ears were still ringing when they walked in the door.

There was an ease of manner to Joe Clarkson. He moved with grace, light as a feather, patting people on the back, snuggling up for photos, and enamoring fans with those famous Clarkson pearly whites. *The Gazette News* was taking every opportunity to snap photos with all kinds of sponsors, advertisers, and fans, and Clarkson's big, broad smile never tired as he shook hands and signed autographs. Francesca faded into the background, making her way over to the bar to get a drink. She felt dehydrated because she was in meetings all day and didn't take the time to take care for herself at all.

"Francesca Milli," she heard a voice say over her shoulder as she was reaching for the glass of water.

She turned to look at a man who looked vaguely familiar. Vaguely.

"Hi," she said. He was extending his hand, so she switched her water glass to the left to shake properly with the right. It was a warm and sturdy handshake. He had piercing green eyes that were big and wide, and a soothing voice that was pleasant to the ears.

"You don't recognize me?" he said. "We accidentally met several years ago."

"You look familiar."

"Jack Thompson," he said. "I'm a sports writer. My first full-time writing job was in Chicago, but now I cover the Blackbirds with *The Gazette News*. But only for a few more weeks—I'm taking over Tom Doland's job at *The Chronicle* in a month."

She scratched her head unapologetically, and shook it quizzically. He further elaborated on their connection.

"Many years ago, you knocked over all my press notes in the hallway at Old Blackbirds Park on my first day as a sports reporter for the opposition during that whirlwind year when the Blackbirds almost made it to postseason."

"Wow!" she said. "That was you? Your hair was a lot longer then!"

"I'm afraid so," he said.

"You're probably still waiting for an apology from me, I would guess. You probably etched my name into your memory knowing someday you'd seek your revenge. Do you plan on tossing a drink in my face to even things up?"

"How did you know?" he said. They both looked at each other for a moment, smirking.

"Jack Thompson," she said, "I'm sorry I scattered your press notes and newspapers all over the hallway at Blackbirds Park years ago when I was in a rush to avoid being late for my shift. Please forgive me," she said with a big smile.

"Interesting…" he said.

"What?"

"You're not at all how I thought you'd be."

"Oh no? What's that? My reputation precedes me?"

"The ballplayers call you a tough-ass."

"I take that as high praise."

"You should. They did say you were pretty witty, too."

"Mr. Thompson," Francesca said, "you barely know me."

"But I will now. I'll practically be living at your ballpark."

"Then I hope we will become excellent friends," Francesca said.

Joe Clarkson spotted Francesca from across the room, waved, and started to make his way over.

Jack turned to her, and once again extended his hand. She stuck hers out for a parting handshake, but then he turned it over, curled it beneath his, brought it up to his lips, and kissed it.

"Nice to finally meet you, tough-ass," he said.

"The pleasure was mine, I think."

Jack walked away in the other direction, where a bald man waited and put his arm around him and led him toward the front of the room.

"What were you talking to Dash about?" Joe asked her after he'd freed himself from a slew of folks who grabbed him at their table, Number 2, right in front of the head table.

"Who's Dash?" Francesca asked.

"Dash Thompson, the reporter."

"You mean Jack Thompson."

"His name's Dash. Where have you been, Frankie?"

Even though Joe called her Frankie pretty regularly, she still hadn't become accustomed to it coming from his lips, even after all these years. And every time he said her name, she couldn't help but think of her father.

She picked up one of the tall, thin breadsticks on the table and took a bite. She looked at Clarkson incredulously.

"The guy's name is Jack. Jack Thompson," she said again.

"I've only ever heard him called Dash. It's his nickname I guess. Not sure why."

"Who the hell knows," Francesca said, becoming worn out from the discussion of a mysterious nickname.

The program started. Francesca looked at her watch. It was going to be a long night. She was tired. She was putting in long hours lately, and she wasn't feeling quite right. She started to yawn, and Clarkson, seeing her yawn, gave her a kick under the table. Wake up, he mouthed to her. She laughed. That was rich coming from him. The ballplayer teaches the professional director some etiquette. It would have been a funny story. Maybe she should have pitched it to Jack—Dash—whatever the hell his name was.

Out of the corner of her eye, she felt someone staring at her. Francesca looked around the room, but couldn't pinpoint the source of the vibe she was feeling.

As the night wore on, all she wanted was to be in her bed. While the banquet surely had a lot of heavy hitters in attendance—corporate executives, entrepreneurs, politicians, and sports figures—she wasn't feeling well enough to be in the mood for it.

Caffeine, she thought. That's what I need. And air.

She excused herself from the table, and slinked over to the bar, where the svelte bartender wearing a tuxedo with perfect posture poured her a Coca-Cola with little ice. Since she was near the door, she took a moment to leave the warm and claustrophobic ballroom in favor of the cooler lobby with vaulted ceilings.

Since the death of her father, she suffered from panic attacks. She knew what they were, and once she understood them, she became accustomed to handling them. Most of them. She could never quite predict when or where she would have one. For no reason at all, she'd be driving along in her car, heavy thoughts weighing on her mind, and she'd find herself unable to breathe. Her hands would tingle, and she'd gasp for air. Several times she had to pull over on the shoulder so she could walk around the car and feel the breeze on her face.

Francesca started feeling that way at the table.

Although the ballroom doors were closed, she could hear the emcee's voice reverberating off the walls as he introduced the next speaker; she wondered if Joe were wondering what happened to her. She sat in the middle of the lavish lobby on the baroque chair, staring at the gargantuan crystal chandelier that hung from the ceiling. She was fanning herself with the program she shoved into her purse, nursing her Coca-Cola.

Those bouts of panic would occur in the middle of the night sometimes. She'd wake up thinking she was having a heart attack. Twice she had to get Sam up because she was freaking out so much, but Sam helped calm her down. Sam read up on how to handle and cope with them, and she was good to her. She was her saving grace right after her father passed away. Francesca kept the attacks a secret from her mother because she didn't want to worry her. Death and heartbreak do leave their marks on the living.

"Are you okay, Francesca?" the reporter was asking her. She knew she was coming out of the attack because she smirked a little at the thought of not knowing what name to call him.

"Yes," she said, not wanting to lie. "I just needed a little air."

The large doors swung open again, and Joe was heading toward them.

"What's going on, Frankie?" Joe asked. "Are you okay?"

The reporter looked at them, first at her, and then at Joe. "Is she okay, Dash?"

"She looks pale to me," the reporter said.

She stood up, wobbling slightly, and put her hands up, one palm in front of each man's face motioning "stop."

"Now wait just a minute you two. Why are you talking about me as if I'm not here?"

They looked at each other. She brought her hands down and bent to grab her purse.

"Is this event just about over, Joe? Because I think I need to go home," she said.

"I can take you home now," he said.

Clarkson grabbed her underneath the elbow, and started to escort her out the door. She turned to see if the reporter was still watching.

"See you at the ballpark, Jack," Francesca called to him.

The drive home seemed interminable. And every time Joe hit a bump or the car hugged a curve, she felt as if she could vomit. She didn't say those words out loud, though. Instead, Francesca just suffered in silence, and every time he asked if she was okay she said she was.

They met at the ballpark earlier, so Clarkson had to drop her back at her car. She had a new one now, not the jalopy she used to drive in those early days with the club. She owned a shiny, black Honda Civic with a moon roof. Things were much better in the car department.

He walked around to her side of the car to open the door for her. She was surprised by his good manners, though Francesca didn't know why she expected that he wouldn't have great manners. He knew how to treat women. The players loved the ladies—and the ladies loved them. Groupies found them in every city, and the women would be lined up and ready for the taking. Sometimes Francesca quietly wondered how many women Joe had actually slept with when she could count her own measly lot on one hand. Hers had all been dalliances she had in college, and one mad, crazy, first love she had in high school. As she was approaching thirty, she tried not to broadcast anything about her love life, let alone its near non-existent state. People probably already wondered what was wrong with her.

"You're okay?" he said, as he helped guide her out of the car.

"Yes, fine," Francesca said. "I think I just might be suffering from exhaustion compounded by dehydration. I may need to actually take a day off and watch soap operas or something. In the six years I've worked here, I think I've only taken one sick day."

"You're due then," he said. "Thanks for coming with me."

"Thank you for going," she said.

The words had hardly escaped her mouth when Francesca felt his warm lips descend upon hers. Joe Clarkson was kissing her.

"Holy crap," she said, as she stepped back and pulled away from him. "What the heck?"

He looked like a wounded animal. His eyes grew wide, as he was obviously surprised by her reaction.

"I just felt—"

"No," she said. "No feelings. We are professionals working together."

"Honestly?" he said. "You felt nothing? Because I sort of think you did."

The truth was, she didn't know how she felt, except sick. She did her best never to allow herself to feel emotion or get too involved with any one guy. That was the deal she made with herself. It hurts less if you don't allow yourself to feel anything.

"Oh, my gosh," she said, throwing her hands up in the air. "This is crazy. Crazy!"

She opened her car door and climbed into the driver's seat. She needed to get away.

"I'll talk to you later," Francesca said.

"Yes, you will," he said.

She hit the gas pedal and found herself exiting the ballpark, her heart racing more than double the posted speed limit.

Ten

"Baseball is love. It's tough to top it."
~Joe Emerson, Blackbirds player, b. 1918-d. 1948

Francesca never did throw up, but she was snuggled under the covers of her cozy bed, the down comforter keeping her toasty warm. She slept. She slept until ten, and only was awake for about fifteen minutes when she called in sick, and continued to sleep. She woke up around one, and decided to make herself some soup.

The doorbell rang.

She looked through the peephole, and found herself opening the door.

"What on earth?"

"I had a feeling you weren't yourself last night. Brought you some bagels with honey, two containers of soup from Tommy's, some Ginger Ale, and these. Think this might help?"

He handed over a dozen yellow roses.

"Thanks, Joe. As you can see, I'm still in my pajamas. How did you know where I lived?"

"What? You don't think we can find out anything we need to know? We're ballplayers. People give us information willingly when we ask for it."

She didn't know what to do; she invited him inside.

He took the bags that he gave her back and found his way to

her small kitchen. Even though her place wasn't exactly the penthouse, it was cute. She spent some time decorating it, so it was comfortable and bright. The galley kitchen was not large, but it had new appliances, new counter tops, and a nice bay window by her table.

"I'll be right back," Francesca said, as he put the goodies on her counter.

She closed the door to her bedroom and changed out of her plaid flannel nightgown into sweats, a bra, and a long-sleeved tee. She brushed her teeth and put her hair in a pony-tail. She slipped her feet into some fuzzy moccasins and even went so far as to pinch her cheeks in the mirror and apply some Chapstick. What was she doing? What on earth was she doing?

When she returned to the kitchen, Joe was leaning up against the cabinets, his sturdy, strong frame dwarfing the sink behind him.

"Sit in the chair," he said. "I'll warm this up."

What the hell just happened over the last twenty-four hours? What in the world was he doing in her apartment making her lunch—bringing her lunch and flowers and looking after her, for that matter? Something was wrong. Something was seriously wrong with this picture.

He sat down across from her and looked Francesca in the eyes. Then he reached for both of her hands and held them on top of the table. His hands were large and coarse. Manly and sexy.

"I know what's going on. You have a professional reputation you need to uphold, and you're worried that if you're with a ballplayer on your team, it could affect your status. I get it."

She was dumbfounded. She couldn't say anything, especially since her head felt heavy, and her stomach was still doing the same flip-flops it was doing the night before.

"And," he continued, "you're afraid—afraid to get into something with me. We could have a good thing here. Can't you see it? We've been flirts and have bantered about for years. Last night, I just thought I'd do something about it, so I made the first move, but you shot me down."

"I didn't shoot you down."

"Yes. You did," he said.

"Okay, maybe a little. But I didn't know—"

He cut her off. "Maybe don't say anything, and just give it a try."

Francesca felt her anxiety start to rear its ugly head again. She heard Isabelle's words invading and haunting her brain. *Don't date players. Don't date players. Don't get emotionally tied up with them. You have a job to do.*

He stood and took the bowl of soup out of the microwave, opened the drawer, found a spoon, and brought it over to her at the table. There was that ease again. There was his effortless style moving around her kitchen. Why did she find a man in command of the kitchen appealing? Clearly there was something wrong with her head, and she wasn't sure she could blame it on the virus or exhaustion.

"Eat up," he said. "I don't like seeing you this way."

"This is nuts, you know," she said.

"Maybe, Frankie. But I think I've always been nuts about you."

Against her better judgment, and forsaking the potential for getting hurt, Francesca agreed to date Joe after the illness passed. However, she did have a condition: to keep it quiet. He agreed, knowing she needed it that way to gain his trust and to protect her professional reputation. There was no need for anyone to know. Truthfully, she didn't want anyone to know.

When Sam called from California to check on Francesca one

night to see what was new, she couldn't bring herself to fully divulge what was going on with Joe. Sam would think Francesca was a hypocrite, and she couldn't bear to hear Sam repeat back to her the words she had said in her earlier days about not dating players. Sam would be relentless about it. She would taunt Francesca no end.

On Francesca and Joe's third date, the first being dinner and a movie, and the second, dinner and a jazz club on the east side, he told her they were going someplace special. Francesca had no idea what he arranged or what he was up to, but her curiosity was definitely piqued. Joe picked her up promptly at six-thirty on a Saturday evening. Spring training was just four weeks away, and she knew she wouldn't see him for a while. Part of Francesca's job was to spend one weekend at spring training, executing media training with the rookies and newcomers, and then offering an overview of what community relations—and the ballclub—expected from the players. Francesca was accustomed to presenting the overview, and looked forward to meeting some of the new players. The club served them lunch, so they were happily fed while she went over their responsibilities as members of the baseball community.

Francesca did have the good sense to ask Joe what to wear for their date, and he told her simply to wear a nice dress. When he came to the door, he was wearing a full suit; he was impeccably dressed and he dazzled her with compliments while Francesca noticed only his smoldering eyes. Had she always been attracted to him? Tread carefully, she thought.

He opened her car door, and she got into his expensive Mercedes. It was a different car than the one they had taken to the banquet. This one was even more meticulously kept than the BMW—freshly polished leather and not a spec of dust on the carpet. The night's selection of music began with Frank Sinatra, as Francesca remembered mentioning to him in passing that Sinatra had been her father's favorite. Hearing Ol' Blue Eyes croon evoked such strong memories for Francesca—she could picture him sitting in his leather recliner, book in hand, listening to Sinatra's voice filling the room. The image of him was still fresh all these many years later.

"So, where are we going?"

"Well, let's see. I deduced from being in your apartment while you were sick for only a short time that you are a movie buff. Am I correct?"

"Yes," she said. "How observant."

"And I further deduce from looking at your vast collection of videotapes that you are a lover of the romantic comedy."

"Right again," Francesca said.

"Figure it out," he said. "Guess."

"You are taking me to see a romantic comedy?"

"Correct."

"You are taking me to see a romantic comedy in a suit, and I am in a cocktail dress?"

"Correct," he said again.

"We are going to a romantic comedy premier," she said.

"Oh, so close, Frankie. So close."

She sat and pondered this secret little date and wondered what he had up his sleeve. She enjoyed the fact that he was making a real effort with this relationship.

"I'm not going to guess anymore. I'm befuddled and enjoying it."

"A befuddled woman. I think I like that," Joe said.

He reached over and placed his hand on her thigh. Francesca already kissed him several times, so the gesture came as no surprise, though she was surprised at how much she liked his warm hand on her body. After their second date and after a couple of glasses of champagne at the jazz club, Joe planted a kiss on her when he said good night at the door to her apartment; he told her he had a wonderful time. She let him kiss her then, and she appeared to have enjoyed every moment of it as well. They lingered there in the hallway for a moment, his hands holding her face as he traced the hair along the back of her neck. After several prolonged kisses, his hands dropped into her hands, and he held them lightly as he started to back away, until only their fingertips were touching. Francesca thought he was trying to woo her slowly and not rush her with his gentlemanly behavior. She wasn't complaining.

The car turned the corner, and they pulled up to the old Majestic movie theatre. A valet had been waiting outside for them. "Good evening, Ms. Francesca," he said as he opened her door and helped her out. Then, he walked over to Joe and held the door open for him, took the keys from Joe, and swiftly made his way inside the car to park it. He probably hasn't parked a car this nice in a while, Francesca thought to herself. The exterior marquis was bright and twinkling; the neon colors lit up the night sky. The Majestic was recently gutted and restored back to its original grandeur of the 1920s. As they walked the red carpet into the lobby, Francesca was struck by the rich and stunning shades that made up the interior of the theatre; golds and reds and velvets adorned the walls. She felt as if she stepped into a by-gone era. All she needed were some white elbow-length gloves and a long cigarette to help finish off the entire retro mood.

"Are we the first ones here?" Francesca asked him. Joe smiled.

From behind the ticket booth came a distinguished gentleman, nattily attired. He walked over to the pair, obviously having heard the question Francesca asked Joe.

"My dear, you are the only ones here for tonight. My name is Phillip, and I'll be taking care of you this evening. Might I escort you to your seats?"

Joe took her hand, and they followed Phillip down toward the front, but not too far. He seated them in the two seats set up in the wide aisle with a small table dressed with a white tablecloth and daisies in a vase.

"These are the best seats in the house," he said matter-of-factly. "Your dinner will arrive momentarily. Thank you, Mr. Clarkson."

"Thank you, Phillip."

"Well, well, well," Francesca said, as Phillip made his way back up the aisle. "You seem pretty pleased with yourself. Renting an entire movie theatre for the night. This must have cost you a week's worth of at-bats," she said.

"Whatever it cost, you are worth ever penny of it," he said.

There was classical music playing in the background. Francesca recognized pieces from Beethoven, Mozart, and Debussy. Within minutes, a staff of two caterers made their way down the aisle. They created a little table in the wide aisle with two chairs and a table on wheels that had a spread of dinner on it. Francesca could hardly contain the joy she was feeling, but she had to conceal the emotions. It was never a part of her personality to be effusive where emotions were concerned—at least not to others. Alone in her apartment, she could cry, laugh, and stomp her feet. But with Joe, she smiled and acknowledged there was an odd fluttering taking place in her stomach.

On the menu were the following: shrimp, a salad, light pasta served with chicken saltimbocca on the side, and plenty of wine. It was going to be a challenge to eat at all, let alone make a dent in the overwhelming assortment of food. But they talked and laughed throughout the meal, and the classical music continued to play.

When they were finished, the caterers came back in and asked if they would like dessert now or after the film. They both agreed that they were sufficiently stuffed, and that they would wait for dessert until after the film. They gave them each another glass of wine and they moved into their seats.

"What are we seeing?" Francesca asked him.

"You'll see," he said. "Patience…"

The screen lit up. It lived up to its name. The restoration was a success, and it was majestic. An old *Tom & Jerry* cartoon played, followed by a *Three Stooges* short. Then it was time for the main feature.

As soon as it started rolling, Francesca knew what it was. She mentioned one day over lunch that she recently became a Cary Grant fan, and was looking forward to checking all his films off her list. She had not yet seen *The Philadelphia Story*, and now it was in front of her, larger than life.

She honestly didn't know what to do with herself.

Eleven

"A pitcher makes a bad decision—he throws a fastball when it should've been a breaking ball. The batter hits the crap out of the ball, and it's a homer. That's just baseball. Sometimes you make a smart decision, and other times, you screw it up. That's the damn beauty of the game."
~ Freddie "The Fly" Montrose, Blackbirds Bench Coach

"Bless me father, for I have sinned. It's been a couple of months since my last confession."

"Go ahead, Francesca."

She was kneeling today. It was the only way she could do it properly. This one needed to feel official.

"I was intimate with a man last night," Francesca said. Oh God. Just hearing herself say that was making her feel as if she had seasick legs.

"Okay, now, let's see. Where should we go from here?" He was thinking.

Father John was hilarious. Sometimes it was awkward telling her darkest sins to a man she'd known for years. Three years older than she, they had played together as kids. Since her father's death, they had become particularly close, and Francesca counted him as not only a priest (which comes in very handy to have a priest as a friend and ambassador), but also as a friend. The best part about him was his complete candor and honestly, and he sometimes had no need for words.

Francesca would always be grateful to him for being there for her family after her father's passing; he had administered the sacrament of the anointing of the sick to him the night before he died. On Sunday, Father John arrived just minutes too late, and was not in the room when he passed. He had been at Sunday morning masses, detained with his congregation, but her family was grateful to see him when he arrived shortly thereafter.

The silence was killing Francesca.

"I know. You don't even know what to say, right?" she said. "I don't even know what to say. This is so unlike me. I'm not a wishy-washy woman."

"Do you love him?" Father John asked. He was more contemporary that she gave him credit for sometimes.

"No…I don't know yet. It's too soon, though he is lovable."

"Is it anyone I know?" Father John prodded. This is when their friendship got interesting, when he became curious and wasn't afraid to ask questions. It led to a certain amount of frankness, which invariably helped the relationship, and the breadth of the confession.

"Yes, well, you know of him."

"Ballplayer?" he asked.

"Mmmhmmm," she said.

"Good one?"

"Yes. Could be a Famer."

"Clarkson."

"Yes."

"Were you safe?" he asked.

Sweet Father John. He wanted to know if she had put herself at risk for pregnancy—or disease. Lord only knows.

"Physically safe. Not sure if I am emotionally safe, however."

Francesca heard Father John sigh.

"Smart girl," he said. "Take it slowly, Francesca, but enjoy building a relationship with someone. You are guarded for many reasons, some of which we have already discussed. All I can advise you is, knowing you, to jump in, but jump in slowly; keep one foot firmly planted on the ground. Now, because he's a potential Blackbirds Hall of Famer and the reason they look like contenders again this upcoming season, you can pray the Rosary, and you will be forgiven. Each of us needs all the help Mother Mary can provide."

Francesca made the sign of the cross, and thanked him.

"Go Blackbirds," Father John whispered as she stood to leave. She snickered.

She envied the woman who could jump in with both feet and not have to keep one firmly planted on the ground. How giddy and delighted she must feel, she thought.

Twelve

"You have no choice, really. When you're striving to be good at what you do,
you have to push it, work as hard as you can,
and not take anything for granted."
~ Joe Clarkson, Blackbirds Outfielder

It was two weeks before Clarkson was to leave for spring train-ing. Francesca decided that, after speaking with Father John, she was going to give a little more and welcome the rather whirlwind relation-ship she found herself caught up in of late. This was not an easy thing for her to do; she tended to equate romance with disaster. To finalities and unhappy endings.

She made her mother's recipe for homemade pizza dough and sauce, and she put two in the oven, made healthy salads, purchased some wine, and rented a movie. The table was set, and she looked around the room feeling pleased with herself. She was not the domesticated sort, but it was fun to play the part, at least for one night.

She took a big step and invited Joe over for dinner.

She also spruced up her apartment. She saw a photograph in a magazine and loved the romantic feel of it. To try to replicate it, she bought a new off-white table for her dining area with matching chairs, tossed some French looking pillows on her white sofa, and put pops of red décor around the room—a vase here, candles there, and a birdcage on the mantle of her small fireplace. She replaced her two ugly lamps that had been hand-me-downs from Cissy with two new crystal ones, and the resulting effect was pleasing to Francesca's eye. For the first time, she saw herself as a woman, separate and apart from being a professional woman, but a woman—one who was desirable and who also desired. This was a new development, and an ideal that she had suppressed for years.

It would be uncharacteristic to say she was totally at ease with the notion of that particular concept, but she was working on it. She also made a vow to herself to let things play out. To not hold back. To see where the path leads, and not to expect it to take her somewhere.

In the simplest terms, she decided to go with the flow. She could do it. It just took effort. A conscious effort, like tying your shoes or driving a car.

She dressed casually, and felt comfortable either dressing up or dressing down with him. Joe took her to some fancy places and they dressed up quite a bit over the course of the last four weeks. She felt things becoming more serious. For the evening's dinner, Francesca decided to wear jeans, her tall boots, and a black fitted knit top draped with a scarf her mother had given her for Christmas. She looked at herself in the mirror as she brushed her long, dark hair, applied a little bit of makeup, and waited for Joe to come over. When she caught a glimpse of herself in the full-length mirror, she was pleased with what she saw, and the corners of her mouth turned upwards ever-so-slightly.

Thirteen

"In baseball, as in life, you have to be giving. If a fan asks you for something, and if it's within your power, you have to do it."
~ Joe Clarkson, Blackbirds outfielder

Joe stopped off at the designer florist boutique and grabbed an arrangement of flowers. Then, he headed to the liquor store for a bottle of Faustino I, an elegant vintage wine from the Basque area of Spain. Despite what his teammates and coaches might say about him, he was capable of being a romantic. He had the power to woo a woman.

Back at home in Texas, people used to treat him as a regular guy—just one of the boys—but once he made it to the big leagues, things changed. People expected more of you, whether it was intentional or unintentional. They expected him to be different because he played ball. He often grew tired of the admiration and the fawning. That's why he appreciated Francesca so much.

With her, things were different.

They'd known each other for years now, and he remembered her wearing that ridiculous uniform that first season he met her. He always found her so amenable, clever, and caring. And she was never intimidated or awestruck by his career—that he played ball. She always treated him as a regular guy. It was refreshing and different from many of the silly girls he found himself dating prior to being with her. Even his former high school girlfriend became enamored and mesmerized by his fame and fortune. With Francesca, his career was always matter-of-fact, and he believed she understood him in a way that no one else did.

He placed the wine on the floor of the passenger seat and began the ride to Francesca's apartment.

In all his life, he wasn't sure if he ever felt this way about a woman before.

In all his life, he wasn't sure if he'd ever been this giving before.

Fourteen

"I may not have any Italian blood in me, but right before a big game,
I eat a lot of carbs—preferably a large bowl of spaghetti."
~ *Zeke Watson, Blackbirds Hall of Famer*

"So, let me get this straight. Your mother and father are both of Italian decent and their parents both spoke fluent Italian, but you never learned it?" Joe asked, as they cleared the table. Francesca's dinner was delicious and filling. They continued to talk as they rinsed the dishes and put the leftovers in the refrigerator. Joe filled their wine glasses and they laughed effortlessly, as the mere presence of each other made them giddy.

"No," she said. "I never learned Italian."

"That seems like a crime."

"Really? Why do you say that?"

Francesca was egging him on, teasing him, as they made their way to the sofa. They clinked glasses, and the whole place smelled of pizza, as the aroma lingered in the air. She lit a candle, the one that smelled of butterscotch, and she admired the red roses he gave her that she had placed on the coffee table in a crystal vase. Joe noticed them, too, wondering if he'd gone overboard. They were massive—elaborate and exquisite—and the table was dwarfed by their enormity. Perhaps they were too much.

"Romance languages...I love the romance languages. I took

Spanish in high school. You know, sometimes Italian and Spanish words sound so similar, you can take a crack at deciphering them."

"That's what my grandfather always used to say," Francesca said in a surprised tone. "He said exactly the same thing. He said that when someone was speaking Spanish, he could often understand the words, sometimes enough to understand the sentences."

Joe smiled at her. "So, seriously, do you understand zero Italian?" He wanted to see where this would go.

"I didn't exactly say that," she said.

"Okay. Let's play a game and see what you know. What does this mean? 'El vino es delicioso.'"

"That's easy. 'The wine is delicious.'"

"How about this one: 'Su apartamento se ve hermoso.'"

"Your apartment is nice?"

"Close. 'Your apartment looks beautiful.'"

He moved closer, an intimate distance from her. "Okay, one more. 'Creo que te amo.'"

He watched her pause. He could tell she knew what it meant. *I think I love you.* Joe had disguised the words in English by using four Spanish words. Just as he began to second-guess whether she knew what he had said, a sly smile crept across her face.

And then, in Italian, not Spanish, she responded in a whisper: "Penso ti amo anche."

I think I love you, too.

In the morning, the sound of rain beating against Francesca's window awakened them both. Joe's arm was around her; he held her closely to him, the bed covers slightly askew. Evidence of passion was littered around the room: stray undergarments sat unapologetically in little piles; mismatched shoes were looking for their matches; and ex-tinguished candles gave off the faintest scent of amour. At one point during the night, Francesca heard her faux, pearl cocktail ring go flying across the room and hit the closet door.

Joe gently kissed Francesca on the forehead as she slept, and the chirping birds outside splashed in the petite puddles that formed on her balcony.

RAINOUT

I rarely threw temper tantrums, but I was looking forward to the Blackbirds vs. New York series all week. I had trouble containing myself because the pennant race was getting tighter and New York was getting hot. When the newspaper came each morning, I checked the box scores, remembering the game play-by-play. I watched either the television broadcast or listened to the game on my radio.

When my dad came into the room that Saturday morning (we were scheduled to attend the 1:05 p.m. game at Old Blackbirds Park) and told me that the game had been cancelled due to rain, I actually threw my glove against the wall of my room, knocking down my bulletin board.

"Really, Frankie, was that appropriate behavior for a ten-year-old?" he asked.

"Probably not," I said despondently.

"Look, I'm disappointed too. I wanted to go to the game, you know I did, but we have to make the best of it."

I couldn't understand how he could be so optimistic and sunny about it; the plan for the weekend, thanks to the weather gods, had been ruined.

"Maybe we can do something else—something else that is fun. Or, we could just blame Grandpa."

"What?"

"Well, that's sort of what I do in my head. I blame Grandpa. I think of Grandpa, and how, if he were alive today, he'd be crying because there was a rainout. Grandpa loved going to the games even more than you and I love going. And since he's not with us any longer and he's in Heaven playing ball with the angels, whenever it rains, I imagine they're Grandpa's tears falling

from Heaven dropping on us. I think maybe Grandpa's crying because he wishes he were here with us, going to the games."

This story made me feel sad, and I started to forget about feeling angry and disappointed. Grandpa did love going to the games. My father told me those stories. Grandpa waited at the mailbox for his father, who was a mail carrier, to come home, and the two of them would go and watch baseball. There was baseball in my blood, and it had been passed down from generation to generation.

"It makes me sad to think of Grandpa crying tears that turn to rain," I said.

"It's just because he misses us," my dad said. "He gets over it."

"When?"

"When the clouds leave and the team plays ball and he gets to watch from his chair in Heaven."

I could picture Grandpa, sitting in a comfortable rocking chair, watching from his vantage point in Heaven.

"Since we can't go to the game, how about a catch?"

"In the rain?" I asked.

"Sure. I think Grandpa would like it."

FIFTEEN

"The thing about baseball is—the damn sport can break your heart. You think you've got it in the bag, and then whamo! The score shifts in the bottom of the ninth, and it's game over."
~ Zeke Watson, Blackbirds Hall of Famer

It was raining. Driving, pounding rain soaked the area, and Francesca was about to fly to Florida for spring training. Dan was taking her to the airport. He would stay behind and supervise the department and its activities while she instructed the media training and hosted the player luncheon.

Francesca was thankful for Dan; he was a quick learner. She trusted him implicitly, and knew that she hired the right person to help her run community relations for the ballclub. There were no tasks too difficult for Dan; he always understood the mission of the department and how to handle the players. He had great intuition, and dealt with the players in only the most professional manner. The two of them complemented each other well.

"Do you have everything you need?" he asked Francesca as she grabbed her luggage from the trunk as quickly as she could. The last time she drove to the airport, her car was towed when she dropped Sam off for one of her trips. Before Francesca pulled away, she realized Sam left her purse sitting on the front seat when she took her luggage out of the trunk. She put her hazards on and left them flashing and ran just inside the glass doors to catch her. Francesca managed to yell her name, and Sam grabbed her purse. However, by the time she returned to the car—maybe a minute or two passed—her car was getting hoisted and was being towed. She chased down her car at the impounding zone and paid an enormous fine, along with the tow fee. Nothing went right after that. Work had been hectic, and it ended up being one of the worst days of her professional life. That was why Dan was dropping her off. She didn't want to take any risks.

"I have everything," she said.

Dan gave her a little hug, and wished her luck.

"See you when I get back," she said, looking at the ominous sky. "If I get back. And don't try to scare me with one of your superstitions."

He laughed. It wasn't so funny to her at all.

Ever since she was little, she never liked to fly. Her family did not take exotic vacations around the world, so she never became accustomed to flying. Her experience was relatively limited. However, there was one trip in particular that stuck out in her mind. They had flown across the country to see the Grand Canyon. They hiked the trails, stayed in a lodge, visited friends in Las Vegas, and then boarded a plane to come back east. With half an hour remaining on the flight, they were met with an explosive thunderstorm. The plane jolted and rocked and bounced. Francesca was petrified. She hugged her mother asking her when it would be over. Her mother assured her that they would land soon and everything would be all right. She was correct; they did make it safely and touched ground, and she was never so thankful or elated in her life. Her father, who had been sitting next to Cissy, gave Francesca a big hug as they exited the plane.

"Whoa!" he said. "Bet you'll always remember that!"

Francesca knew he was just trying to make light of it, but years later at Cissy's graduation, when he made the toast, he said, "We've had some great times and some bumpy times…and I mean that literally, right girls? Remember our flight home from Vegas?"

Moments like that were far more fun to remember than to actually experience, but it did make for good stories.

Little did Francesca know that four years later, her father would be dead, her mother would be alone, and she would be getting on a plane in bad weather about to suffer a flight by herself in the teeming rain, turbulence and all.

It was at times such as those that she missed her dad. She wished she could have called him and said, "I'm nervous about the flight," and he would talk to her and calm her down. She was a firm believer that girls needed their fathers to be around for them in good times and in bad. He was a calming force in her life, and she missed that aspect of him.

The truth was that it didn't matter how old Francesca became; she knew she would always miss her father.

She was clenching the tote bag she held on her lap so severely that her knuckles were white. The woman next to her with silver hair and blood red fingernails leaned in and said, "It's going to be fine, you know. Once we're up, the rain and storms will be below us."

"I hope you're right," Francesca said.

They were on the runway, waiting for clearance. At any minute, the big bird was going to ascend toward Heaven. She just hoped she wasn't going to be its next customer.

In the end, the woman had been right. She was so tired from the long week, that once they were up above the clouds and the flight was smooth, she actually dozed off for a few seconds. Never a romantic, or a dreamer, when she closed her eyes, a sense of calm came over her as she pictured seeing Joe on the field. She smiled to herself. For a few moments, she allowed herself to imagine him in his uniform, jogging in from the outfield, greeting her with his warm, beaming smile. Francesca also couldn't wait to feel the Florida sunshine on her face knowing chills would run up her spine when she heard the sound she loved so much ever since she was a small child: the sound of the crack of the bat.

It was spring training—and she was about to be a part of it all.

Sixteen

"Every day, a new opportunity presents itself. Take it."
~ Vince Rogers, former Blackbirds Manager

It wasn't Joe who came trotting across the field when he saw her. It was Zeke.

"Hey, Sunshine! Glad you made it!" He had a glove in his left hand, while he tossed a ball up and down in his right. He was the team's new batting coach, and Francesca found it nostalgic to see him back in a uniform after all these years.

"Was there any doubt I wouldn't make it?" Francesca asked.

"Well, you've admitted to me on several occasions that you have a fear of flying."

"That's an understatement," she said. "There were storms when we took off, and if it weren't for the little old lady next to me who, bless her heart, tried to calm me, I might have passed out from fear. But her sweet little face kept me from losing it. I didn't want to upset her."

"I never think about flying," Zeke said. "It's second nature now. When you fly for your job, it just fades into the background."

"Well, I'm here, and that's all that matters."

"Not on Valium?" he asked.

She punched him playfully on his arm. "No. No Valium."

He laughed. Zeke's favorite pastime wasn't baseball; it was teasing her.

"When are you doing your shtick," Zeke asked.

"I love when you call it that. It makes it sound like I take a dog and pony show on the road, like an old Vaudeville act I do with a hat and cane."

He looked at her and winked. "You said it, not me."

"Tomorrow at noon. Please tell me you won't be there."

"What? And miss seeing you scare the shit out of the rookies? Never!"

Francesca sat in the stands with her notebook. The sky was clear and it wasn't particularly humid in Florida. That was the amazing thing about the state: you never knew just how hot or how humid it was going to be. However, just to be safe, she pulled her hair into a ponytail and sat with her sunglasses on as she watched batting practice. The team was playing a game in a little while, but Zeke had them in the cages taking swings. Joe saw her as he came out of the dugout and gave her a little wave along with the multi-million-dollar Clarkson smile. She appreciated that he kept their situation quiet. She wasn't ready for any of it to go public. Not yet, and maybe not for a long time. Their relationship needed to stay professional while Francesca was instructing the players on community relations and organizing them for the upcoming weeks when they returned home. She had to tell whole team about the Kick-Off Luncheon that the club sponsored and organized with the city; they were all expected to be in attendance.

The list of items on her "to-do" list grew quite long in the thirty minutes she sat and watched them hit. She was making notes and working through her list when she felt a tap on her shoulder.

"Mind if I join you?" Jack Thompson was standing above her, holding his hand over his eyes to block the sun.

"No, not at all," she said. "Enjoying spring training?"

"It appears that way, though I'm not sure some days what the heck to write about. No offense, but your team looks sluggish," he said. "I hope they snap out of it. It's way more fun to write about a winning team than a losing one."

"Really? Sluggish? No worries. They'll get it together. We've got Zeke now to help with the hitting, and he's a real motivator."

"Yes, that should make a difference. So, you look well—better than the last time I saw you at the banquet."

"Right. Forgive me. I wasn't feeling well that night. I stayed in bed for a couple of days after that and missed work."

"Yes, I know," Jack said. "I stopped by to check on you, and they said you were out."

"You did? No one told me."

"I didn't leave a message or anything. I just stopped by your office."

"Sorry I missed you," Francesca said.

At that moment, they both heard the sound—the sound of a broken bat—and they turned their heads to watch Joe's ball soar out of the park and over the outfield wall.

"Holy crap! That was a bomb!" Jack said. "He hasn't hit one like that since I've been here. That was his best hit by far."

"Guess you've got something to write about now," Francesca said, trying not to say it too proudly. She wanted to believe Joe hit that dinger because of her presence, and she kept her eyes focused only on him as he rounded the bases, watching his every move from behind her very dark, Jackie-O style sunglasses.

It was the top of the ninth inning, and the sun began to set behind the ballpark. The way the light hit the roof made it seem as if Heaven itself were shining down on it, forming imaginary halos around each ballplayer's head. There was a peaceful quality to this time of day, and the fans had filled the seats, dressed in their black and red and white, the official Blackbirds' colors. Little children wore their jerseys, and adults sported the team's top players' numbers. Number 6—Joe Clarkson. Number 7—Lee Daniels. And Number 27—Gregg Maloney.

When the team won the game, the players and coaches began to file into the dugout, and some fans headed toward the field for autographs. Francesca followed the crowd down toward the field. Freddie Montrose—otherwise known as The Fly—called to Francesca. The former stellar shortstop served as the bench coach and was an important community liaison. He was gruff, probably in his late forties, but Francesca loved his playful demeanor. Everyone did. There were absolutely no pretenses with Freddie.

"How goes it, Francesca?"

"Not too bad, Freddie. We miss you back home. There's nobody around to do all our community appearances since you and Zeke are here now."

"We'll be back soon enough," he said. "Don't forget—I'm better at those things than Zeke. He runs his god damn mouth too much."

"Awww. That's not nice to say about one of your best buddies."

"I say it to his face! He knows he talks too much. And about himself!"

Freddie reached over and handed Francesca his unopened box of Cracker Jacks.

She hesitated to grab them. "I didn't spit in them! Take them!" he said teasingly. "The friggin' things get stuck in my teeth."

The hotel was quiet. It was perched on a little knoll, with a rolling front and back filled with palm trees. The way they swayed in the breeze, rocking gently to the earth's own rhythm, was calming. The grass looked like a perfectly manicured golf course, neatly mowed and lush. Francesca sat on the lawn in a glider, the lights of the resort twinkling just enough to give it its own personality, its own charisma. She breathed in the evening air. The players were arriving back to the hotel after showering at the ballpark, and many of them were probably already out on the town—gallivanting—or worse. She didn't want to know. The only time she saw Joe was when he was on the field, but she was waiting for him now. She changed her outfit at least five times before deciding on the turquoise dress with the open back and the silver platform sandals that gave her a little height.

When she finally saw him saunter out of the back hotel doors and make his way over to her, she felt her heart skip a beat. What was it that made her think about him differently now, even though they had known each other for years? It was their intimacy—the way he made her feel special. Their level of intimacy had grown, and she found herself opening up more.

And then there was the letter that arrived only four days after he arrived for spring training. She wondered if he had written it on the plane. *I've never felt this way about anyone, you are so special to me … you make me so happy—happier than I've ever been before. I hope we never lose what we have.* Joe had written those words to her, and she carried the first love letter she ever received around in her purse ever since she opened it. She read it countless times over, sometimes reprimanding herself for acting like a fool—like a crazy, love-struck girl. And yet every time she tried to stop, she reminded herself that it was okay to feel that way. Those beginning stages of euphoric love, which she heard stories from friends who've been through it, were worth savoring.

As he approached her, wearing jeans and a dark shirt, she could smell his cologne, the scent that would linger blissfully on her sheets after he left her apartment. The one that made her feel slightly off-kilter. The one that made her realize she looked forward to seeing him again. And again.

"Hello there, lovely," he said when he approached her and kissed her lightly on the cheek, making sure not to arouse suspicion.

"Hi there, handsome," she said. "Nice hit today. Did you get any splinters from it?"

He held up his hands for her inspection. "I think they're in good shape. No damage done."

He put his arm around her, and then thought better of it because they were out in public. She wished they could just walk away together arm in arm, but she was determined to continue to protect their privacy and her professional reputation.

"I made a reservation at a quiet little place the next town over where no one will go," he said. "Are you ready?"

"Yes," she said.

The restaurant boasted twinkle lights that hung from the ceiling, plants and tropical trees, and the open-air roof. Greenery was spread throughout the restaurant, and light music played in the background, the view of the Gulf Coast just to the right out the open window. If you wanted to impress a woman, you took her there, where there was no doubt about your intentions of being romantic. Joe had picked well, and the food—fresh fish and mango salsa—was savory and stimulated the palate. Francesca sipped her champagne.

"Do you know what weighs on my mind sometimes?" Joe asked.

"Whether you'll try to hit one opposite field or how you can avoid making an off-balance throw?"

"Yes, smart-ass. Those thoughts do cross my mind, but I look at retired players and wonder what the hell I'll do when it's all over. You're lucky. You have a career."

"Yes, I do. But don't think I don't wonder about the future, too, you know," she said. "But it's not one of my big downfalls. I tend to go the other way."

"What do you mean?" he asked.

"Too often, I live in the past. Sometimes I dwell on things that should have been or could have been."

"Maybe I can help you with that."

"I'd be thankful if you could," she said. "I often torment myself with the 'what ifs'."

"Such as?"

"I often wonder what it would have been like had my father lived. Sometimes I find I keep it stored inside. It's all in here," she said, pointing both hands at her chest. "Locked down. And I'm regularly concerned about my mother."

"That must have been difficult. I don't know what I'd do without my dad. He's been such an influence and supporter in my life."

"So was mine," she said. "Don't ever take that for granted."

When Francesca and Joe pulled into the parking lot at the hotel that night, their bellies full of delectable food and expensive bubbly drinks, they were giggling like schoolchildren trying to pull one over on the teacher. Their arms were wrapped around each other as they sauntered back into the hotel lobby, and then they promptly let go of each other as they strode closer to the elevator, just in case anyone were to be around.

"Are you coming to my room or am I coming to yours?" she whispered to him much too loudly, the residual effects of the champagne making her silly as they waited for the glass elevator to float downward toward them. Joe loved when she giggled and was funny. Right then, at that moment, he pretty much loved everything about her.

"I'll come to yours, Frankie, just in case anyone comes looking for me."

She relished how he played along with the game—a secret kept in the night. Their secret. This thing that was happening was all theirs.

The elevator doors opened, and they exited the elevator, keenly looking around the halls to be sure no one had glimpsed them as a pair. Francesca opened her purse and removed the key to the room. She fumbled to open it at first, and then she heard the click. The two of them pushed the door open with such force, they almost knocked each other over, their muffled giggles threatening to shatter the silence. They did not reach to turn on a light—the room was already glowing from below, the open curtains allowing the twinkling from the resort to illuminate the intimate space. Within seconds of closing the door tightly behind them, their clothes were off, tossed carelessly in piles all over the floor, and as Joe playfully attacked her, kissing her neck and shoulders, Francesca smiled, feeling the warmth of his rugged hands roam all over her body, and she reached to lock the door and slide the chain across the mount.

When morning arrived, reality hit. Joe had to get to the field for batting practice; they were scheduled to play an early afternoon game, and Francesca had to prepare for her presentation.

She was lounging beneath the sheets as she watched him dress. She realized she liked watching him, still wrapped up in the euphoria that was last night, and couldn't help but wish the two of them had nothing to do all day but stay right where they were, curled up together.

It was at that moment, in a blissful, dreamy state, that her cell phone rang. She knew who it was, and so she answered, as she watched Joe put his shoes on and comb his hair.

"Hey, Cissy. Are you calling because you wish you were free as a bird with me here in the Florida sunshine?"

"No. Mom's ill. She's in the hospital. Francesca, I think she may have taken too many pills or something." Her voice was panicked and she sounded desperate.

Francesca's heart sank. What was she saying?

"What?"

"She was supposed to meet her friend Connie for lunch and didn't show up. Connie knocked on the door and found her throwing up on the floor of her bathroom, half unconscious."

Francesca didn't know what to say, what to do. She just felt sick, as if her body were collapsing, as if there were no bones in it to hold her up.

"What's wrong?" Joe said.

"Who's that?" Cissy said in a surprised tone.

"I'm coming home," Francesca said.

"I'm here at the hospital," Cissy said. "And I'm scared."

"I'm getting on the first plane out of here and coming home," Francesca said again.

Joe sat down next to Francesca on the bed. "What's going on, Frankie?" he asked.

"My mother's ill, and I have to go home."

"How can I help?" Joe asked.

"Tell Zeke to call me when you get to the ballpark."

He kissed her, told her everything would be okay, and then left her room in search of Zeke and the ball field that was calling him.

"Love you, Frankie," he had said.

In a mad frenzy, Francesca threw things in her suitcase and packed up her laptop. In the bathroom, she scooped her toiletries and tossed them right into her luggage. She took the elevator down.

The sympathetic and cooperative woman working the hotel's front desk called the airline to see if she could book Francesca on a flight back home as soon as possible. There was an eleven-forty-five available. She would just barely make it.

In a matter of minutes, she was checking out and waiting for a cab.

Francesca would not be making the presentation at noon. She needed to call the manager, Kevin Desmond, and cancel on him. And she needed to call Dan.

Just as the cab was pulling up, Freddie saw her.

"Where are you headed?" he asked.

"I have to leave, Freddie. My mom...my mom...she's sick..."

She couldn't get the words out as he stood there looking at her. Then laconic Freddie Montrose took Francesca in his arms and let her cry. He let her sob, and she felt herself clinging to every fiber of him. In that gesture, two people who worked together for years and never shared a serious, personal, intimate moment both knew how serious the moment was, and Francesca appreciated him.

He opened the door to the cab, kissed her on the forehead, and helped her climb inside.

"You don't worry about anything here. Zeke and I can present your talk. I'll tell Desmond. We can tell the guys what's expected. We know better than anyone, plus I've heard you give the damn thing about five or six times now."

Francesca nodded, grabbing a tissue from her purse to wipe her eyes. "Take the laptop. My presentation is on it. I'll have Dan email you the details. Have one of the assistants or David set it up for you in the auxiliary clubhouse."

"Got it. Now, no more. You just worry about your mother. There is no need for any anxiety about your job."

He closed the door, and Francesca instructed the cab driver to take her to the airport, as fast as he could.

Two flights in the span of twenty-four hours. Francesca couldn't help herself from feeling nauseated. What had her mother done? Was she depressed and no one took notice of it? Did Francesca neglect to see it?

The thoughts were overwhelming. She wanted them to go away. She wanted to wake up from this nightmare. Two parents, one dead, one in the hospital. She felt as if she aged in a matter of minutes when Cissy told her over the phone.

Her mother was taking medication to help her sleep. That much she had told her. But had she taken too much?

There were unanswered and troubling questions, and they were drowning her in thought. Perhaps she did not look after her well enough. Had she slipped away without Francesca noticing it at all?

She wasn't sure about anything.

She didn't even notice that the plane took off, bound for Bay City.

ROOKIE

One September afternoon, a dog appeared at our front door. I never saw him before that day. My father called him a mutt, and I asked him what that meant. I was only nine and never had a pet.

"A mutt is a mongrel dog—a dog that is a mix of different breeds like poodles, labs, cocker spaniels, labs, and others. A mutt is also a person who is foolish. And this dog is definitely a mutt," my father told me.

I didn't fully understand it, but I knew that dog looked skinny and sad. My father allowed me to keep it for a while, at least until they spread the word in the neighborhood that a dog was without its rightful owner. The dog wore no tags.

Weeks later, my father finally announced that I could keep the "mangy thing." I fed him and took him to a dog groomer to have him trimmed and properly clipped. He loved to play fetch, and would often let me throw the ball to him. He also enjoyed the rubber newspaper I saved up to buy for him at the pet store. It squeaked, and he looked adorable carrying it in his mouth back to me. He would catch it endlessly, and I would often become tired far before he would.

I named him Rookie.

Six months later, right after I turned ten, I brought him outside on his leash and attached him to the tree on the front lawn so he could enjoy the fresh, clean air of the springtime sunshine. I ran down the street to a friend's house to play, and I didn't come home until dinner.

When I returned, Rookie was gone.

I never found him.

After shedding what seemed to be every tear I possessed, my father finally, several weeks later, relented and said I could get another dog.

When I went to pick one out at the pet store, I was adamant.

I wouldn't get a male dog. It had to be a female.

I had been right. That sweet collie, Sadie, never broke my heart.

Seventeen

"I made three errors in one game. I'm embarrassed to say I think it's a club record. Who the hell does that?"
~ Joe Clarkson, Blackbirds Outfielder

Cissy was standing in the waiting area staring out the large picture window that looked out onto the courtyard when Francesca arrived. The hospital was austere and smelled like a combination of antiseptic and rubbing alcohol. Even the attempt at yellow painted walls couldn't disguise that it was a place where the sick were cared for, whether it was night or day. The sterility added to its sense of foreboding, and it quickly reminded her of the long stays her father endured there. Francesca hoped—even prayed—that she would not step foot into that place but for happy times, such as the birth of a friend's baby.

Cissy began to cry when she saw Francesca approach, and when Francesca saw Cissy, she feared the worst. It was one-thirty in the afternoon, but she was there.

"I feel like such an idiot," Cissy sobbed.

"How's mom? What's going on?"

She reached for Francesca and clutched both of her elbows with each of her hands.

"I'm so sorry," she said. Francesca felt herself start to panic.

"How's mom?" she said, yelling and pulling herself from Cissy, forcing her to look her in the eyes.

"She's fine," she said. "Dehydration from the flu, and then the idiot tried to take a sleeping pill. I'm sorry I made you come all the way home."

"She's fine?" Francesca asked, wanting to hear it one more time. "Fine?"

"Yes," Cissy said, wiping her eyes. "The doctor just saw her. She had the flu for five days and didn't tell anyone. She forgot to cancel with Connie for lunch, but thank God she didn't. None of us knew how sick she was."

"Good Lord!" Francesca said. "That woman is going to get it from me. And I'm throwing away any sleeping pills I see in her house. I almost had a heart attack on the plane. All I kept thinking was why she tried to kill herself. But she wasn't trying to kill herself."

Cissy flopped down on the couch and shook her head. Francesca took a deep breath and then sat next to her.

"I guess I can't see her now?"

"She's sleeping."

Cissy, who by her birthright, was supposed to be older and wiser, looked as if she just suffered a nervous breakdown, and needed Francesca to offer strength in this time of urgency. She put her head on Francesca's shoulder, and they sat there together for hours until they were able to see their mother when she awakened.

There was an IV in her arm, her face was pale and drawn, and for a moment Francesca felt a sadness overcome her. Prior to walking in the door, Francesca had trouble finding empathy for her mother because anger enveloped her. Her mother was propped up, and Cissy sat beside her on the edge of the bed. Francesca could not sit, and instead paced the floor.

"What in the hell do you think you were doing not telling any-one you were sick?" she asked.

"Francesca!" Cissy shouted.

"No—I don't care if she gets mad at me. I'm furious with her! I went away to Florida and you didn't even tell me you weren't well? Why would you keep that from us?"

"I didn't want to worry you," she said.

This was the consequence of her mother's lack of sound reason-ing and judgment; it ended up putting her in the hospital.

"That's a logical argument! You would rather I get pulled back from my job after receiving a panicked call from my sister and have to fly round trip in one day when I hate to fly, leaving me to freak out on the plane, not knowing what is wrong with you? Thanks, Mom. Thanks for keeping it from us. Glad you decided not to worry us."

The irony was almost comical, yet Cissy allowed herself to side with their mother.

"Francesca Milli! You apologize to Mom right now! She's in the hospital!"

"Really? Oh, I thought we were all at a carnival together."

That sarcastic, biting comment shut them all up. Francesca stared at the two of them—always close, always those two against Dad and her.

But she had done it. She had silenced them and rendered them mute. Or so she thought, when her mother ceded.

"Francesca is right. I worried you far worse by not telling you than if I had just told you I wasn't feeling well to begin with. I'm sorry, Cissy. I'm sorry, Francesca."

Francesca walked over to her without another word needing to be said and kissed her mother's forehead.

"What was it you always said to us when we were growing up?

'Always learn from your mistakes?' Let this be a lesson to you, Mother Dear. We've already lost one parent. We have no intention of losing another in the near future," she said.

It took two full days for her mother to become fully hydrated. Cissy left the morning her mother was to be discharged from the hospital. She needed to get back to Cam and Emma, and Francesca pledged to drive her mother home and to stay with her for a few nights until she was back to her old self.

The Blackbirds sent a colorful and fragrant flower arrangement to the hospital, which Francesca put in the backseat of her car when they left.

She had not heard from Joe at all, but Zeke called after hearing the news from Joe. When Francesca relayed the story to Dan, he booked the first flight he could get at her urging to spend time with the players in Florida. One of them had to be there to set up appearances and get the luncheon details organized. She could count on Dan. She could even hear it in his voice that he was excited to go, and even more excited to be there once he arrived.

Isabelle left a message saying she called the ballpark looking for her, and Dan answered the phone. He filled her in on Francesca's situation. After she heard the full story, she sent an overly generous fruit basket to the house for her mother.

Connie stopped by hours after Francesca tucked her mother in on the sofa with a tuna casserole made especially for her mother; the bottle of wine she carried in the house was meant for Francesca.

As for Freddie, he called every couple of hours. Francesca had talked to him after he and Zeke gave the talk with the slide show, and he said it went well. Not as well as if she had presented, he said, but well enough. He left a morning message asking Francesca to call him after she got her mother settled in back at her house.

The kindness of others. Who knew?

Three days later, a care package arrived at Francesca's mother's house. Replete with a fuzzy throw blanket, boxes of tea and biscuits, two paperback novels and two movies, Francesca had no choice but to read the card aloud to her mother when she opened it.

"Mrs. Milli—I hope you feel better soon and know that Francesca will take great care of you. All the best, Joe."

"Joe who?" her mother asked.

"Joe Clarkson," Francesca said.

"Joe Clarkson, the ballplayer?"

"Yes."

Her mother stared at her and silently put the pieces together.

"Nice of him to care," she said, raising her eyebrow with a smirk, and left it at that.

Finally, after a lot of mother/daughter heart-to-heart talks about taking care of oneself, Francesca found herself able to return to the office after spending most of her days working from her laptop at her mother's. She still wasn't fully comfortable leaving her alone for the entire day, but her mother's strength was returning, and the doctor told them it could be up to a week or two until she was completely back to normal.

"Who's normal?" Francesca's mother jokingly said to the doctor. "You'd be hard-pressed to find one completely normal person in the whole town!"

Francesca could tell her spirits were returning because she was becoming lighthearted and funny again. But Francesca did as she promised—she flushed every sleeping pill she could find down the toilet and told her never to take one again.

The day at the office was hectic and consisted of returning over two-hundred emails and phone calls she received during a week's absence from work. Doing as much as she could from home, it was not the same as being in the office. Opening Day was two weeks away, and the chaos level was at its normal high.

She heard the message on her machine when she finally made her way back into the office after being away for several days. "Hey, Frankie, it's Joe. I hope your mother is doing better. Freddie told me she's making a strong comeback, thanks to you. I miss you. Hope to talk to you soon. Call me."

Very generic, yet sweet, she thought. Why hadn't he tried to contact her at home? She didn't want to become one of those obsessive girls who checked her voice mail every two minutes, and she also had no intention of becoming a conspiracy theorist, but it did strike her as odd that he remained in the background for that extended amount of time she was playing nurse to her mother. Perhaps he didn't want to interfere when he knew she had priorities. He called, that's what mattered, and he did care.

She took a quick call from the vice president of operations about Opening Day festivities, when her other line rang. She could see it was Dan. She would call him back.

When they finished discussing the logistics of the children and the banners, the bands and the player introductions, she saw her line ringing again. Dan. The relationship she had with the vice-president was a good one, so she asked if she could call him back. Dan was calling from Florida and it must be important.

She dialed Dan back immediately.

"Hey Francesca," he said.

"Hi Dan. What's wrong?"

"Well, this isn't easy for me to...um...talk to you about," he began.

"Just say it! We've known each other for years. What's going on?"

"Are you sitting down?"

"Yes. I'm at my desk. What's up?"

"It's really none of my business—none of my business whatsoever—but..."

"What is it?" She was raising her voice now. "Stop dancing around it, Dan, and get to the point. It's okay. You can tell me anything."

"Is there any truth to the rumor that you and Joe Clarkson are an item?"

"Jesus!" she said. And she knew. He opened his mouth. He broke his promise.

"Is that a 'yes'?" Dan asked.

"What the hell is he saying, Dan? And you must be honest with me. Completely honest."

"When he heard about your mom, he made some comment to Freddie that you two had been together."

"Freddie! I'm going to kill him. Who else has Joe told? Jesus!"

"I don't know. As far as I know, just Freddie, not Jesus."

"Humor? At a time like this! Really?"

"It's your business, Francesca. I just thought you should know since you've always been so protective of your reputation, and as not just your colleague, but as your friend, I felt I had to tell you."

"Dan, thank you for telling me. I know it wasn't easy for you. Now, go find that son-of-a-bitch and get him on the phone. I want to speak to him!"

"I'm on it. Stay in your office. They haven't gone out for batting practice yet."

She slammed the innocent receiver down with all her might. She should never have trusted him. She should never have been that open. Never trust men, she thought; they always let you down.

Her hands were shaking and her blood was pumping so hard, she thought she might have an out of body experience—or throw something through the window. What behavior would she have to exhibit to execute a full-blown temper tantrum. Kick the door? Pound the wall? Throw some of her desk accessories around the office? The rage she felt was unprecedented. She never actually wanted to strangle someone before.

Minutes later, the blasted phone rang. She let it ring twice before she picked it up.

"Hello," she shouted.

"Frankie—" he started to say, but Francesca wouldn't allow him to use that sacred name that had been her father's to use, and her father's only. She should never have allowed him call her by that name in the first place. How dare he!

"Francesca to you! Listen to me clearly, Joe Clarkson. You will make sure you straighten this little thing out with Freddie and whomever the hell else you decided to tell. I should not have to hear that there's gossip flowing—and from your mouth—in the clubhouse! I thought I could trust you to keep this quiet. I'm fuming, so angry with you—I better not hear one more remark about us. My reputation was impeccable until I got involved with you, and I won't have you destroy it!"

"Frankie—Francesca—I'm sorry. It just slipped out when I told Freddie that...I think...I love you. It was in no way meant to be harmful."

For a second, Francesca felt like she might believe him, give in to him simply because he uttered the word "love." Holy crap! What was it about the word love that brings out the best and the worst in people? Why did he feel the need to talk? And yet, a part of her believed that on some level he might have loved her.

"Go fix it, Joe. I don't want to be the subject of tabloid talk in the clubhouse. These players have to respect me. I have to earn their respect and keep it."

"I'm sorry," he said. "I said something in confidence. I didn't mean for anyone to know."

"Oh, and Freddie is your confidante?"

"Well, yes, sort of..." he began. "I don't know if anyone else knows."

She cut him off. "Just fix it. What don't you understand about privacy? This was not meant to be common knowledge for anyone but you and me for now," she said.

She slammed the phone down.

On the other end of the line, Joe was left holding the receiver in his hand knowing that the complexity of what just happened was not something that could easily be fixed. Nor was it what it seemed to be on the surface. He was in a real pickle, and as Freddie said a few days ago, it would take great love to get out of the complicated hole he had dug for himself. He and Frankie were still in the honeymoon stage of their relationship when everything was perfect and dreamy and new. He liked the way her skin felt and the way her eyes twinkled when they talked; he liked the way she could discuss baseball, directly and without putting him on a pedestal; and he loved her wit and air of confidence.

Her qualities all appealed to him; he hadn't ever met anyone who could go head-to-head with him like she could. And she had a sweet side. What had he done? If he could turn back the clock and take it all back, he would not have put himself in this predicament. However, the reality was clear, and in his gut, he knew his mistake would be a hurdle, if not an obstacle. This was his concern. Joe wasn't sure Frankie would—or could—overlook the ramifications of his actions with ease, or with a heart full of understanding.

Eighteen

"I try to lead my life off the field the same way I lead it on the field: with honesty, integrity, and determination."
~ Joe Clarkson, Blackbirds Outfielder

Francesca put the newspaper down and couldn't help but to cackle out loud. Her assistant, Claire, came running.

"Are you okay?" she asked. "You scared me."

"Oh, yes, I'm fine," Francesca said. "Just reading a bunch of bullshit in the newspaper." She flicked the newspaper with her fingers.

Her assistant walked out of her office door with a nod, and went back to her desk. Francesca sipped her coffee, which had become cold as she sat there mesmerized by the snow job Joe Clarkson was able to pull over on Jack Thompson.

It was so flattering, she hardly recognized Clarkson in it at all.

She picked up the newspaper again, having to read the line over and over to herself, which articulated the following:

Joe Clarkson exemplifies what it means to be a committed member of the community. He is connected, and is always eager to meet fans from all over the Blackbirds metropolitan area. He believes in being committed to every facet of his obligation, and loves the trust he has built with his fans. "I try to build relationships through baseball, both on and off the field, and they mean the world to me," he said.

Brilliant, she thought. How absolutely brilliant of him.

Claire poked her head in the office again. "I ordered all the sandwiches. You want them delivered to the conference room, right?" she asked.

Opening Day was one day away, and Francesca and Dan were scheduled to conduct the final training session with the part time assistants. Dan popped his head in through the door.

"I'm heading to the clubhouse to drop all this off," he said. He stocked a cart full of welcome kits they put together for the team, and a copy of the first edition of Blackbirds magazine, in which they were all prominently featured in full color.

"Thanks, Dan," Francesca said.

It was two weeks since the debacle at spring training, and she was feverishly getting everything organized for all the Opening Day festivities. There was so much to consider, including the day's entertainment, the volunteers, the kids who would hold the flags, the bands that would play on the corridors, and the multitude of balloons they strategically placed all over the ballpark. Francesca was the chair of the Opening Day committee, and they all worked together to get the ballpark ready and make sure the game-day personnel were on point. The weeks leading up to it were tiresome, and she came through the door to her home at between ten and eleven o'clock for the last two weeks. There was one plus, however; she lost about seven pounds because she didn't have time to eat.

Her mother was doing much better, and she was planning on attending the game tomorrow. The weather report was cheerfully optimistic: partly cloudy, with a high of seventy degrees. It was a little warmer than last year's Opening Day, so the kids from the inner city schools who had been selected to hold the flags during the on-field pregame ceremonies wouldn't be too chilly. She actually thought about things like that even though she had no children of her own. But when she did allow herself to think about the future, she couldn't imagine a life without children in it.

Joe and she had not had contact since that contentious phone call, and as well, she told no one about it. Thankfully, her mother didn't bring up Joe's name up at all.

She only had thirty minutes until lunch, so she decided to accomplish her last few tasks before the afternoon was spent initiating the final training session. She dropped off a couple of packages to the mailroom and then stopped at the restroom for a quick break. She was hoping Dan would be able to do the last hour on his own, offering the assistants one last instruction time in the control room and press box. David, the public relations director, had already written the press notes, and Dan was going to show the team of assistants how to run them off and where the set would be placed in the press box for the reporters.

Francesca forgot something on her desk, and bolted through the double doors that lead into the very busy communications suite. The area consisted of her department of community relations, public relations, Blackbirds productions, and publications. They were a pretty tight-knit group, and they all genuinely liked and supported one another. And even though she felt humiliated by Joe, not one of her colleagues mentioned it. She wasn't sure who knew about it and who didn't. Quite frankly, she appreciated that if people did know, they were letting it die a quiet death.

When she pushed through the double doors with force, once again on a mission, she did it again. She knocked poor Jack Thompson to the ground.

"Oh, my gosh!" she said, trying to help him up. "Jack, I'm so sorry."

"I swear to God, Francesca, you are trying to kill me!" he said, laughing.

Francesca heard a couple of snickers come from the public relations folks, whose offices were right near the double doors. She offered to help him up.

"I didn't see you! I'm sorry! I was in such a rush to…"

"Let me guess," Jack said. "Were you possibly late or forgot something?"

"Bingo!"

"This is going to cost you, you know. I'm an innocent bystander. All I was doing was picking up my press credential," he said, smiling, and holding up his press credential as evidence.

"Yes, I know. I deserve to be punished. Tell me what I have to do to make it up to you."

"You can buy me a beer after the game tomorrow in the press box."

"Happy to do it, but the beers will be free then," she said. "Compliments of the ballclub."

"Look how lucky you are!" he said. "See what a cheap date I am?"

After a very harried, but successful day, she found herself back at her desk answering emails and returning phone calls. As the director of community relations, she was one of a handful of people in the office at that late hour, including the receptionists at the front desk who had extended hours that night. Therefore, there was no reason to question why the switchboard called her at eight o'clock the night before Opening Day to come to the reception area. A woman wanted something dropped off to the clubhouse for a player.

She trudged down the hall in her high heels, her feet tired after walking all the way around the ballpark with the assistants. Minutes prior, she sent the assistants on their way home to get some rest for what would most likely be a very exciting first Opening Day for them.

"Hi, Francesca," Emma said, one of the front desk receptionists. "This is Jessica. She would like to drop this care package off to her boyfriend as a surprise for tomorrow."

Jessica, tall and blonde, wearing heavy mascara and lipstick, was standing behind the counter, sealing the envelope to the card, and sliding it into the area of the basket that had an opening. The package was adorned with an abundance of ribbons, of course in Blackbirds colors. It was substantial and looked expensive as it was filled with lots of food, nuts, fruits, and chocolates. It was wrapped in cellophane.

"Hi," she said. As Francesca moved closer to her, she realized just how tall she was. As a diminutive person, Francesca never let another person's height intimidate her. She was quite used to being on the small side, but this woman made her feel unpolished. Her curled, bleached blonde hair cascaded past her shoulders, and she wore lots of jewels around her neck.

"I'm Francesca Milli, director of community relations. I assume this is for one of the players?"

Francesca didn't recognize her, so she presumed she was a relatively new girlfriend or the girlfriend of a newer player. As part of her job, she worked with the players' wives and partners over the course of a season. Community relations assisted with many fundraisers over the years with the Blackbirds Wives Organization, and they raised money by organizing food drives, publishing cookbooks, and planning special fundraising events for hospitals and charities.

"Yes, it's for Joe Clarkson," she said, as she moved from behind the counter to shake her hand. It was then that Francesca noticed a belly growing under a very tight shirt.

Within an hour, she was knocking on Father John's door.

A BROKEN BAT

High school is meant to be a time to enjoy life, be free from restrictive commitments, and have fun one last time before venturing off into the working or collegiate worlds. High school—the time for football games and bonfires, senior proms and ski trips, weekend parties and friends for life.

He sauntered into my life one Tuesday morning when he entered my homeroom class two weeks after the first day of class; he moved into town from the south. He had no accent, because he grew up with a father whose business moved the family around a lot, so he sounded just like everyone else. He had a soft mustache, blonde and light, and his eyes were hazel, and dazzling. I would often wonder if the other girls took notice of him, because he was sweet, outgoing, and conversational. Something inside me leapt when he walked through the door wearing Levi's jeans and fitted tee, his arm muscles filling out the sleeves. His slip of paper was in his right hand, and he offered it to Mrs. Wills, the homeroom teacher.

"Class, this is Johnny Mulaney, your new classmate."

He sat directly behind me, as both of our last names began with the letter "M," and we ended up talking and flirting. One day he surprised me and asked me to go to dinner. I accepted. We became inseparable.

I never meant to fall in love with him.

But I did.

I confided in him, trusted him, and gave all of myself to him, including my heart, which I always protected. We seemed to need each other and filled each other's voids; the relationship had been intimate and wonderful, much to my own surprise.

The intensity of my father's sickness worsened later that senior year of high school. He became ill, and when the Leukemia diagnosis came, I was not ready to hear it, let alone have to cope with that type of disease attaching itself to a member of my immediate family.

I was sick with worry—we all were—spending nights and week-ends with my father, trying to get him well. If only we could get him well.

One Friday night, after dating for over nine months, my father had fallen asleep, and I decided to go talk to Johnny. I just needed his support, to feel his arms wrapped around me. When we talked earlier on the phone, he said he would be home all evening and to call him if I wanted to get together. I didn't call, but instead decided to go over unannounced to surprise him.

He was not alone. Katie Gregg was there. My classmate from school had moved in and taken the opportunity to romance my boyfriend. I don't know how I didn't see it coming, and he had allowed it to happen.

I wasn't worried about her; I had no vested interest in my friendship with Katie. It was Johnny who had broken the bond. He splintered it like a broken bat, and I experienced heartbreak for the very first time. It came from the organ whose job it was to pump blood throughout my body and keep it going, which explained why I ached with pain and felt as if I didn't want to go on. I cried for days, ridiculous tears falling, falling, falling as I kept crying, crying, crying. I tried to keep it all to myself. How can a heart break and bleed and yet not make any noise?

When my dad went into a short remission, he asked me about Johnny.

"I haven't seen Johnny for a while. He's well I assume?"

"I assume," I said, "though we both know what happens when we assume."

"Did you assume too much about him?"

"Yes," I said. "He's with someone else now."

"Do you miss him?" my father asked genuinely.

"How can you miss someone when it was all wrong?" I asked.

"You've got a point there, Frankie, but don't let it sway the way you

feel about men in general. We're not all bad guys."

"I know that, Dad. It's just…"

My dad waited patiently for me to simultaneously gather my thoughts and prevent tears from falling.

"I don't know how I can ever love someone again," I said.

"You will. And when you find the right person, you'll know it. You'll know it from way down deep in here," he said, pointing to his heart. "And it will feel just right."

Nineteen

"I never dreamed the team would let me go. I had a great season
and was batting close to .300. It was a shock.
But when isn't it a shock to get released?"
~ Sparky Davis, former Blackbirds first baseman

Francesca was furiously knocking on Father John's door, her knuckles turning red from the incessant pounding. She didn't know where else to turn, and he knew her as well as anyone.

He answered the door in sweats, holding a steaming cup of coffee in his hand.

"Francesca," he said, "is everything all right?"

"No, John, everything is not all right. Do you have a minute for an impromptu confession?"

"Is it a confession you need or a friend? Am I serving you as John or Father John?"

"Both."

"You know I always have time for a good confession and never close the door to a dear friend," he said.

"Well, I didn't exactly use the word 'good' when describing the confession, now, did I? I can't promise you that."

"Come in," he said, "and stop your gibberish."

She visited his home at the rectory many times. Their friendship was always strong, even when they were younger. They became even closer during her father's last fleeting days on this earth. It was actually Father John who told her to take her dad to a ballgame, despite the wheelchair and the difficulty of getting him there. He said it would do him good, and it ended up being something Francesca would never forget and would never regret. Though it was incredibly painful for her to watch her father's physical state deteriorate and watch him use every ounce of energy to do the smallest of things like take a sip of water, she brought her father to the game nonetheless; she would always treasure those moments they shared as dusk fell on the ballpark that night, the last game they would see in person together.

"Coffee?" he asked, heading toward the small kitchen area. "Or would you prefer a glass of wine maybe."

"Definitely wine. Is that okay?"

"No problem at all. Jesus was a big fan of it."

He poured her a glass in one of his crystal wine glasses, and Francesca sank into his small leather chair, worn but cozy. He was reading, and the book had been turned upside down and been kept open to mark his page on the table.

"Is it any good?" Francesca asked him, pointing to the novel.

"I'm just a big Grisham fan. I pretty much read anything he writes," he said.

"I like him, too," she said, "even though he's a man."

"Ah, I see," Father John said. "So now we're getting down to our theme of the night: 'Trouble with Men.' What's the confession?"

She nodded and sipped her wine. "Is it wrong to hate some-one…a man? Because right now, I feel hatred building up inside of me."

"Jesus doesn't like hatred, nor do I. It's not like you," he said. "What's happened?"

"I think the problem is me," she said. "I'm no good with men. They all seem to leave me."

"Who has left you?"

"Well, in high school, first it was Johnny, then it was my father, and all the other guys I've dated in college, and now it seems to be Joe."

"Clarkson, huh?" Father John raised his eyebrows.

She nodded.

"I assume it got more serious since the last confession?"

"Unfortunately," she said.

"That's a shame. He's a good hitter."

"Oh, dear Lord. Not you, too."

Father John fell silent for a moment.

"After several weeks together, things were going pretty well. But now it appears he has a very pregnant girlfriend he neglected to tell me about. I got suckered in, Father John. I even allowed myself to start to fall in love with him."

"And you're sure he's the father?"

"It appears that way."

"Sweet Lord Jesus," Father John said. On his brow, little beads of sweat started to form.

"Have you no advice to give, John? Have you nothing to offer me?"

"Only this: Hating someone for their actions is bad. It's very bad. You can be angry, because in time you will overcome that. However, to reflect back on what you said earlier, your father did not leave you. He died. Given the choice between life and death, I'm quite certain he would have preferred to have stayed with us on our dear planet a little longer."

"But the fact remains, he's not here. Not when I need him."

"No, Frannie, he may not be, but your loving mother is. Perhaps this is something you can talk with her about. Get her opinion. See what she has to say."

"She's better at that with Cissy. We don't talk about men in depth," she said. "I can't trust men. I just can't. It's over for me. What did the Raven say in Edgar Allen Poe's story? 'Nevermore.'"

"But you're here trusting me," Father John said. "And the last time I looked, I was still a man."

"Yes, but you're like a direct line to God. I'm here to listen to you tell me what God thinks I should do because apparently following my own conscience is not working."

"You know the expression, Frannie: time heals all wounds. You must breathe and consider that maybe it wasn't meant to be with Clarkson. There are bigger fish for you to fry, my friend. You are being looked after, and you must trust in the events that pass before you. There is a reason for all things. It's just that sometimes it takes a little while to figure them out."

For a long time after that comment, the pair became pensive as they listened to the quiet ticking of Father John's enormous grandfather clock while the sounds of Ella Fitzgerald played softly in the background, almost as if in a whisper. Francesca sipped her wine, allowing it to warm her insides, and she breathed deeply. After the time of introspection passed, each of them in their own meditations, she cleared her throat to break the silence. However, it was Father John who had more to say.

"When I think about what you've told me, Frannie, your high school guy—Johnny—he wasn't right for you anyway. You two were young, he was immature, and you were dealing with something that no kid her age should have to deal with. And Clarkson now, well, he's a big time ballplayer, which might come with a big ego to boot. He doesn't know what he wants, and you shouldn't be the one to try to help him figure it out, because in the end, you know who you are and what you want. It's just going to take some patience to wait for it to come along."

But what Father John failed to realize was, Francesca wasn't actually waiting for anything. She was never one to wager that she would marry by a certain age and have kids and live in a house with a white picket fence. He was probably right. In the long run, could she see herself with Joe? In fact, that night at the movie house, while she had a great time, something felt awkward through all the elaborate courting. She had never been a needy or high-maintenance type of girl; she didn't need jewels and furs, champagne and caviar.

And yet, she did what she swore she wouldn't do—she fell for him. It had taken years, she thought, to allow herself to feel emotion, and now the energy she had put into that relationship felt wasted. If Francesca allowed herself to be completely honest, she came up empty handed. She actually had no idea what she wanted in a man at all.

Or was that statement untrue? She thought again, and perhaps it was. What she wanted was a man like her father—someone kind, supportive, unselfish, and caring to a fault. Someone who made her laugh and helped her look at life with joy.

She was sitting before one of those types of men, disguised as a priest, but who was wholeheartedly a caring and kind man, so they did exist. She knew that.

She just wasn't sure if one existed for her to believe in.

She wasn't sure.

She just wasn't sure anymore.

TWENTY

"He wouldn't know a strike if it hit him square in the face. There's a reason our blood boils and we turn our freakin' hats backwards — it's because of jackasses like him calling the games!"
~ Kevin Desmond, Blackbirds manager, who was fined for his comments regarding umpire Tim Walley's controversial call at the plate

Opening Day arrived. Everything went smoothly—so smoothly, in fact, that Francesca kept waiting for something urgent to happen, but nothing ever did. The copiers ran perfectly and the assistants got the press notes up to the press box on time; the performers for Opening Day were all accounted for and strolled the concourses and the sidewalks outside the ballpark; the brand new scoreboard looked clean and crisp, and to her knowledge, no typos appeared on the screen; and the corsages for all front office female personnel were delivered and the carnations had been dyed exactly the right shade of red of the Blackbirds logo.

Francesca did not see Joe Clarkson. She had every intention of avoiding him all day. She did, unfortunately, get a glimpse of Jessica in the stands looking as primped and polished as ever, and the tight shirt she was wearing showed off her growing bump, which looked more noticeable today than it had when she first met her only a few, short hours ago.

When she felt completely famished after having not eaten at

all that morning, surviving only on two cups of coffee, she headed for the press box lounge to grab some lunch. Dan was already there waiting for her, so she stood in line for her "usual" on Opening Day: a hot dog with mustard and relish. It wasn't at all fancy, but that particular food signified "Opening Day and baseball" to her. Her father and she both clamored for hot dogs, peanuts, Coca-Cola, and Cracker Jacks on Opening Day. As cheesy as it sounds, they always waited until that moment to have a hot dog vowing not eat any at all during the off-season, further enhancing the enjoyment of it after a long winter.

"I see you've got decadent taste, Ms. Milli," Jack said. He had snuck up behind her by entering from the press door. He was staring at her fully loaded hot dog.

"The best baseball food in the world," she said. "And I'm going to top it all off with a high-caloric, non-dietetic carbonated drink. Care to join me?"

"I'd love to—and I will—after the game. But the beverage of choice at that time will be a Budweiser. Remember? You owe me one."

"How could I forget? I almost killed you twice and must pay for my mistakes."

"That's right," he said. "So be ready to ante up."

She laughed.

"Two attempts at injuring me call for a real beverage," he said. "Now, I've got to get back and cover the game. That's why they pay me the big bucks, you know." He winked.

"See you after the game," she said.

She hoped she would not open a door in his face or send his laptop crashing to the floor when next they met.

Kevin Desmond was ejected from the game. Francesca, along with forty-seven thousand other people stood in utter shock as he ran out to homeplate, turned his hat backwards, and screamed expletives in umpire Tim Walley's face. Francesca had never seen Desmond's face get that red before. When he used the "F" word consecutively and inappropriately told the ump that Ray Charles could have made a better call, he was tossed from the field, ejected during Game One of the regular season. Never in all her years had she witnessed behavior like that on Opening Day. It was the start of the season, and although baseball was not as gentlemanly a sport as golf, it was considered a more mannered sport than many others. It made Francesca wonder if there wasn't something else going on in Desmond's life. It takes balls—or as her grandmother would say, *coglioni*—to argue that way and risk being tossed out in front of a packed house on such a ceremonial day.

Dan and Francesca stood in awe, embarrassed as the ballpark erupted with boos. Their colleagues in the control room, who were responsible for the in-game entertainment, were trying to handle the tense situation by playing light music, but unfortunately, the noise from the crowd was drowning it out.

"Unbelievable," Dan said. "Why did he let it go that far today of all days?"

"No clue," Francesca said. "What do they say? Bad publicity is sometimes as favorable as good publicity. Not sure that's true, but look at the fans. This place is electric."

They stood for a moment at the top of the stairs with the ushers behind home plate. Their credentials that they wore allowed them to go anywhere in the ballpark, and the ushers were always amenable, allowing them to sit in empty seats or stand in the back of the row with them as long they didn't obstruct the view of the fans.

Even though Desmond was ejected, it did something to spark the team, as they were down by a score of 5-1 in the bottom of the 5th inning. By the time the top of the order came up to bat, the Blackbirds managed to get one man on base. By the 7th inning, the Blackbirds had tied the game, despite the manager's forced disappearance.

It didn't take long for the Blackbirds to pull it together under the direction of bench coach Freddie Montrose. The Fly knew this game—maybe even better than Desmond. He knew exactly how to motivate the players, and Francesca suspected that one day, he'd get his day in the sun. Perhaps he would be named a manager with the Blackbirds or get an offer from another club.

Kirk Johnson, the left-handed hurler they acquired from San Francisco, shut down Detroit and the antics that ensued looked like a championship win. The team congregated on the mound, jumping up and down, their arms around each other, smacking each other on the back, rejoicing in pure celebration.

It was at times like these that Francesca felt the deep pang. Her father would have loved this Opening Day's chaotic, yet perfect ending. Back at the office afterward, employees were high-fiving each other, smiling, laughing, and talking about Desmond's ejection. David was still down on the field setting up interviews, most of them with Freddie, but he ordered up a case of beer for the offices with a note attached that said, "This is our year!"

Everyone was having so much fun rehashing the drama of the day's events, that it completely slipped Francesca's mind to meet Jack for a drink until he tracked her down by calling the office line.

"Francesca, it's for you," one of the assistants called.

"Hello?" she said.

"Are you trying to get out of this because your boy was ejected?"

"First, no. And second, he is not my boy. I'll be right up."

She grabbed the keys off her desk, locked the office door behind her, and began the walk to the press box. She arrived out of breath from the quick pace she kept the entire walk there. He was still in the main press area, seated at one of the counters, writing his story. He saw her enter, and winked. That was his thing. That little wink of his. He held up his finger as if to say "be with you in one minute," and Francesca moved to the press lounge to wait for him.

She was well acquainted with most of the local media, as they covered most—if not all—of the Blackbirds 81-home games. There were several beers on tap, and remembering Jack mentioned Budweiser, she selected it and picked a table near the window.

"Hey, Francesca," Dom Longfellow said, as he watched her set the beers on the table. He worked for Blackbirds Radio as the sports director. "Gotta love your team today," he said.

"Sure do. If today's any indication of how this team might play this year, it may not be as painful as last season," Francesca said.

"I'm certain it will be a good year. I've just got that feeling. Clarkson looks good—real good. A dinger with four RBIs and that tremendous outfield catch. Not too shabby for day one."

She nodded and bit her tongue.

Jack walked in and sat next to her with a sigh, stretching in his chair and getting the kinks out of his shoulders.

"Glad you made it," she said. "Bet you had a lot to write about."

"You can say that again. Thanks for getting me a beer."

"You did say a Bud, didn't you?"

He nodded. "I like a woman who pays attention to the details," he said, and grabbed his glass, taking a sip.

Francesca looked at him and he was smiling at her. She knew they were close in age—maybe he had a couple of years on her—and he was clearly one of the youngest reporters in the press box. His hair was dark, and he had a dimple on the left side when he grinned. Something told her that there was a lot to learn about Jack-Dash Thompson. As he sat there peering at her over his still somewhat foamy beer, she smiled back. For a minute, neither of them said anything.

"You look nice today," he said. "I like the corsage. Nice touch."

"Thank you," she said. "We always get them on Opening Day. Do you want anything to eat?"

"No thanks," he said. "I ate earlier. So, how was your day over-all?" he asked.

"Good until all hell broke loose on the field," she said. "But on our end, things ran rather smoothly."

"Well, that's how it goes when you have a competent woman at the helm," he said.

"I like this," she said, sitting back in her seat and crossing her legs, looking at him across the table. "Two nice compliments in the span of two minutes. I'm starting to feel really good about myself."

He laughed. His eyes twinkled when he did, and he reminded her of someone, but she couldn't quite put her finger on it. There was something familiar about him. Something warm and friendly.

"Everyone needs someone to pump them up. That's why I have Dom," Jack said, leaning back far enough so Dom could hear.

Dom was sitting behind them, and Francesca didn't notice that he was eavesdropping on the conversation, but Jack did. He was mess-ing with him, but all in good fun. Dom got up from his table and made his way back for something else to eat.

"So, I've been meaning to ask you, where does someone our age go out and have fun in this city?" Jack asked.

"Honestly, I'm the wrong person to ask. I think I've been out three times in the last six months, and they were so unimpressionable, I can't remember where I went. You'll have to ask some of the assistants. They go out a lot more than I do."

"What, are you not invited to their outings?"

"Yes, they invite me, but it can be uncomfortable because I'm the boss, and now I'm a little older than they are; I don't want to compromise my position by becoming too familiar, you know?"

"I can understand that," he said, "but you've got to live a little."

Francesca knew he was right, but he hardly knew her and was offering advice.

"And what, pray tell, makes you such an expert on social lives?"

"Oh, God. I'm not an expert at all. In fact, I have little to no social life, except for with other writers who travel with the team. I usually end up spending so much time with them that I'm surprised they don't buy me chocolates and flowers."

"Very funny," Francesca said. "You can have a social life, you just need to make time for it, not find time for it."

He motioned for his reporter's notebook, took out his pencil, and said, "Will you go on the record as having said that?"

She laughed.

"You may want to heed that wonderful advice you just offered," Jack said.

"Tried it, but it didn't work," she said.

"What? With Clarkson?"

Francesca's mouth dropped open. She was mortified. Jack-Dash Thompson knew about it? And if he knew about it, then everyone knew about it. She suspected news of it was being plastered all over the clubhouse or churning through the rumor mill. She was rendered speechless, just like that, and her face turned a deep shade of red.

He put his hand on her forearm. "It's okay. You don't have to be embarrassed…"

"Oh my God!" she said, whispering the best she could, trying not to draw attention to what was happening at the table by the window. "Honestly, that really is none of your business, and I have absolutely no intention of discussing it with you."

She got up from her chair and began to leave. She turned on her heels, her body taking over for her mind, as she walked over to the trash can, tossed her beer into the garbage, and marched out the door, cognizant that she was being watched every step of the way.

Seventh Inning Stretch

"I start getting concerned if we're down by a few runs when I hear the
Seventh Inning Stretch song, and when I do, I know it's 'game on.'
In my mind, from that point forward, everything matters."
~ Duke Milton, Blackbirds Catcher

I probably always knew I would be a sports writer.

Actually, that's not entirely true. I didn't always know. I found writing again after I was cut from "A" ball. When the manager released me, even though my dream was to play ball, I knew my professional career was done. I could play ball, I reasoned, but it would most likely be in a men's recreational league. When I got the news that Sunday afternoon, I threw a couple of bats around and kicked the locker with all the force I had. I bruised my big toe and swore I would put playing ball behind me.

It was fortunate for me that I enjoyed writing and wasn't too bad at it. As a journalism major in college, I wrote for the school news-paper. The portfolio of clips I saved helped get my foot in the door at *The Tribune*. I was a stringer for a while, covering local high school games, and then I got my big break—a chance to cover a big league game when my colleague had surgery on his rotator cuff.

When I saw my first by-line for a major paper, it did send me. I won't lie about that. By Jack Thompson. I kept that first paper. It's hanging over my desk in a frame in much the same way that people who start a business hang their first dollar they make.

Once I got a taste of sitting in a press box, discussing the game I loved with other professional enthusiasts, I latched on to it at that point. Plus, I knew what I was doing and could talk shop as good—if not better—than others. I'd been in the trenches. I knew the rules and rigors of the game.

Still it would pain me when I'd watch a pro game sometimes—I knew I wasn't as good as those big leaguers, but still I wondered. Could I have spent more time in the batting cages? Could I have fielded a few more grounders? Could I have bulked up a little more in the weight room?

Life on the road covering the team wasn't always easy. It was limiting if you wanted to have serious friendships or relationships. I spent lonely nights hanging out in bars and hotel rooms and running for connecting flights. Once I got the job covering the Blackbirds, I bought myself a nice condo on the water downtown. Additionally, I made a pledge to myself: to slow down and attempt to have a social life. It had been a while.

I met people daily on the job—sad ones who had given up the opportunity to have a family or those who desperately missed their families while on the road—to be a sports journalist. While some were happy, not all were, but I wasn't complaining. I just vowed never to be like the unhappy lot. It was tough to find a middle ground. It's true—it was my choice not to be in a relationship, although I hoped I would not be alone for the rest of my life. Additionally, I couldn't bear the thought of putting my future wife—and potentially kids—through the agonizing notion of having me as an absentee husband and father. The job required me to travel eighty-one nights a year, minimum. And the other eighty-one nights would be spent in a ballpark in your hometown. And though some might have considered that an "ideal" setup that could lead to a successful marriage playing into such romantic notions as "absence makes the heart grow fonder," I believed it was hard on all three parties involved: the kids, the mom, and the dad.

My father played minor league ball. His career lasted a mere six seasons, and he made it to the big leagues for 181 of those days. But he was a smart man and knew when to get out of it; he inherited a little bit of money, just enough to purchase and run a car dealership having sacrificed attending college, and he's been doing that ever since. I knew he missed the game. It was a fraternity of brothers, all there for the purpose of playing baseball. Swinging a bat; running for home; catching balls that were shot up into the glare of the lights. It didn't matter. He wanted to be playing on that field.

I guess the same was true for me. It was my goal to go further than my old man did, but there were so many others who were better. If you're one of those people who sits in the stands or watches the game on television, let me assure you, those guys are way better than you can imagine, and at times I wanted to spew a few obscenities at jackasses who liked to coach from the stands or call players bums or worse. Baseball isn't an easy game to play, and only the best would rise to the top. Players who could rip the ball and those who could field the ball at that caliber were worthy of playing to sold-out crowds and allowing their name to be a household one. Those guys were worth the money they were paid. If the owners were willing to pay it—and it appeared they were—then across the board, those guys got paid for doing their jobs. It's a rough life, and it's high pressure. However, I saw what the game had done to families—both good and bad—either ripping them to shreds and causing major fallouts between the players and their loved ones or watching them have unbelievable support from those closest to them.

Roll the dice. Some people handled it better than others.

I just knew—even then—that I wasn't willing to take the risk. I had an idea of how long I would do the job, and, like my father, would also know when to get out. Plus, when Sarah died, right there in my arms, I vowed I'd always be there for someone, come hell or high water.

I probably won Sarah over not by telling her I was going to cover baseball as an occupation, but because I told her I was going to write as an occupation. She had the biggest crush on Nicholas Sparks—anything he wrote, she read, and then she would talk about it for days. She was an avid reader, so it was no surprise she was going to be a teacher.

We met in line at the Registrar's office during our junior year of college when we both had scheduling problems. It took the two of us sharing a course booklet to get us to talk. Once we did, we never really stopped.

Sarah lived on one side of campus, and I lived on the other side, but once we got together, we essentially lived in each other's rooms. We studied together, ate meals together, and attended events and happy hours together. Initially, I was drawn to Sarah because she was sweet and shy. She wasn't pushy or outspoken, but kind and respectful, but once you got to know her, a little devilish side came out. She was funny—and she made me laugh.

I decided to move to Chicago to start writing for *The Tribune* after my baseball career was over; she said she wanted to come with me. Even though I would be on the road a lot, we were committed to each other and decided to give it a try. We'd been together for a while at that point, and I knew I wanted Sarah in my life, not just as a temporary part of it, but for the whole of it. I asked her to marry me one cold, windy night before Christmas. We would have married on Christmas Eve the following year.

That summer, however, as she was planning our wedding, orchestrating every detail of it, we made a commitment to represent the newspaper at a black-tie fundraiser in the city. We lived on the outskirts, and had driven in for the event that night.

As we made our way home, someone intoxicated and driving on the other side of the road crossed the median and hit my car, forcing my own car into a tree. I could barely move, but I could see Sarah was struggling. I unclasped my seat belt and cradled her in my arms as she winced in pain.

"Hold on, Sarah," I called, "help will be here soon!"

I could feel the blood dripping off my own forehead, but the damage I could see that had been done to her caused me to panic, and then I saw flashing lights and heard the ambulance. I thought she would be saved.

"I love you, Sarah," I said, frantically, as the medics were taking me out gently and trying to calm me. Another set was working on her. "I love you—"

I'm not sure she ever heard me.

Naturally, after the accident, it took me a while to come around. My parents and my sister from the East Coast tried to help me pick up the pieces after Sarah's death and funeral. They provided meals and put their arms around me on the couch as we sat silently and stared ahead at the television. Weeks later, when I did come around, I threw myself into my work. It was all I had at that point. I'd lost my fiancée, and yet my career was taking off. It seemed sacrilegious to be conducting interviews and watching baseball. The story of Sarah's passing garnered quite a bit of media attention because the gentleman who hit us had been convicted of drunk driving, though he had no previous record. I was quoted in stories, and although I was angry and devastated, once I saw the man—who looked just like any one of us—it pained me to know his life was equally as miserable. He was going to have to live with the fact that he killed someone. Drinking and driving never mix, but I could be honest with myself enough to know there were a few times when I shouldn't have put myself behind the wheel of a car. My emotions were all over the place, and yet from somewhere deep in me, I felt compassion for what he was going through. A father of four with a wife, he attended a similar event that evening, and made the wrong choice to get behind the wheel. The consequences he faced for that choice were surely going to ruin the rest of his days on this earth. I resolved that to be significant punishment, though I will never stop missing Sarah. But interestingly enough, the loss of her didn't stir as much anger as it did an interminable sadness and a void that I was certain would never be filled again.

I attended church as a child and even into my teenage years, though I would not have called myself a religious person before. Nonetheless, I went through the motions, and I definitely had my beliefs, but I never needed help until a tragedy of that magnitude took hold of my life.

Getting through it was something I could not do alone, not if I wanted to survive. I'd never needed help like that before, but when I did recognize I needed it, it came in the form of two men who were ironically and inexorably tied to baseball.

Damian Gaynor was a star centerfield for Chicago. He was agile and fast, and made stealing bases look like the norm in baseball. If you glanced at him quickly, you may have mistaken him for Ricky Henderson. He was with the team for a while, and I wrote about him constantly for the paper because he was a clutch player. Plus, he was generally known in the clubhouse as being a pretty nice guy. Raised in the south by a boisterous minister and his active and effervescent church wife, he learned of the accident and reached out to me.

"Jack, you know you need to reach out for help. It's there for you if you ask for it," he said, putting his arm around me in the clubhouse one day. "My Baptist father can sit and listen to your problems. He can talk you through it."

"Thanks, man," I said, "but I'm Roman Catholic."

"Then you need to reach out to your Pope," he said.

"You mean priest?"

"Pope, priest…any one of those guys will do. You're hurting, man. I want to see you get back to yourself. You lost a great thing, it's true, but you're young and you got a lot of living to do," he said.

I wasn't really sure why Damian felt compelled to console me, but I appreciated it. He was the only player who addressed the situation at all. Damian became a friend to me. I met his father. He offered kind words and invited me to dinner. He told me to reconnect with my church, to find someone I could lean on who would help me get past the death of Sarah. I was thankful for the advice, but it was Damian I was most thankful for during that ordeal. He and I became close after that. There's a certain bond that forms between people sometimes, especially after a tragedy strikes. For whatever reason, there are some friendships you know you will never give up on and that you'll cherish forever, no matter what.

I'm sure Damian's father would be pleased to know that I did seek help at his suggestion, and it did come to me because I found the courage to ask for it.

I went to church that following Sunday before the afternoon home game I was scheduled to cover. I quietly asked the receptionist at the ballclub where the Catholic players went to church, and she gave me the name of a congregation nearby where the priest was connected to the team. The church bulletin had been handed out after mass, and I waited patiently until the congregation cleared before I approached the priest. His name was Father Brian.

"Excuse me, Father," I said. "By any chance, would you have a moment?"

The priest put his arm around me gently. "I always have time," he said. "Would you like to come to the parish office?"

"That would be fine," I said.

He was an older man, with grey hair and crystal blue eyes that seemed to be full of kindness. I don't know if it was because people wearing robes just looked holy or because they're nurturing by nature, but the second I met him, I felt as if someone understood my heartbreak.

He offered me a chair, and I sat down. He sat across from me, gently crossing his legs beneath his vestments.

"I can tell something is weighing heavily on your mind," he said.

"Yes," I said. I could hold it in no longer and broke down into tears, sobbing, mumbling that it had been my fault and that my fiancée was dead because of it. When he calmed me down, I realized he knew my story because he read about it in the newspaper.

"I know the story, my son," he said, placing his hand on my shoulder. "It was not your fault."

I was still kicking myself for putting my big foot in my mouth. I should never have mentioned Clarkson's name to Francesca.

Francesca was the only woman I found remotely interested in talking to since Sarah. I'm not sure if the initial attraction was the result of the way her doe-like eyes seemed to look deep within me when I talked to her, or the way her shiny, dark hair swung a bit when she spoke, but there was something exceptionally intriguing about her. Nevertheless, it was probably pointless. I put up walls and barriers that were tough to break down, as a few women who tried to get in afterward could attest. As the years passed, I became lonelier and realized that at some point I'd have to let go of Sarah and the accident. It was a tough endeavor. The story line would never change: I lived, but Sarah did not. I asked myself the same question over and over and over again: What exactly was fair about that statement? Nothing. And I've learned it takes a certain amount of acceptance, and an ability to forgive yourself, if you have a shot at having any sort of a life after losing someone you love. It took me years to grieve for Sarah, and I suppose I may continue to do so all the remaining days of my life.

I barely knew Francesca, but I detected there was something vulnerable about her. During our few conversations, I could sense it. Deep inside her, I suspected there was something there that she doesn't talk about. Could she possibly be a little bit broken like me?

How often we take relationships for granted and waste hours and minutes and seconds being angry or bitter toward friends and family. As a grown man who had suffered enough, I saw its uselessness, and I questioned why people said and did some of the things they said and did only to regret them later. My mother used to say that God created apologies so they could be delivered, received, and accepted.

I pissed Francesca off by mentioning Joe Clarkson earlier, even though I don't know at all what happened between them. I just guessed.

Intuition told me something was going on between them that night at the banquet. A reporter has instincts, and I perceived something deeper than a casual working relationship was developing. Perhaps Clarkson was in love with her. What happened after that night, I don't know.

The truth is, I haven't dated in a long, long time, and admittedly, I'm out of practice. I suppose I went about checking her potential availability in the wrong manner.

That, my friends, was a strike out.

TWENTY-ONE

"Somebody let me know when Clarkson finds the sweet spot,
for God's sake!"
~ Kevin Desmond, Blackbirds Manager, prior to the
press conference following the game

One thing you didn't do as the community relations director was to make Kevin Desmond's players late. He hated tardiness. If you so much as showed up on the field one second late for batting practice, he barked at you, swallowing you whole. Sometimes those barks were worse than others, but he and Francesca always maintained a mutual level of respect for each other. Or so she thought.

Rumors were flying, and then the Blackbirds acquired a player named Damian Gaynor from Chicago much earlier in the season than they expected. Gaynor was a solid hitter who kept raising his average every year. He was batting .300 with Chicago until he was traded. The Blackbirds needed his bat and his speed, and it seemed all the baseball operations folks were pleased with the trade.

Francesca was meeting Gaynor for only the second time, and was headed toward the clubhouse, her script in hand. From their first interaction following the press conference, he had agreed to do a public service announcement for kids about staying away from drugs. Francesca had learned from her counterpart, Gretchen, in Chicago, that he'd been a big supporter of drug education in the schools there. She told

Francesca he'd probably be willing to continue his course of action with Bay City if the Blackbirds had a similar program. When Francesca asked him after his short press conference if he'd be willing, he was quite amiable and agreed to do it. She arranged to shoot the public service announcement—the PSA—and now Gaynor was set to do it before batting practice.

The shot was set up in the infield, with the outfield wall and scoreboard in the background. It was a beautiful day, and the clouds looked as if they were painted in the sky. It was crisp out; there wasn't a trace of humidity in the air. The shoot went extremely well, and Gaynor was a natural at reading the cards. In two takes, he'd created a strong message: "Hey, kids. Listen to your parents, your teachers, and those who love you. Stay away from drugs. There are more important things to do with your life in this world. Stay healthy, play sports, do well in school, and be an inspiration. You have the willpower to do it. Be a sport, and stay away from drugs." He gave the camera his sparkling smile, flashed his one dimple, and Francesca was confident they just recorded a strong message for kids. That's what the club was there for: to spread messages that children and adults would understand and to make their club one of the best outreach organizations in baseball.

What she didn't mean to do, as the video crew was packing up and Gaynor was shaking hands, was piss off Desmond. Like a bat out of hell, he came over to her, pointing his fingers, shouting at the top of his lungs: "Francesca—don't you make my players late. Don't you dare make my players late for batting practice! You hear me? You hear me?" Reporters were on the field taking notes as they watched batting practice, but for a moment, it all got quiet and still. All eyes were on her. She was the focus of all of their attention, and she could feel the stares, some of them snickering, some of them feeling badly for her. All she could do was move her feet.

She ushered the video crew off the warning track and into the home plate exit. She thanked them, trying to hold her head high while simultaneously attempting to disguise the humiliation that was building. As predicted, she knew one day she'd have her ass chewed out for something. She just didn't expect it to be quite so public.

Gaynor trotted off to his outfield position and vanished from sight. He didn't look her in the eyes, but rather ran out onto the field looking straight down at the grass. Lucky him, she thought. He didn't have to reap the wrath of Desmond.

As she was getting ready to go up the press elevator, still shaking, she ran into Jack. They acknowledged each other in the elevator for a brief moment, and then the two looked down at the carpet as others entered. It had been a couple of weeks since they'd had contact, and Francesca was feeling a little guilty about her tantrum in the press lounge when she walked away. She pretended to look at her notes, as if something of great import had been written on them, her hands still trembling slightly from the incident on the field, and the elevator doors opened. They both got out.

"Francesca," he called, as she darted off in front of him, her heels clicking on the cement as fast as they could go. She had no choice but to turn around and acknowledge him.

"Yes," she said.

"Hey, I'm sorry about what happened out there with Desmond."

She was mortified once again. He had seen it? She hadn't seen him on the field. "Don't worry about it," he continued, "he's a total hothead. He's screamed in my face and other reporters' faces countless times."

"Thanks," she said, nodding. "That's helpful."

"I'm also really sorry about the comment I made the other day. It truly was not meant to be intrusive. Reporters are just curious by nature, that's all."

"I understand," she said. "It's just..." She had to collect her thoughts for a moment. She wasn't used to opening up to anyone but Father John, and occasionally her mother. She struggled, embarrassingly so, until she found the right way to say it. "It's just that I don't usually discuss my personal matters at work."

"I understand. Really, I do. Probably more than you know."

There was something about the way he said those words that made Francesca believe that he knew something of hurt or mistrust or broken love. She wasn't sure what it was, but saw it there for an instant, and she felt sorry for her actions.

"It's not a problem, really," she said, trying to brush it off and lessen the degree of awkwardness that was standing between them. "Let's not talk about it again. It was ridiculous of me to overreact. Next time, I'll buy you a real beer without all the dramatics," she said. She caught herself and realized she was inviting him out.

"That would be great. When?" he asked.

"How about Thursday," she said. "It's an off day. Meet you at Shamrock's on 41st? Seven o'clock?"

"Luckily for you, my calendar just happens to be wide open that night," he said.

Francesca spent some time back at her desk cleaning up piles of work, hanging her head in shame, and wondering if Desmond felt badly about the spectacle he made of himself and her. No doubt she would not receive an apology from him. He was notorious for being an asshole during post-game interviews, especially when the team lost, as they did today. Joe struck out three times, and while they played well in the field, their bats were silent.

Her desk was piled high with requests: there were requests for player appearances from organizations all over the city. When the team was playing well, the requests were doubled—tripled even—and it required meticulous organization and conscientious, pragmatic decision-making to pick the places where the players were most needed. The guys traveled during the year, and it was often difficult to match their schedules with events. Honestly, Francesca's department did the best it could. The club's efforts made some members of the community extremely happy and then, with no malicious intent, disappointed others. However, Francesca and her team did their best to try to minimize disappointment where they could by offering the mascot or items for auction to help raise money for various organizations.

She worked while the ballpark emptied and traffic dissipated, though it was tough to focus. She was happy for the distraction of dinner with her mother in an hour, so she was just biding her time. She was watching the post-game show and highlights on the television in her office. Desmond was as ornery as ever during the question and answer segment with the reporters, responding in his ever-glib, snide and sarcastic style. He probably hadn't even thought twice about chewing her out earlier, and she dared to guess it would even cross his mind.

As she was organizing her desk and shoving paperwork into her briefcase, there was a light rap on her office door. She turned around to see someone she had not expected to see standing in the doorway.

"You got a minute?" he asked.

She was caught off-guard and didn't know what to say. He was freshly showered, and she could smell the scent of his cologne wafting in from the doorway.

"I suppose," Francesca said, turning to him and folding her arms across her chest.

The old Clarkson smile was gone, and he looked more wounded

than anything. He shut her office door behind him and sat down on the couch under the window, turning his head to peer outside.

"Always a good view from here," he said, looking across to the field.

"One of my perks, I suppose," she said.

She leaned against the wall, staring at him. They hadn't been face-to-face since the end of their romance, which took place during spring training. She wouldn't answer any of his calls for the past three weeks.

"Look, I'm sorry about—"

"No need to be sorry about her. I should have known better. I should have known there was someone else. I never even asked if there was. How stupid I was—"

He cut her off with his hand raised, and stood.

"For me, there was no one else," he said.

"Do you take me for a stupid woman, Joe?"

"You are not stupid. Just let me speak," he said. "All I want you to do is listen."

"Why should I?"

"Because I'm asking you to," he said.

She huffed, then walked over to her desk chair, folded her arms, and sat down. The expression on her face told him to start speaking.

"Jessica—Jessica was my high school girlfriend. We've been on again and off again for years. For years! Honestly, I don't even know why I…I didn't think about what I was doing. I got carried away, maybe even sentimental, when I went home for Thanksgiving. We hooked up, but that was before you and I—"

Francesca stood and interrupted. She couldn't hear it. "There is no you and I," she said.

"You're not letting me talk, Frankie."

"I told you not to call me that!" Her blood was boiling now.

"Please, let me finish, Francesca. I was with her before you and I started seeing each other. I didn't know she was pregnant. She purposely kept it from me, not wanting to tell me because she was keeping the baby regardless."

"You didn't know?"

"No! She only told me recently. I got the call when I was at spring training, right after you left. She kept it from me all this time. It appears she didn't know for sure it was mine. She was seeing someone else back home."

"Good grief," Francesca said. "Musical beds back in Hillsboro, I suppose."

"Frankie—Francesca—I didn't know how to handle it. I've been upset about it. I mean, it's a pretty big mistake to make," he said.

"Yes. And now you're engaged apparently."

"No, we're not, but that's what seems to be going around. And now there is a soon-to-be child involved in my mistake."

"Yes," she said. "Pretty big mistake, I'd say."

There was a momentary pause, and the two of them looked at each other without saying a word. She could feel his eyes on her, looking at her, searching her, as if a burst of forgiveness and understanding might come bounding from her soul, her mouth. Francesca let the silence hang in the air as she collected herself and spoke calmly, but firmly.

"Listen, Joe, I honestly don't know how you want me to respond. It's disappointing. I'm disappointed. What do you want from me?"

"I just wanted you to listen. I'm sorry. You mean everything to me. Our relationship was just taking off, and I'm now caught up in a big mess. I'm sorry this happened. I couldn't face you. I suppose I was biding my time trying to come up with a solution. I even talked to Freddie about it. He was the one who told me to straighten things out with you."

"Is that why Freddie knows about us?" she asked.

"Yes. I felt I could tell him and it wouldn't go anywhere."

He was doing a good job of trying to save himself from Francesca's wrath, but she couldn't help but sink the already tottering ship.

"You should have spoken to me about this sooner. You could have told me what happened and not tried to hide it. Some people now know we were together—people I work with—and I look like the idiot girl who allowed Joe Clarkson to get into her pants. You are going to be a father to a child with a woman you've known for ages. You should have come clean with me, Joe. You're no dummy; you just acted like one."

She grabbed her purse, and started to walk toward the door.

"Come on. I've got to go. I have dinner plans, and I don't want to be late," she said.

He got up dejectedly, and walked toward the door. Francesca flicked the light switch off, and shut the door behind her. He pulled her close to him, and she was shocked when he did it.

"You must believe that I care for you. I so badly need you to believe this. When I said I never felt this way about anyone before, I meant it. Won't you consider sticking with me on this?"

"And what would you have me do? Help raise your baby?"

"If you care for me, you'd consider doing whatever it takes to make it work between us."

Francesca would not consider anything at that moment except leaving it all behind. It had become a nightmare, and she was tired from it all. She couldn't think about it another second. This was why she had stayed away from men, and until getting involved with Joe, had pretty much sworn them off altogether.

"Thank you for the apology. I appreciate that you finally talked to me about it. Unfortunately, though, something has transpired that cannot be undone, even if it took place before you and I became involved. We can't make this go away, and I'm already weary from thinking about it."

He nodded. His eyes could not hide his sense of confusion and regret. Three strikeouts during the game and an apology gone wrong. He stood there waiting—seemingly hoping—for her to change her mind. She stood firm and did not speak once the words hung in the air, a transparent, yet weighted divide standing between them.

For a second, she almost felt sorry for him, almost told him so, almost reached out to hug him, but she didn't. She let what he said resonate with her, as she again heard the words that he "cared for her" instead of the more meaningful and heartfelt and powerful words—that he "loved her." And moreover, his retreat from her life and subsequent actions reinforced what she suspected she might already feel and believe. Something wasn't right.

"Goodnight, Frankie," he said, "and I hope you'll change your mind."

She turned to go, and he turned in the opposite direction. She watched as he moved away from her, the space between them increasing with every step he took as he followed the hallway toward the door to the parking lot marked *Players Only*.

Francesca's mother was waiting for her at the restaurant. The team had played a Sunday afternoon game, and despite the strange occurrences, Francesca did not want to cancel on her mother. When she walked toward the table, she noticed how good her mother looked. Rosy cheeked and smiling, she pulled out Francesca's chair for her. It was a cozy Italian place on the edge of town with candlelight and white tablecloths with fresh flowers. Sinatra played softly in the background. It had been one of her dad's favorite places. Francesca felt the sadness overwhelm her. All of it. It was too much to bear, but she fought back the tears.

"Look at you!" her mother said. "You clean up well."

"Mom, you know I do actually dress nicely for work. I'm all grown up now. No more torn Levi's and sweatshirts. I'm a big girl."

"Well, I like it," she said. Her mother took a look at her and knew. "What is it? Something's wrong."

"Well, to start, I was humiliated by the manager today for making a player late for batting practice."

Her mother spread her napkin across her lap attempting to be cheerful and supportive. "Oh, like he's never been late to anything before," she said.

Francesca loved when her mother stood up for her, even in her little ways. It was her way of demonstrating her solidarity.

"So how's life other than that at the ballpark? I ran into Father John," her mother said. "Is everything okay with you personally?"

Isn't it a priest's job not to tell of another's woes? Isn't that in itself a sin?

"I'm fine," Francesca said, but her words were not matching her emotional state, and before she could restrain herself, tears started to puddle in her eyes, and then they were streaming uncontrollably down her face. Francesca's mother reached into her purse right away and offered her a stack of tissues, trying to hide that she was surprised to see emotion of this nature emanating from her daughter.

"Oh, my poor girl. What is it? What's gone wrong?"

Francesca had to take a moment to get herself together. What had she become? She could usually handle difficult challenges without shedding any tears; she could always manage things herself. Why was she feeling so off-kilter? She took a second to pull it together, and was thankful they were seated in the corner, in a position where her face was looking out a window and not into the main dining room.

"I was seeing one of the ballplayers a little bit—it got a little serious, though I really should have listened to Isabelle and should have avoided any sort of intimate relationship at all costs—and when he went to spring training, things fell apart. That's it. There really isn't any more to it."

"Clarkson? The one who sent the flowers to me?"

"Yes, him," Francesca said. She dabbed her eyes with the tissue, and composed herself. She was beginning to feel embarrassed by her own behavior. She had turned into a silly girl. Francesca hated silly girls.

"So you two are not together now?" her mother asked. "Things are over?"

"Well, yes. The icing on the cake is that his former girlfriend is pregnant...with his child. So no, we're not together."

This time her mother couldn't mask her surprise. The two of them had reached unchartered territory; Francesca never asked for her opinion on love and romance and her mother never really offered it, mostly because Francesca never gave her the chance to do so. Her mother looked as if she didn't know how to respond. But she did.

"As your mother, I can see that your life is full, no matter if there's a ballplayer—or boyfriend—in it or not, Francesca. Don't go looking for love or forcing it, and don't mourn for it when it isn't right. It will come when you are ready, and not before that. There are many fish in the sea as you are well aware, and you haven't needed the support of a man yet. I'd say you're doing just fine."

"That's not necessarily true, Mom. I needed the love and support of Dad."

"He gave you all the love and support he could give until he could give no more," she said, "and look how his influences have paid off? You are a strong, independent, successful woman. And the last time I looked, you didn't get here with help from any man—including your dear father. You got here on your own. As your father would say, that's a 'sweet spot,' my dear."

Her mother was using her father's words—his baseball analogies—again. Unable to contain herself, Francesca began to sob again, this time more vigorously; right in front of her mother, she continued to weep. It had been a taxing day. From being yelled at by the manager, to Joe's apology, to interacting with Jack, to now sitting and having a frank discussion with her surprisingly supportive and proud mother, it was about all Francesca could take. Perpetual tears continued to fall. She was unable to stop.

While she continued to sniffle and dab at her runny mascara, the stack of tissues strewn on the table, Francesca's non-judgmental mother came around to Francesca's side of the table and gave her a little hug and a kiss on top of her head.

Francesca smiled through her blubbering. How long had she not appreciated her mother, Francesca wondered.

DISABLED LIST

I was sixteen and learning to drive my father's old car. It had been sitting in the driveway for years, impeccably kept, my father holding on to the paid-off vehicle so it could be my car to drive when I got my license. Apparently, my father and mother tossed a coin to see who had to take me driving to practice that day. My father had won the toss. He had the patience of a saint, the fortitude of a teacher, and the mouth of a sailor.

"Holy shit balls!" he said when I backed the car into the fire hydrant that sat at the foot of the driveway, cracking the rear bumper.

I couldn't get the car out of the long driveway. Pathetic. I hit the yellow hydrant as I was in reverse, and when I'd stepped on the brakes and then put the car into drive, I heard the rip, the tear.

My father hopped out of the car from the passenger's side to inspect the damage. I could see him in the rear view mirror.

He pounded on the window and told me to get out of the car.

"You've got to see this," he shouted.

I stepped out from behind the wheel and closed the door behind me. I walked over to him as he stood there, admiring the damage, stroking his chin and puzzling over it. I didn't know what to expect.

"Well, I've got to hand it to you, Frankie," he said. "You beat the shit out of this car, and we didn't even hit the road. You should get a damn medal for that!"

I looked at him and started to laugh. It was difficult not to. The rear bumper was hanging from the car, and the yellow paint from the hydrant streaked the backside of the black vehicle, making it look like tiger stripes. It looked like a "Sanford & Son" car now.

"I'm sorry, Dad," I said, trying to hold back my giggles.

He put his arm around me, shaking his head in disbelief.

"Come on then," he said, pushing the bumper back into place the best he could and giving it a little kick with his foot. "Let's take this heap of crap out for a spin and see what else you can destroy before we have to put it on the DL," he said.

Twenty-Two

"What do I do on my off day? Exactly what most ballplayers do—rest,
watch television, and if it's nice out and my spikes are clean,
I play golf."
~ Zeke Watson, Blackbirds Hall of Famer

An off-day was something to be cherished. When there are one hundred and sixty-two games in a baseball season and eighty-one of those games happen to be played at home, you work a hell of a lot of nights and weekends, including every weekday from eight-thirty until around six in the evening. Everyone knew that the dinosaur days of a true nine to five job were gone, and a position working in sports with a long season only made you work longer and harder. Some days seemed endless, especially when a game went into extra innings and you saw the clock strike midnight and your team was still playing. And you were still in heels. And there was a tied score.

Those days were the culprits of lost sleep and long hours: extra-innings and rain delays. Some were never-ending, stretching from the early hours of the morning until well past midnight and into the sunrise hours of the next morning. Only those who loved the game as much as she did could exist on a steady diet of little sleep and didn't pay attention too much to the reality that they seemed to live where they worked. She often joked that she should just move her dresser and toiletries into her office; there was no reason to leave the ballpark on some nights other than to catch a cat nap, shower, and change into fresh clothes.

Francesca stood in the back of the press box that Wednesday night, a box of popcorn in her hand, as she slowly placed one piece at a time into her mouth, clandestinely observing Jack. He had not seen her, as he was much too focused on his work. She had plenty of her own to do, but knowing she'd be spending the next evening with him, and not knowing at all what to expect, she decided that what she needed to do was her homework. She equated it to studying for a test. You can learn a lot about people by watching them in their work environment.

She heard the PA announcement: "Now batting, Joe Clarkson, Number 6."

Of course he was batting. Clarkson always seemed to step into the batter's box whenever she was watching. Just to torture her.

The first pitch came in high and near the ear, and Joe backed away from it, afraid it may have been intended for his head. The second pitch hit the dirt at the catcher's feet and almost got away from him. The third pitch was a fastball straight down the middle, and Joe, having raised his grip a little higher on the bat of late, took that ball for a ride, way down the left field line, just inside the foul pole for a two-run homer. The fans were standing, clapping, and chanting "Joe, Joe," and Francesca moved her eyes away from the celebration that took place on the field, to watch Jack take in what had just happened. He jotted down a note on a piece of paper, looked back at the field, and then turned his attention to his computer, where he typed, what she guessed, was a segment of his story. He took a sip of his Coke, scratched his brow, and leaned back in his chair, folding his arms in front of him. She wondered what he was thinking as he ran his hand through his thick head of hair and stared straight ahead at the field in front of him.

The ballpark's speakers blasted Kool & The Gang's "Celebration," as the fans continued to stand and clap their hands, Joe's picture and replay of the homerun front and center on the video board.

One could get a bit of an ego from hitting baseballs around and out of ballparks. The adulation that comes from wearing that team's uniform—and being handsome while doing so—was enough to make anyone's head swell. Women swooned over Joe's rugged good looks, though she did wonder sometimes if he would command as much attention if he worked in any other career that did not require a professional uniform, such as that of an accountant, a restaurant manager, or a fisherman.

Joe came out of the dugout, only briefly, and tipped his hat to his adoring fans. They were satisfied and sat back down in their seats.

Jack leaned over to the reporter next to him and said something into his ear. Then, they both folded their arms in front of them simultaneously, and chuckled.

She wished she knew what he had said. She was perplexed for a moment, and then shook it off. Francesca straightened her skirt, tossed her popcorn into the trash, and headed out of the press box and onto the concourse.

Men, she thought.

The team got a break on Thursday because of a scheduled day off. Francesca understood why a baseball team would need a break—a rest from play—but she thought it might be nice if once in a while, the front office got a day off too. At one point, she went three weeks straight working crazy hours, and barely found time to get herself to the supermarket. Not only did they not get a day off, but the next morning after a late game, they were at their desks by nine in the morning. If only she didn't love her job so much.

She popped into the Dunkin' Donuts near the ballpark and bought herself a low-fat blueberry muffin and a large coffee. She was running a little late, but she didn't feel any guilt for it; the homestand was a long one, and this weekend would mark the second of two straight weekends she worked.

Part of her wished she had not made the plans with Jack for that evening. What she really wanted to do was snuggle on her couch and watch a movie—all by herself. Curling up under a soft blanket was something she rarely had time to do, yet she sometimes yearned for that quiet time alone. Her very public job required her to talk to people all day long, whether on the phone or in person. She had to be detail-oriented and extremely organized, which she was. However, some nights her greatest desire was to do nothing, to say nothing. Melting into her couch was a treat whereby she could therapeutically not talk about baseball for a while. She wondered what Joe would do with his time off. Had they still been together, would she have taken a day off and spent it with him?

This was ridiculous. She hated wasting time thinking about a man. Senseless. There relationship was too new to judge, but new enough to suffer debilitation already, and that's what she couldn't get past. Cutting the relationship off now was the best for both parties involved.

She had the ability to rationalize anything—and everything. Some things are not meant to be. You have two different lives…could the two of you endure your job and the entirety of his career? Francesca envisioned herself as a Looney Toons cartoon, with a devil and angel character sitting on each one of her shoulders…love him…don't love him…stand beside him…don't stand behind him…forgive him… don't forgive him…trust him…don't trust him. She should not have to feel badly about making a decision. She chose not to be involved. It was as simple as that.

And yet a nagging question tugged at her heartstrings: what kind of a person was she to leave him in a situation when he had asked her to be there? What kind of a girlfriend—or friend—was she?

Perhaps, she thought, she was she none of the above.

Back at the ballpark, everyone was tired. Faces grew weary from the pace at which they worked, and it wasn't even close to the halfway point in the season. It was the end of May, and the weather was just starting to become consistently warm. However, the last few days were chilly, and the upcoming weekend called for a significant amount of rain. Weathermen were using words like "Nor'easter" when describing the amount of rainfall that was expected to drown Bay City over the next few days. The clouds outside Francesca's window were camouflaging the blue sky, and she took a moment to pause from her work and appreciate the beauty of what was outside her window.

The knock at her door startled her.

"Sorry to scare you," Freddie said.

"No, no problem. I was just taking a breather."

"Mind if I come in?"

"Not at all," Francesca said. "I have your schedule of appearances right here waiting for you. See how on the ball I am?"

"You're always on the ball. How's your mom doing?" he asked.

"Oh, very well," Francesca said. "She's back to normal, if anyone can really be called normal."

"Glad to hear that," he said. Although he had never met Francesca's mother, he always asked about her since the scare in Florida. Francesca appreciated that he cared and continued to inquire.

She reached into her "out" box and extracted Freddie's paperwork. It was deep in the pile, but she color-coded each player's itinerary so she knew whose was whose. He was scheduled for a card show at the Convention Center and a hospital visit uptown over the next week. All the necessary information was attached, including his contact's name and phone number as well as directions to the location.

Freddie walked over to her maroon, leather guest chair and sank into it. He was wearing jeans and a black tee, and the little bit of grey in his hair dusted his temples, though they looked more silver today than grey. His skin was well tanned from all the time in the sunshine, and the lines around his eyes had deepened over the span of years Francesca had known him. He was a distinguished looking man, and he kept himself in great shape, as Francesca had seen him in the player weight room on the days when the front office staff was allowed to use it. She took advantage of that benefit and joined other colleagues in the quest to keep in shape. Freddie was a teaser, and even though some people found him gruff and curt, Francesca only knew him as a teddy bear. She was getting the impression that he had something important to say, and so she took his cue, and sat back in her chair behind the desk.

"I hope you don't mind my candor," he said. "And I know it will seem like I'm butting in where I really don't belong."

"Go right ahead. You know I respect you and value you."

"Joe's a damn good guy, you know?"

"Yes," she said. "I was beginning to see that."

"Well, he's still a damn good guy. We have a solid friendship, and he turns to me on occasion when something's bothering him."

"I just recently understood that to be true a few weeks ago."

"Yes, but…"

He paused. He was thinking. Francesca saw him hesitate, pause, and then shake his head from side to side.

"Oh, I shouldn't interfere…never mind, Francesca."

He started to get up out of his chair.

"I think you should say what you came to say," she said gently, raising one eyebrow in encouragement. He slowly sat back down. "Whatever you have to say, I have probably already thought before," she said.

He scratched his head, and then repositioned himself in the chair. Whatever was on his mind, it appeared it wasn't going to be easy for him to share.

"Let me say this: Joe seems to really care for you. I just wonder if that's enough."

Francesca leaned back in her chair and crossed her arms. She allowed her mouth a small grin. Freddie just articulated out loud the one thought that had played over and over in her mind since their discussion in her office. He just happened to say it out loud. Sadly, she couldn't have agreed with Freddie more.

"Thank you, Freddie," she said.

He stood up to leave, and then held one hand in hers, and placed his other hand on top, a meaningful gesture. He pulled her closer and looked her in the eyes. Then, in a whisper, he said, "I loved my wife, but I realized too late that my actions didn't indicate that I did. And now she's gone and happy with someone else. I could have made her happy—should have made her happy—but my happiness was more important. And life on the road—it isn't easy on any relationship. Part of me feels as if I'm betraying him by saying this, but I've known you a lot of years, too, and I'm just worried. The situation is…delicate. Do you understand what I'm saying?"

"I'm afraid I do," Francesca said.

Twenty-Three

"I loved playing in Bay City. There was always a certain romance to it."
~ Freddie "The Fly" Montrose, Blackbirds Bench Coach

Jack stood in front of the mirror. He changed his clothes at least five times, and still wasn't happy with what he was wearing. He felt ridiculous, and finally acknowledged that his palms were sweating. Although this wasn't necessarily a "date" where he would be picking up the woman and driving her in his car, he was still meeting her for drinks. Therefore, since he hadn't been through this process in many years, he decided he would call it a date nonetheless. He stopped and looked at himself in the mirror. He felt foolish, like an indecisive teenager. He finally decided on the blue and white striped button down—not too casual, not too dressy—and a pair of trousers he picked up at Banana Republic. His dark hair was tamed more than usual with a comb, balm, and a dash of spray, and he finished it all off with a splash of his favorite Calvin Klein cologne.

He'd never been to Shamrock's, but knew exactly where it was. It was in a part of the city called The Village, though it was tiny in comparison to Greenwich Village in New York City. There were lots of pubs and restaurants and boutique shops that lined the main street called Hamlet Road. He dined at a couple of them in that vicinity when his parents came to visit. He walked up to the pub door and went inside. There was Irish music playing, and it was surprisingly busy for a Thursday night. Francesca was sitting at a table for two next to the bar, and she waved him over.

"Am I late?" he asked.

"No, I think I'm just early," she said.

"And anxiously awaiting my arrival?" he said, more as a question.

"Indeed," she said. "You look nice."

"Thank you," he said.

He pulled out his chair and sat down. She was drinking a Guinness, and when the waiter came around, he followed suit and ordered the same.

"I like the atmosphere in here," he said.

"Good, right? And there's live music on Thursdays, but they won't come on until nine."

"As long as it's not Karaoke, I'm safe," he said.

"Afraid to sing in public, Mr. Thompson?" she said, grinning.

"Quite the opposite, I'm afraid. The public is afraid of my singing."

The waiter asked if they'd like anything to eat, and they decided on some Corned Beef Poppers and an order of Killarney Cabbage Rolls. They were laughing at themselves.

"When in Ireland, do as the Irish do," Francesca said.

"That's always been my motto," Jack replied.

The lights in the place had been dimmed, and the small, white twinkle lights around the bar area were draped over a mahogany carved structure that supported glasses, wine bottles, and some imported beers. It was rich in color. Francesca liked the quiet, but unique comfort of the place, but it was by no means a dive bar. There was a richness to it that made her feel comfortable. She leaned in for her napkin, and caught a whiff of Jack's cologne. The scent of him reminded her of…

"Here's to getting to know each other better," Jack said. They raised their glasses and clinked them together. "I promise not to put my foot in my mouth tonight, and if I do, please know it's not intentional."

Francesca smirked at him. "It's fine. I totally overreacted. Someday, I'll tell you all about it."

"If and when you want to talk about it, I'm happy to lend both my ears. Some people only lend one, but both of mine are available gratis."

He was funny, Francesca thought. And he didn't try hard to be; he just was. He was charming, actually.

"So, tell me a little about yourself," Francesca said.

"Why do I feel like I'm on a job interview? 'Let's see how this guy handles a question that could take hours, and see if he can whittle it down to a few, mere sentences.' Okay. I'm up for it. I'm up for the challenge," he said, smiling.

"I'm sure you are. Or, Mr. Reporter, I could ask the questions in Barbara Walters's style, and you could provide the answers."

"And they must be truthful answers?"

"Ethics and journalism are supposed to go together, aren't they?" she asked.

"In the normal sphere, one would hope so. But I know some pretty shady characters in my field."

"Tell me about your childhood."

"Let's see. I grew up in New York State. My dad owns and operates a car dealership, and my mom has a thriving, albeit small, art gallery in town. I have two sisters, Jen and Mel, who call me 'Mom's Favorite,' because, well, let's be real, it's true, and I've never owned a dog."

"Count yourself lucky there. All they do is break your heart. Now, what do you do for fun?"

"I don't have time for fun, unless it's cold out and baseball season is over, in which case, I catch up on a lot of books and movies I haven't seen."

"Favorite book?"

"*The Boys of Summer.*"

"Ah. No surprise there. That's to be expected. Besides baseball, what's your favorite sport?"

"Who said baseball was my favorite sport?"

Francesca looked at him with a doubtful face. "I think *The Boys of Summer* says it all."

"Okay, yes, it's my favorite sport. I also like to play tennis."

"Do you ever wish you could be a professional athlete?"

"I already tried that. It didn't work out so well. That's why I'm a writer."

"No, you're a writer because you're a good writer. What sport did you play?"

"I played Double A ball. Couldn't get out of the minors. I wasn't big enough."

"You're kidding. For what team?"

"The Starlings."

"My dad played for the Starlings for a short bit way back when," Francesca said.

"So did my dad," Jack said.

Francesca almost choked on her beer. And then, it clicked.

"Is your father Bradley Thompson?"

"Yes."

"My dad's name was Archie Milli. They played together."

"That seems impossible," Jack said.

"Not really...they played ball together, but only for one year. My dad was injured in a construction accident that affected his hand, and he never made it back onto the field. He had to leave that career behind him. Broke his heart, I think." She was brushing the hair off her face, absolutely astonished at this coincidental revelation. She exhaled.

"God, it's a small world," Francesca said.

"So, do you know the whole Starling team roster? I think I've only looked at my dad's stuff a couple of times. I mean, I knew his stats, but I didn't know all the guys on the roster. That's remarkable. I probably should have paid better attention."

"How can you say you love baseball, yet you don't know this stuff? Your dad had a great season in 1957. He batted .323 that year, and he led the team in stolen bases."

Jack paused a second to look at her. He was in disbelief. A smart cookie who knew minor league statistics. He was amazed.

"What?" she asked.

"Don't you think this is weird? Our dads played ball together, and you're a stats wizard?"

"Only when it comes the Starlings and that one season! My dad taught me about all the guys on the team. I was eight and I memorized all their averages. Pete Therault hit for the cycle that year."

"Remarkable," Jack said.

"And I have my dad's things in a box at my mother's house. I'll have to get them and show them to you. He has a whole collection of pictures he took. My father's hobby was taking photographs. He shot a ton of them. I bet there are some pictures of your father in that box. I haven't looked at them since…"

Jack looked at her and waited. There it was. There was the thing that made her vulnerable…made her like him. They had both suffered from a loss. He could sense it weeks ago. He wondered if she had sensed the same.

"His death was agony for me. It still is all these years later," Francesca said, looking up, choking back tears. "Anyway, you will have to come see the photographs. I'll get them from my mother tomorrow.

What are you doing this weekend?"

"Covering the games. And you're working."

"Not Sunday night. We have a day game," Francesca said. "You have to come over for dinner after the game. I'm not much of a cook, but I can throw something together. I have so much to show you."

She could feel herself becoming nostalgic, hopeful, and thankful all at the same time. This guy she had nearly knocked down and who nosed into her business with Joe Clarkson had a connection to her father through his own father. She felt like rejoicing and telling the world that her father's memory was alive and well.

Because someone from back then knew him.

By the end of the night, they had spent most of their time smiling and laughing, especially when they tried to sing an Irish song when the microphone was passed around the room and neither of them knew the words to "My Wild Irish Rose." They giggled as they tossed the microphone like a hot potato to the next victims, trying to get rid of it as quickly as they could.

When they were full from food and feeling foolish about their awful singing, they decided to take advantage of the gorgeous night and fresh air, a little teaser of warmth before the cool, torrential rain would hammer down on them over the next couple of days. Jack insisted on paying the bill despite the fact that Francesca organized the night.

"I'm just glad I had something to do tonight, are you kidding?" he said, signing his name to the credit card receipt. They put their light coats on and headed toward the front door. The night air felt refreshing after being in a bar for several hours.

"Do you want to take bets on how long it will be before the umps call the game tomorrow night?" Jack asked her.

"They'll wait a while since it's a Friday. They'll let it rain, and then they'll call it."

"I know," he said, "but play along, what time will they call it?"

"I'm guessing nine-thirty," she said.

"I say earlier. I say they call it at ten after nine."

"You are trying to beat me by twenty minutes?"

"No. I'm being twenty minutes more optimistic than you are."

She shook her head and rolled her eyes. The street was a long one, well lit by retro looking lampposts, and it butted up to a small, crackling creek at the end that wound its way through the center of the city to the river. Their goal was to make it to the bench at the end, feel the warm, humid breeze that had started to blow, and admire the moonlight that was streaming through the low clouds as it hung low to the earth, as if suspended by a string.

They began their walk, still talking, discussing a variety of things such as what it's like to live next to college students when you're almost thirty and feeling way beyond them in years, some of the young, up and coming stars across the big leagues, and how working in sports requires a tremendous commitment, when rather naturally, without any thought, Jack reached for Francesca's arm and slipped it through his as they continued to walk in the evening air.

As he exited Mon Ami, a pricey French bistro in The Village and stood on the step while he placed Jessica's cotton wrap around her shoulders, Joe Clarkson saw two figures walking arm and arm across the street. He watched Francesca Milli toss her curled hair, look at Dash Thompson with her big, happy eyes and broad, beaming smile, move closer to him, and lean her head into his shoulder.

"Is everything okay?" Jessica asked.

"Yes," he said. "Just fine."

At the end of the night, Jack walked Francesca to her car. She wasn't sure what was making her feel the way she did at the moment. Was it the beer? The good conversation? The way they were connected by the Blackbirds and the Starlings? Or was she trying to make herself feel better about herself by quietly getting back at Joe?

She was tired of trying to rationalize everything, and at that moment, she didn't really care about the nature of any of it. This was a first date, and she wasn't engaged or married, so she reminded herself that she had the freedom to feel the way she wanted to feel. She hadn't felt anything for such a long time before Joe. She worked, and worked. She kept her feelings for anything locked away. For how many years? Perhaps her emotions were playing catch up, all the while confusing her and making her feel slightly off-kilter. She allowed herself to be cordoned off from the world; how was it that she would permit herself to feel anything again. For anyone?

There was a quiet sex appeal to Jack Thompson she hadn't noticed before. Or maybe she wasn't looking before. Nevertheless, she could pinpoint it: there was something in his eyes—the way he looked at her and focused on her, the way they danced with delight over silly conversation, the way they teased and understood—that made her feel special. He was highly appealing at the moment, and she didn't want the evening to end.

After reaching the end of the sidewalk and pausing for a few moments near one of the benches, they decided walk back to the car. There was mist in the air, that light, whispery kind that can precede a heavy rain storm. Jack linked their arms together once again, and he walked her back to her car, which was parked only a few spaces away from his. Their feet were keeping the same pace, and she noticed something inside her was lifting; she felt unusually comfortable. The time spent together had been easy, replete with good conversation and laughs. It made her wonder if she laughed enough, breathed in life enough, and was thankful for life enough. She could have been angry for what happened with Joe, but she wasn't. He had awakened something in her that had been serene and afraid and closed off for years. Perhaps that's why she was not about to waste any more time moping and silently regretted the years she had locked herself away from others, keeping her feelings pent up and unavailable. She looked at Jack, and in a moment of—what was it? bliss? euphoria? lust? attraction?—she leaned forward to kiss him. His lips willingly met hers, and his hands found her face, held it gently, and she, in turn, put her arms around his neck and pulled him as close to her as she could. The moment seemed to last for minutes, each of them breathing gently then harder, while Francesca tried to contain herself. When they reluctantly and slowly pulled apart, they looked at each other squarely in the eyes and smiled.

She would not forget the breeze that evening, the warmth of his hands as they lightly touched the back of her neck and moved her damp hair away from her face to look at her—smiling, twinkling—as the gentle rain tickled them both, leaving them feeling revived and aroused and giddy as they said goodnight.

Jack drove home recounting every detail, from beginning until end. He had just kissed a woman in a meaningful way. This was a first. Something deep down in his gut knew that when he dared to become involved again, it would have to feel as good—if not better—than it did with Sarah. There was not much significance in this statement at all except that he had kissed a couple of women he'd been fixed up with after

Sarah's death, and during both encounters, he felt absolutely nothing. This time it was different; he was awakened in the keenest sense, as if a part of him that had been in the dark for many, many years had just opened the door to blinding sunshine.

It reminded him—if only briefly—of what having love in your life can do for a person. It was then that he realized the empty hole that had been part of his life for all these years.

Francesca blared the radio on her ride home. She was singing out loud to "Why Can't This Be Love," one of her favorite songs by Van Halen. She was a big fan of rock music, and this song reminded her of the ballpark, as the ballpark deejay would often play it during batting practice. It also reminded her of living with Sam, when they would play air guitars and stand on the bed mouthing the words to the songs.

As she approached her apartment, she saw a figure standing near her door. From a distance, it gave her pause, but as she moved a little closer, she recognized who it was and her heart dropped.

"Did you have a nice night out?" he asked, as he saw her rummage through her purse for her keys.

"What does that mean?"

"I saw you on your date with Dash."

"See now, that's the thing. Why do you keep calling him Dash? His name is Jack."

"Dash to me."

"I'm going inside to dry off a bit. Would you like to come in so we can talk about this?" She put her key in the door and opened it wide for him to follow her inside.

"Yes," Joe said. "I'd very much like to talk about this."

She ushered him in, asked him if wanted anything to drink,

and went to change her clothes. She peered at herself in the mirror, but was unable to hold that gaze. The two of them sat on her living room couch. Not as they used to, though. In previous months, they would have snuggled up together, her head resting on his chest, he with his arm around her, her right leg draped over his legs. Now, he was at one end of the furniture, and she was at the other. There was an uncomfortable silence until Joe spoke.

"I guess you gave up on me that fast, huh? I must have meant nothing to you at all."

"I went on a date, Joe. He didn't get me pregnant. Lighten up," Francesca said, trying to refrain from raising her voice. But as the words left her mouth, she realized how harsh they were.

"Ah, I guess you got me there, Francesca. You got me. Yes—I messed up. I screwed it all up. And now I'm in a sticky situation. What am I'm supposed to do? I made a mistake. Does this mean Jessica and I are bound together forever?"

"Maybe you should have thought that through before you hopped into the sack with her. There's always a risk. And how would she feel hearing you talk about her this way? As if she meant nothing to you, when apparently, she meant something. She had to have meant something."

"Maybe. And maybe she should have told me about the baby instead of keeping it from me. I can't help but resent her for that."

"Father John would not like to hear you say that you resent someone. You shouldn't do that."

"Who is Father John?"

"My direct line to God." He looked at her full of doubt. "He's my friend who also happens to be a priest. It comes in handy sometimes, you know?"

"I may need him," he said despondently.

"You may. And he'd be pleased to meet you. He knows all about you and me and your stats. Big fan, Father John is. Loves the Blackbirds."

She couldn't help but smile during this conversation. There was something so teenage and naive about the premise of it. Life was simple when you broke it down. Be nice to people. Be kind. Don't hurt anyone intentionally. Try to do the right thing. Be gentle. Give of yourself. Give love when love is needed. That's what it's all about.

She moved closer to Joe and sat beside him, their legs touching. Then, she leaned into him and wrapped her arms around him, giving him a big hug. He was not expecting such a gesture. He responded by putting his arms around her tightly, giving her a big squeeze at first, his hands caressing her back, and they sat embraced in silence like that for a very long time, neither one of them saying a word.

They had started as friends, after all; perhaps they would end that way.

TWENTY-FOUR

*"This field can bounce back in no time. We don't want the fans to be
disappointed, so we try to avoid as many rainouts as possible.
Our state-of-the-art drainage system helps the field to recover.
By tomorrow, you'll never know it rained."*
~ Pat Gallagher, Head Groundskeeper, Blackbirds Park

The rain fell from the sky, unrelenting, since the night before, a strong, steady rain, with drops the size of dimes. The sky darkened, and night came earlier than normal over the ballpark. The house lights had been on since four, even before the gates opened, as devoted fans in slickers made their way into the ballpark grabbing hot dogs and eating at picnic tables under cover on the concourse. The bars inside the ballpark were packed with loyalists drinking the hometown brewed-beer, "Gusto," while eating peanuts and French fries. Everything was sopping wet, and the shiny tarp had been on the field since the previous evening.

Francesca was in the press box watching the pellets of rain make puddles on the tarp while the ballpark's speakers blared songs like "It's Raining Men" and "Purple Rain." She was making notes as she often did, scribbling her checklist as she sat in the back at the counter. She had to talk to Damian Gaynor about his upcoming appearances, and she wanted to ask him if he would kick off the reading program in September at one of the neighboring schools at an assembly.

She wondered how Joe was today. It wasn't that she was insensitive. She did care. And she did love him, but in what way? They talked only briefly afterwards, making mostly small talk, until he went back home, the two of them feeling unsure about their respective situations, and each other. It was funny how it came to this, she thought, to holding on tightly, but knowing letting go was probably the best. So much for the idea of following your heart—sometimes following your head was really what mattered.

Her laptop finished booting up while she was making her daily notes. The reporters were in the clubhouse, so she had a few minutes before she went down there to tidy up a few loose ends.

She opened the Google bar and typed in his name: "Jack Thompson, reporter."

She saw the link to the newspaper and his blog, and then she saw his job at his former paper, and the headline that read: "Sports Reporter Jack Thompson's Fiancée Dies in Automobile Collision."

She swallowed hard, and exited Google immediately. An overwhelming sadness came over her, and she felt as if she might cry.

She powered down her laptop and scooped up her things, her mind racing, wanting to know more about the story. When she was in the privacy of her own office, she would read it from beginning to end.

"How are you doing today, Francesca?" Fred, the press box attendant asked her. A retired gentleman who served in Vietnam, he was standing in the back, making sure all the press notes were readily available for the media. His hair was snow white, and he wore a uniform.

"Oh, good Fred, good," she said. "Think they'll call it early?"

"Well, we're here now. We might as well play ball."

"That's a very positive outlook, but it's not looking good. I'm predicting a double header tomorrow," she said.

Jack came in the door and saw Francesca right away. He grinned, and she could see the sparkle in his eyes. He waved.

She waved back, and stood and waited for him to come over to where she was standing with Fred.

"Good to see you in the rain," he said.

"Good to see you, too," she said.

"A bet's a bet, and a winner's a winner," he teased.

"But we didn't bet anything except bragging rights."

"I'm content with that—and dinner—if you are."

She blushed because Fred was still standing there, listening. "Surprisingly," she said, "I'm quite content with it all."

At that point, Fred became uncomfortable, feeling as if he shouldn't be a part of the flirty conversation that was unfolding. He fidgeted and mumbled something about needing to make a phone call about a bad electrical outlet and walked away.

Jack moved a little bit closer to Francesca—an intimate distance—and placed his hand on her right elbow. He leaned in even closer and said into her ear, "I had a great time last night. Looking forward to Sunday."

She pulled back a little so she could look directly into his eyes, smiled, and said, "Ditto."

They called the game at precisely eight-thirty that night, but Francesca was behind the closed door of her office reading the tragic news stories of Jack Thompson's fiancee's death and had the volume on her television so low she couldn't hear the game. He had been in the car with her—driving. A drunk driver hit them, crossing into their lane. Jack swerved, attempting to avoid a collision, but he couldn't maneuver the car in time. Sarah was pronounced dead before the ambulance arrived at the hospital.

Francesca looked out her window that faced the ballpark as streams of fans were leaving after the announcement came. Neither she nor Jack won the bet because the umpires called the game much earlier than anyone imagined; the radar was showing steady bands of rain that were expected to continue until morning. Down the rain came, dancing against her window. She had half a mind to see what Jack was up to tonight, because after reading those stories, she felt so sad for him and couldn't imagine what that must have been like for him. She never imagined he'd dealt with such tragic circumstances. She was reminded of something her father used to tell her when she was a teenager: Don't judge people. You never know what they are privately going through. She picked up the phone to call him, but then placed it down, deciding she didn't want to come across as pushy, and hoping that he would talk to her about Sarah when he was ready.

She picked up the phone again. It rang three times before someone answered.

"Hi, Mom. Feel like having company tonight?"

"I just saw they called the game," her mother said.

"What? Are you watching?"

"Honey, I've been watching all the games. I think I might like baseball after all."

Francesca chuckled. "Be over in a little while. I need to find that box of Starlings' stuff Dad had. I have to show it to someone."

"Really? Who?"

"I'll tell you all about it when I get there."

She logged out of her computer, grabbed her briefcase, turned out her lights, and walked, umbrella in hand, alongside the thousands of disappointed fans as they all called it a night.

Her mother was already in her pajamas, a robe tied around her waist with her matching slippers. Francesca's mother loved to match everything, from the colors in her wardrobe, to the colors in the house. She blended and coordinated them constantly, and as a whole, had a pretty good eye.

"Got your hair cut, I see," Francesca said to her as she walked through the door, planting a kiss on her cheek.

"Do you like it? No too Posh Spice, right?"

"Well, it is a little edgy," Francesca said. "Makes you look younger."

"Then it's working," her mother said. "I made you a little sandwich, and there are some of the hard pretzels you like in the pantry. Want something to drink?"

"Just a soda," Francesca said.

Francesca removed her raincoat and hung it on the banister. She kicked off her rain boots and headed toward kitchen where she decided to eat that sandwich. She never ate dinner in the press box that night because she spent too much time reading the stories about Jack's tragedy in her office. She was hungry. She grabbed the pretzels and poured herself a Coke.

Her mother emerged from the basement holding the box Francesca remembered so well.

"Is this the one you're looking for?" she asked.

"I think it is," she said.

"So, what's going on?"

"Well, remember that little talk we had about Joe, my ballplayer?"

"Yes," she said.

"Well, I met someone else. Actually, I've kind of known him for a few months, but we recently started talking. He's a sports writer for *The Chronicle*, and his name's Jack. We actually went out on a date last night—I guess you could call it a date—and we had a great time. But during our conversation, he told me his father played for the Starlings. I told him Dad played for the Starlings for a season, and I told Jack that our fathers played on the team at the same time. Isn't that unbelievable?"

"It's quite remarkable. What was his father's name?"

"You mean 'What is his father's name?' His father is alive and well and owns a car dealership in New York State."

"Bradley Thompson?"

Francesca looked stunned. "Yes," Francesca replied. "How did you know?"

"I guessed," she said. "He was Dad's favorite."

"What do you mean?"

"Dad loved him. They were pretty close that year. Bradley Thompson had a tragic story, and Dad was there for him as his friend. He lost both of his parents in a house fire a week before the season opened. Devastating. Then Dad had his own injury, and we lost touch when Dad left the minors. We used to socialize with Bradley and June."

"Remarkable," Francesca said. "What an odd coincidence."

Francesca grabbed the box and made her way to her mother's carpeted living room floor, where she opened the lid and began to go through it. There were notes, scraps of papers, box score clippings, actual lineups, and photographs all thrown in it. When she lifted the team photo that was taken out of the stack, Francesca stared at it. She knew exactly what Bradley Thompson looked like. She spotted him in the middle row, two from the left. He was standing directly behind her dad who was sitting on the bench.

"There he is," Francesca exclaimed, looking at the photograph, and noticing that the resemblance was uncanny. Francesca had always thought Bradley Thompson was a handsome man, even as a young girl.

"And your Jack?" her mother asked.

"Well, he's not exactly 'my Jack,'" she said. "But he is coming over for dinner on Sunday."

"And what about the ballplayer and the baby?" her mother asked.

"That would make a good book title, Mom: 'The Ballplayer and the Baby.' Maybe I'll write it one day," Francesca said. "He's a mess. He came over last night after he saw Jack and me out on our date. Funny, though, I didn't see him…nevertheless, he is obviously not happy about his situation and is even more distressed that the woman didn't tell him she was pregnant right away, claiming she was scared to because she wanted to keep the baby. They were high school sweethearts and apparently dated on and off afterwards. He originally wanted me to stand by him, but I don't think I can do it. And I think he's confused. My gut tells me that I don't think either one of us would be happy in the end."

"A gut feeling should not be ignored," her mother said. "A gut feeling is an instinct, and instinct can lead us down the right path."

"How very profound, Mom," Francesca said.

"I like to think so," she said.

Francesca had a hunch and didn't think she—or their relationship at that moment—could withstand the demands that would end up being the remnants of their relationship. What had begun as friendship and evolved into a pretty passionate couple of months didn't make a solid foundation for the rest of your life. She felt the right thing to do was to let him go.

"Oh, my goodness," Francesca said, holding up a photograph of her dad with Bradley. "I cannot wait to show this to Jack on Sunday."

"I hope I get the chance to meet him sometime," her mother said.

"I don't see why you wouldn't," Francesca replied.

Francesca's mother reached for her forearm and held it, a token of appreciation for that moment of pure candor and opening up. Francesca could sense that her mother was quite pleased. She had a daughter who needed her, and Francesca had a mother she could confide in.

On Saturday, the first game of the double header started on time despite the lingering clouds and mist that hung in the air at Blackbirds Park.

Sometimes after a substantial rainfall, the players bemoaned the condition of the outfield; they claimed the field didn't drain as well as the groundskeeper said it could and left a swamp-like feel to the field. Francesca had heard these types of mumblings from players on numerous occasions when they discussed the conditions. However, none of them besmirched the short porch in right field that allowed pop flies to become home runs. No, indeed; they quite liked that a lot.

Francesca waited at the front gate to meet Willie, a small child of no more than eight years old, who was battling cancer. His family's written request to the ballclub was read by one of Francesca's staff assistants who showed it to her during the weekly meeting they would hold to discuss community events and requests. Willie's story brought Francesca to tears right there in that meeting. He had been diagnosed with cancer at the age of five, and his parents said he liked baseball since he was two. He had been hospitalized several times, and his big wish was to meet catcher Duke Milton. His parents sent photographs of Willie wearing Duke's jersey and number, and a couple of shots of him in full catcher gear from his youth league. Despite his battle with the disease, he still played baseball, and his treatments were helping, but he was not in full remission. "Maybe if he could meet Duke Milton, Willie's idol, he would have a role model and something to live for. We have to try everything we can," his parents wrote in their letter. There was no denying this child his wish of meeting Duke, for Duke himself had suffered a similar ordeal when he was a small child, enduring surgeries to remove tumors from his legs, which, in time and with treatments, eventually healed. Willie needed to meet someone who had been through it and survived it well, and in moments, Francesca was about to make that dream a reality for Willie and his family.

She saw the family approach the gate, outfitted in Blackbirds gear, the tickets Francesca's staff mailed to them in their hands. The usher scanned the tickets, and Francesca walked up to them, fully stocked with goodie bags for each member of Willie's family. Willie was holding his sister's hand as they came in.

"You must be Willie," Francesca said. "I'm so glad to meet you," she said, bending slightly to meet his eye level.

"Thank you," Willie said. "I'm glad to be here. This is my sister, Molly."

He was so polite for a little boy. His eyes were sweet, and after meeting him, Francesca could see he was a special child. She swallowed hard. It was difficult to watch cancer attach itself to someone so young and innocent. Francesca couldn't wait for Willie to meet Duke.

"Hi Molly," Francesca said. "These bags are for you two, and these two are for your parents. It's so nice to meet you both. I'm Francesca Milli."

Willie's parents' faces wore the expression of pure gratitude, and Francesca could sometimes find herself becoming emotional with the parents as they would tell their stories, but she didn't want Willie to see her cry. So she tried to keep it upbeat.

She hugged Willie's mother. "I'm so glad you all were able to come and that we can help. Duke is very excited to meet him."

"We can't thank you enough," Willie's mother said.

Then, Francesca led the way to the elevator that would take them down to the clubhouse. There was a holding area—a private room for "meet and greets"—where the players could feel comfortable mingling with families who were going through tough times, and a place that wasn't too public. The room was furnished with sofas, Blackbirds artwork all over the walls, and a small kitchen area with a fridge where complimentary drinks were at the guests' disposal. The television was tuned into the team's network so guests didn't feel out of touch with pregame or the game if they were waiting in that area.

"Can I get anyone something to drink?" Francesca said as the family made themselves comfortable in the room.

"Sure!" Willie said. He opted for a Coke as his mother said, "Just one, Willie, okay?"

"Okay, mom," he said. "Molly, you want one?"

They decided to split it, and Francesca poured two cups of Coca-Cola. "Help yourself to some popcorn too," Francesca said. "And parents, help yourself to anything. I'm going to go get Duke."

About five minutes later, Francesca returned with Duke, and she'd never quite seen a reaction like the one she saw from Willie. Without hesitation, Willie bolted across the room, reached for Duke, and hugged him exclaiming, "Thank you for coming! I've been so excited to meet you!"

Duke bent down and gave him a big hug back. He was a strong, sturdy, burley guy from California, with dirty blond hair and blue-green eyes. He had a low, soothing voice, and he signed Willie's ball and glove. He talked with him about his batting stance, and Willie asked him how he decided he wanted to be a catcher. Francesca couldn't help but notice that at that moment, Duke Milton looked like he was twelve, talking to his buddy and catching up with a long, lost friend.

This is what it's about, thought Francesca. This is what it's about.

Duke said goodbye to Willie and his family, and Francesca held the door open for them as they exited the room. She was planning to escort them to their seats. Just then, Joe came in from the field, jogging down the hallway. He saw Francesca and called to her.

"Francesca," he said, somewhat breathy. "Who do we have here?"

Francesca was surprised to see him engage in this manner. She typically had to make a request for a player to do something before a game. His interest in meeting the family was somewhat unprecedented. She introduced him to the parents, then to Molly and Willie.

"Wow," Willie said. "You're a lot bigger than I thought!"

"Thanks," Joe chuckled. "I'll take that as a compliment."

"Your arms look strong," Willie said.

"Well, they're not swinging the bat the way I wish they would," Joe said.

"What do you mean? You just homered the other night. Choking up on the bat is really helping you," Willie replied. "I wish I could hit a homer. That would be awesome!" Joe smiled, impressed by the kid's observation.

"So, who did you just meet?"

Willie grabbed his ball that had been autographed by Duke, and then pulled his glove out of his bag, telling him all about it. "Would you like to sign my ball, Mr. Clarkson?"

"Ah, sure, Willie, but you can call me Joe."

"Ok, Joe."

Joe took the ball from him, and Willie's father produced a ballpoint pen for the signing. Francesca watched how Joe talked to both the kids, and then very nicely, excused himself to head to the clubhouse to have his ankle taped.

"Cheer loudly," he called as he was backing away from them. "We need all the cheering we can get!"

And he was off.

That night, after the double header, it was Duke Milton who hit a bouncing single up the first base line that got past the first baseman, allowing Milton to drive in Clarkson who was standing on third, to win the second game in extra-innings. Tired fans exhausted from two back-to-back games left pleased. The Blackbirds held tough to win both games, something they hadn't done in quite a while.

Francesca was glad to have worn flats that day; she was on her feet nonstop, having to entertain a group of dignitaries in the Owner's Box along with the owner's wife during the first game after seeing Willie and his family to the seats. Prior to the second game, she escorted the winners of the Blackbird drawing contest onto the field to watch batting practice. Joe swung by those folks as well and introduced himself to them. Francesca watched him in awe as he schmoozed and charmed them all, smiling for pictures and signing whatever they put in front of him. He knew how to work the fans, and that old Clarkson smile was in full swing. He even went so far as to wink at her and whisper in her ear, "Can I stop by after the game? I want to talk to you."

Her curiosity was piqued. Yes, she would be there, she said. She was intrigued by his latest approach to talk.

Dan was sitting on her couch in her office when she entered.

"What's up?" she asked.

"A group is going to Cagny's Ale House. Want to come?"

Francesca typically passed on these types of offers, but not tonight. Tonight, she felt like going, felt like being a part of things, and felt like getting away from the burdens of work. Jack had been right; she didn't take time out to play and have fun. She needed to do that for herself. She couldn't remember the last time she went out with colleagues, enjoyed their company, and allowed herself to laugh. What she had allowed herself to do, instead, was to make a lot of silly excuses.

"Sure. I'll meet up with you," she told Dan.

"By the way," he said, "I ran into Willie and his family on their way out today. That kid had a great day and was beaming. Good call on that one, right?"

"Yes," she said, feeling herself get a little choked up. "Great one."

Fifteen minutes later, as she was powering down her computer and making her checklist for Sunday's game, Joe appeared. The offices were quiet, and the ballpark had emptied rather quickly.

"So I was thinking about what happened on Thursday night when I was at your place," he began.

"What?"

"We have a thing. You might not want to admit it, may prefer to be in denial, but we've got something pretty good despite the situation I'm in right now. But, I think we can work through it. I want to work through it. Why are you giving up so easily?"

Francesca was not expecting to hear those words.

She just looked at him, not sure at all how to respond. Months ago, Father John had told her to go with her feelings, to take one step at a time. Was she giving up when she should be holding on?

Joe didn't feel like waiting any longer for her response. He walked over to her, grabbed her hands, and then he kissed her, just the way he thought she needed to be kissed—the way they had kissed in spring training when they stayed up until three o'clock in the morning, rolling around in the bed, unable to keep their hands and mouths off each other.

At exactly that moment, Jack, feeling encouraged by Thursday night's date and his flirtatious exchange with Francesca on Friday evening in the press box, came down the hallway with an unusual pep in his step. He had decided earlier to see if Francesca was going to go to Cagny's for a beer. He had been invited several times by David to join the crew for a drink after the games. He wondered why he never joined them.

When Jack turned the corner and faced Francesca's office, his heart fell as he witnessed Clarkson and Francesca in an intimate moment, their lips locked in a kiss, Clarkson with his muscular arms wrapped around her torso. Embarrassed and caught off-guard, he turned and walked quickly down the hall, praying no one saw him, pretending he saw nothing. Pretending he felt nothing.

You couldn't compete with a ballplayer. Everyone knew that. What woman in her right mind would choose a lowly reporter to a good-looking, strong, charismatic baseball stud? This was a no brainer for Francesca, and Jack was no fool. He could see with his own eyes that their affair was not over. Something was still there between them.

Not only was his ego bruised, but Jack was confused by what he had seen, because just a few days ago, he'd seen Joe leaving in his car with that woman who was carrying his child. Everyone knew about it now.

And yet Francesca apparently still felt something for him.

He opened the heavy wood and etched glass door. The lights inside were dim, the woodworking around the bar was dark, and the noise from inside was inviting. Music played, people chatted, and the atmosphere seemed perfect. Embrace this, he thought, as he walked through the front door. Give it a chance.

"Jack," called David, raising his hand in the air. "Over here! Come join us!"

Jack was determined not to miss out on the night. He had been invited and had accepted. He promised himself he would get out more and he didn't intend to ignore his own advice. He needed to feel alive again, and despite what he had just seen, and that his heart had just sunk to his lower extremities, he was convinced that having beers with colleagues was far better than going home by himself.

Alone. Again.

Fielder's Choice

I remember my father became very angry with me one sunny after-noon after visiting the ballpark. The heat was oppressive that day, and the two of us had been sweating all through the game because our seats were in direct sunlight. No amount of water could cool us off as temperatures hovered around ninety-eight degrees. It was fortunate for us that my mother had lathered layers upon layers of sunscreen on me, and I'd worn my favorite Blackbirds visor. My skin wasn't burning, but it was so hot I could fry an egg on it.

The game didn't go well that day. Zeke Watson struck out three times at the plate, each time leaving men on base. The humidity was choking the fans as much as Zeke had choked in the batter's box during that fateful loss.

"Dad, please, please, please can we stop for ice cream. I'm so hot," I pleaded.

My dad liked my suggestion, and I was pretty certain he wanted ice cream just as much as I did. He just didn't say so.

We pulled up to Lots of Licks Ice Creamery, which was only about five miles from our house. We loved the logo of the place—a large, cartoon tongue licking the tip of an ice cream cone—and we mimicked it as we ate our cones.

The line was long, but my dad and I braved the heat again, trying to find some shade as we waited in the winding queue.

"What flavor are you going to get?" he asked, trying to bide the time.

"Butterscotch," I said.

"Sounds good," he said.

"Well, maybe mint chocolate chip. I'm not sure."

"Either one sounds like a good choice."

One by one, people ordered their ice cream, until finally, about twenty minutes later, it was our turn.

"Do you know what you want?" he asked me, after the clerk greeted us.

"Still thinking," I said.

"You've had twenty minutes to think, Frankie. It's time to make a choice."

I was still thinking, so my dad ordered first.

"I'll have chocolate and vanilla in a cup with fudge sauce and sprinkles," he said. "Frankie?"

"Coconut," I said.

My dad turned to tell the clerk what I wanted, but before he could, I spoke.

"Wait…no I want Rainbow Sherbet," I said.

"Ok," my dad said.

"She'll have—"

"Wait—I think I'll have Butterscotch."

"Is that your final answer?" he asked me. "There are lots of other people behind us."

"Yes…no…I'm not sure," I said.

My father was getting frustrated, and ordered for me. "She'll have the mint chocolate chip in a cake cone." He grabbed his wallet and paid quickly.

We found a spot in the shade, and my dad and I sat down on a bench, my father juggling both his ice cream and the handful of falling napkins he grabbed.

"I understand it's hot out and our brains probably aren't working properly, but you can't hold up a line like that when making a decision. You have to learn to make choices in life—some good, some bad—but the point is,

it's your choice and no matter what, you have to live with it," he said, trying to impart some worldly wisdom through the oppressive heat.

When I had no feedback to offer, he decided to use a baseball analogy to further drive home his point.

"You know how when you play infield and the batter hits the ball up the middle, the man on third starts heading for home, and the man on first heads for second? When you grab that ball, you have a choice to make. Do you take the chance and throw it to the catcher to stop the runner from scoring, or do you go for the double play? Kind of like that. You want to be in control of your choices. Any choice in life you make is a gamble, but you have to make the best one you can, because you are the one who is going to have to live with the outcome."

"Honestly, Dad, I have no idea what you're talking about," I said.

"Someday you will," he said. "Someday."

Twenty-Five

"No two players are alike. It's all about individuality. It's about setting yourself apart, doing the best you can, but always acting as a member of a team. It is a team sport, after all."
~ Freddie "The Fly" Montrose, Blackbirds Bench Coach

Francesca woke up that morning and reflected on what happened last night. She reached across her queen bed with her eyes shut, thankful that there was no one there beside her, and she felt relief. She didn't allow herself to fall under Joe Clarkson's charming little spell, no matter how hard he tried to woo her, or how sexy he looked. He sweet-talked her; he kissed her; he told her they were meant to be.

Francesca could have easily allowed herself to grow limp in his arms or become enamored with his winsome small talk. His eyes shifted from her eyes to her mouth, and then back to her eyes. Careful now, Missy, she thought. She looked him squarely in the eyes as she began to take a step back from him, and then he kissed her. She gently pushed away from him and was adamant.

"I can't do this," she had insisted. "It just doesn't work for all parties involved. Besides, have you forgotten how much you pissed me off?"

Joe didn't take no for an answer easily. He wanted her, and he wanted to show her that this good thing didn't have to end.

It was Dan who had saved her. He got caught up in listening to a disgruntled fan in the lobby and was trying to help quell the gentleman's frustrated emotions by gathering up some goodies to help smooth things over with the fan. The man had turned red-faced and animated as he described how the drunk man in front of him had spilled beer down his back—and down the back of his daughter. Apparently, a fight had broken out and they had both become victims of immature young men resorting to throwing both punches and beers. He and his wife were not happy, and the daughter looked out of sorts, but Dan's attempt to appease them had worked. He invited them back as his guests for another game in the future, promising a quick behind-the-scenes tour, and offered them Blackbirds memorabilia, which brought a few smiles to their faces. After he escorted them out through the lobby and the switchboard had shut down, he decided to check one last time to see if Francesca was still interested in going to Cagny's.

Francesca heard a knock at the door. "Dan, come on in. I was just talking to Joe about our guest, Willie, and I was just getting ready to lock up. Thanks for coming to get me." Her voice sounded nervous, unlike her own.

"Hey, Joe. Ah, sure. No problem," Dan said, realizing by her tone that she wanted to be rescued from the moment. Dan had not caught them in an embrace, thank goodness. They were just sitting there talking when he arrived. Dan was almost as broad as Joe, and about an inch shorter. How had she never noticed this before?

"Are you sure you won't change your mind?" Joe asked one more time.

"Not tonight," Francesca said, straightening her blouse. "I'm good. I'll see you tomorrow, Joe," she said, and then she patted Dan on the back, the two of them walking out the door together, Joe heading in another direction.

"What's going on?" Dan asked in a whisper when they were in the elevator alone. It was his understanding that they no longer were an item.

"Joe's tremendously persistent, that's all. There's nothing—nothing anymore."

"And you're okay, right?"

"Right," she confirmed.

"Good, so when I tell you what I saw, you won't hold it against me, right?"

"Oh crap," Francesca said. "What now?"

Jack Thompson rolled over and scratched his head cursing the gargantuan, throbbing headache that pounded right above his temples. The light was coming through the draperies at just the right angle and it caught him in they eye, blinding him momentarily. He was afraid to sit up for fear his head might shatter into a million little pieces. His stomach churned, and he felt unusually hungry, though the idea of eating at that moment was not a good one.

In an effort to drown out his sorrows, he downed one drink too many, and took a cab home. His car was still at the ballpark because he had walked over to the bar. Francesca never showed up last night, despite that the public relations director insisted that she would. He imagined what had happened. He could envision it, and played the scenario over and over in his head. Ballplayers and women—women loved ballplayers. He'd seen it with his own eyes; there were groupies in every city. Yet, he knew Francesca was different. At least that's what he surmised, but what did he know?

Obviously nothing.

When Dan showed up at the bar, much after the rest of them, David asked where Francesca was, and he said she was too tired and had to go to bed. It had been a long day. Oh, she went to bed all right, Jack thought. Just not alone.

And now it was Sunday morning, and he was supposed to be going over her house for dinner. He would cancel. It wouldn't be right. He couldn't get involved any more than he already had or take a chance on her any longer. He almost allowed himself to fall for her, and he took an emotional beating last night, much to his chagrin. He would bounce back; he knew he would. If he could survive the death of his fiancée, he could survive one, early-stage heartbreak. No sweat.

He shuffled out of bed and turned SportsCenter on right away. He walked into the kitchen, opened the fridge, took out a Gatorade, opened his bottle of Ibuprofen, and desperately swallowed four of them in one, large gulp.

Most headaches go away in time, he thought.

Joe Clarkson's alarm went off at nine in the morning. He liked to sleep in when he could, but he had to report to the ballpark soon, and he didn't want to be late. He prided himself on his rituals and the way he was a responsible member of the team. Now, at thirty-one, he was a veteran player, and he was beginning to feel older, his injuries taking longer to heal than they did when he was in his early twenties. He needed to have his ankle taped; it still wasn't feeling the way it should. He stumbled out of bed and turned on his coffee maker.

There was a loneliness he felt that morning. The rain had disappeared and the sunshine was bright as it came streaming in through his high-rise condominium. Joe loved living in the building, high above the city, where his views of downtown and the water stretched out before him.

He stepped out onto the balcony and breathed in the air. Way down below, the city was coming to life, and in the distance he could hear the faint sound of church bells ringing. His coffee was steaming hot, and he took a sip, trying not to burn his tongue.

For a second, he felt he was being unfair—to Jessica, to Francesca, to his unborn child. He felt selfish. For the past ten years, he'd been playing pro ball, and the only thing that had mattered was his career. It was the one thing he was passionate about. He loved it more than anything. And then he allowed the thought that he tried to keep at bay again and again to take center stage that morning: What would he do when it was all over? What would he do then? Retire? Never play again? Take up golf? Try coaching? Move to Arizona? Go home to Texas? He wasn't getting younger, and there were no guarantees as to how long his already sore arm and knees would hold up. And now there was a child who would soon be in the picture who needed care no matter what. Francesca said those words out loud last night, and it was the first time Joe really considered how his life was about to change. He was going to be responsible for someone else now, someone other than himself. How was he going to take care of another little person? Francesca was right. Everything had become much more complicated, and at some point, he needed to sort it all out.

Those were big questions that couldn't be answered as the breeze warmed his face when he had to get ready for a game. He was swinging the bat a lot better lately, and as that kid Willie said yesterday, choking up a little has helped. He would stick with that for a while. No need to adjust anything when things were working to your advantage. He wished he could say the same for his personal life.

He stepped back inside the condo from his balcony, and closed the sliding glass door behind him, leaving the morning's questions to be answered at another, more convenient time.

Francesca got her morning cup of coffee and sat on the carpet of her living room in her pajamas that Sunday morning with tears streaming down her face. Why was she crying again? What was happening to her, a woman typically in control of all emotion who could keep her feelings tucked inside like the contents of her father's box of stuff, which now was all around her, spread out on the carpet?

Dan told her about Joe, that the night before, he saw him leave the ballpark with a whole entourage of people, and then later ran into them at Club 21. Some of Joe's teammates along with several younger women—possibly some of them groupies—were all hanging together at the bar. They were having a good time after the game, drinking and sitting at the bar. Jessica was not with him. Having Jessica there might put a damper on Joe's social life, Francesca thought. Then again, maybe it wouldn't. But Francesca knew this for sure: it was the kind of thought she didn't want to have herself now or for future years to come.

Regardless, what Dan shared with her solidified that she wanted not to be involved with Joe on a romantic level any longer. She wasn't sure if there would be trust issues, but she wasn't willing to find out. Freddie had been right. Joe might care about her in his own "Joe" way, but it was not enough for Francesca. In fact, she probably knew it all along, even when she dared to dabble and throw caution to the wind and be one of the participants in a fleeting, whirlwind romance. And even if it was over between them, she learned a lesson about herself: she was alive, a woman with feelings and love to give even though it had been locked up inside of her for so many years as she protected herself from ever feeling hurt again.

She appreciated Dan's candor. He was a good, solid friend and colleague, and she needed to appreciate him more. The next time he invited her out with his girlfriend, Tammy, she would go. She needed to spend more time outside of the office with them. She only met Tammy on one other occasion, and they had spent the night laughing together at a hat party, as they giggled over some of the most ridiculous hats they had ever seen.

She realized what was lacking in her life—companionship. Men in a male dominated sport and industry surrounded her in the boardroom, the office, and the field, and now, apparently, in every thought she had. She missed two people in particular that morning as she resolutely sat on her floor intently looking at one photograph after another of her father's short-lived life in baseball: Sam and her mother.

When was the last time she picked up the phone to call her friend? Sam was an energetic ball of outrageous fun. She missed her antics, sarcasm, and candor. She decided to call her next week to see how she was doing. She would finally tell her all about Joe and Jack. Why had she kept everything to herself for so long? Too often she was afraid to speak of her relationships for fear that the mere act of telling another human being resulted in its demise. She blamed herself for being too wrapped up in her own life over the years. She would fix that. She would fix that soon.

As for her mother, her father's absence remained a void. His death left a vacancy that had yet to be filled. How was her mother able to forge ahead? It had been ten years ago today on a similar warm and sunny May afternoon that he lost his battle, and Francesca lost the most important man in her life. But so did her mother. And now, thinking about her mother spending so much time alone made Francesca feel sad and miserable for her. She was far too young to spend the rest of her time by herself. Francesca needed to make more of an effort to see her mother. Maybe they could get together when the season was over. Maybe they could go visit Cissy and the kids and they could all spend some quality time as a family, perhaps even head to a resort for several days.

She held up a picture that she didn't remember seeing before. It had been inadvertently stuck to another photo, years of humidity in storage most likely the culprit, and Francesca gently pulled them apart, hoping she wouldn't tear the sepia images.

The photograph was mesmerizing. A professional had taken it; she knew this for sure because it bore the insignia "Johnson Photography" embossed on the bottom right-hand corner. Her father had rounded third and was in a full-trot run, heading for home. His face was focused on home plate, but there was nothing but pure contentment on his youthful face.

She returned everything to the box and ran the water for a shower. She knew where she needed to be that morning.

The large doors were just about to close when Francesca slipped through them as the organ was playing loudly. She dipped her fingers in the holy water and made the sign of the cross, and then slowly walked down the main aisle to where she typically sat when she went to church, the pew second from the front. She made eye contact with Father John. He gave her a little nod, and the corners of his mouth turned up ever so slightly. She knew he knew the significance of the date. Father John had admired her father as well, and shared many Sunday meals with all of them, as they laughed, talked baseball, and enjoyed conversation around dinner tables fit for kings.

She sighed. Ten years ago she delivered a sentimental eulogy for her father right there on that altar. She hoped she had paid proper respect to him, but she knew as well as anyone, that mere words cannot describe a person, though she did the best she could. If you really wanted to know someone, you had to take the time for them, understand them inside and out, and love them no matter their faults, no matter their mistakes.

She felt a tap on her shoulder. "I thought you might be here," her mother whispered.

Francesca slid over so her mother could sit next to her and placed her hand on her mother's thigh.

"I'm glad you're here," she said to her mom, and gave her a peck on the cheek.

Twenty-Six

"There were times I thought the fans hated me, but then you go and do
something you hadn't planned, like hit a home run or drive in three runs,
and you're back. They forgot you were in a slump to begin with."
~ Bradley Thompson, Starlings Outfielder, AAA Ball, 1960

Francesca and her mother had a conversation with Father John following mass. They were standing outside the church on the steps, the pavement still damp from the rain the day before. The church bells began to ring as robins flew by, chasing each other around in circles, then up toward the sky. People were still milling around, enjoying the sunshine of the day's weather, a slight breeze blowing steady, but warm. Father John was speaking highly of her father, talking about him warmly, reminiscing about days gone by.

"I'm going to the game today," she said, directing her statement to Father John. "I didn't tell Francesca, but I wanted to go. Connie and Jim are taking me," her mother said.

"I'm so glad you're coming today! I may even be able to sit with you for a bit. Slow day at work. Not much going on, and then Jack's coming for dinner. Why don't you both come for dinner too?"

Father John couldn't help but pipe in. "Francesca is making dinner? The Lord does work in mysterious ways! Let me never question that again," he said. Her mother chortled the loudest at that one.

When she stopped giggling, she asked Francesca, "Won't we be in your way on your date?"

"Date?" Father John said. "Oh my. I need to attend this dinner. Crashing dates is my specialty."

Francesca laughed. "Please do. I want you both to come."

After Francesca twisted their arms for a bit and swore they would not hinder the date, Father John and Francesca's mother agreed to come, and they said they looked forward to it.

"Sorry I'm a little late," she said to Dan when she arrived a little breathless to her office. "I had something to take care of this morning."

"No sweat," he said. "All is under control. I'm off to meet the guests. Let me know if you need anything today."

"Nope," she said. "Nice and quiet."

For the first hour after she arrived at work, she wrote her weekly manager's report that was due for Monday. The meeting took place at 9 a.m., at the beginning of each week, and the team of front office managers would update each other on their department's weekly happenings. Francesca's list always tended to be one of the longest, because it was her job to keep public relations up to date on all the player and mascot appearances. Additionally, many of the programs that originated from her department needed volunteers, and she often solicited help from front office employees across the board. Employees in accounting, for example, liked to help out with the player clinics for kids because it was an opportunity to meet them and get to know the players besides just printing their paychecks. In fact, she needed about ten volunteers in two weeks when they would promote a new field in the city that had been refurbished for Little League play. The mayor was scheduled to come, and two players were responsible for the ribbon cutting along with him. There were many community events scheduled for the next few weeks, and Francesca had a lot of organizing and coordinating to accomplish. She sat and typed her report, putting it in order by date and importance.

Just as she was saving and printing her work, her office phone rang.

"Francesca Milli," she said as she spoke into the receiver.

"Hey, it's Jack," he said.

"It's Sunday, and you know what that means, right? You—you poor thing—are going to be subjected to my cooking," she said, flirting with him. "Honestly, you have a right to be concerned."

"Actually, I don't think I can make it," he said.

"Why? Are you okay?"

"Yes, it's just, I'm not sure it's a good idea."

Francesca was puzzled. Why wouldn't it be a good idea? Two nights ago in the press box prior to the rain delay, he said he was looking forward to it. They had looked into each other's eyes, still feeling amorous from the night before. They had flirted in the press box. He had whispered in her ear.

"Well, guess what? I don't really know why you are saying that, and clearly you're not going to explain it to me, but the truth of the matter is it's a great idea. Whether you believe it or not, I've got another couple joining us for dinner, so leaving me without a date for my own dinner party would be a pretty uncool thing to do. Don't you think?"

"Isn't there someone else you might like to invite?"

"Not really," she said. "I invited you."

Jack was baffled as he sat there talking to her, hearing her voice over the receiver. She was playful and fun, and she still wanted him to come over. He scratched his head that continued to throb, though it wasn't as bad as it had been three hours ago. Hydrating himself with a combination of water and soda was helping. He didn't know what to say or how to say it. What would he say? I can't get involved in a love triangle? I don't want to be the other guy? It sounded so childish and insecure. So, instead of speaking, he said nothing. He just listened to her light breathing on the other end of the line.

Francesca swiveled in her chair with the phone to her ear, playing with a ballpoint pen as she clicked it and then unclicked it again over and over. She could hear the commotion in the press box and the reverberation of the sound system playing pregame music, but Jack continued to say nothing.

"Do you have a pen in your hand?" she asked, trying to bring the conversation back and be light about it all.

"Yes," he said.

"Write this address down: 24 Beaumont Avenue, Apartment C in the Towerlight Complex off Surrey Road." She heard a player make contact with a ball, as the sound of it echoed through the receiver. The team was still taking batting practice, and the volume of the music in the ballpark had become louder. "Got it?" she asked as she sat there twirling her hair, trying to process what was happening on the other line. Only seconds passed, but his lack of response seemed endless.

"You there, Jack?" she asked.

"Yes," he said.

"If you decide you might like to venture out for some mediocre food tonight, which you seemed eager to do two nights ago, I might add, that's where you want your car to end up. Please come. I have lots to show you, including some photographs I think you'll love, along with two very nice people for you to meet."

He thought for a second. "Okay," he said.

"Okay, you're coming, or okay, you'll think about it?"

"Yes," he said, and then hung up the phone.

Clarkson's bat was hot that day. Red hot. Smoking, red hot. He hit a single, a double, and a home run. He attributed it all to his new stance and grip. Each time he stepped into the batter's box, he stared down the pitcher—all three of them he faced—as New York's pitching staff couldn't find its rhythm. The pitchers' arms seemed sluggish, and the balls were floating in and over the plate, ripe for hitting.

Duke Milton hit a two-run homer, and the Blackbirds ended up winning by a score of 8-2 that sunny afternoon.

Francesca listened to the last inning of the game on her car radio. She left early to stop at the market for dinner, knowing her guests would be arriving in three short hours. Her place needed a quick dust and vacuum, and she wanted to have time to prepare the roast. It was marinating in the refrigerator since last night, and she needed a variety of fresh vegetables, salad fixings, and a dessert she ordered from the bakery up the road. She could do it. She could manage it all in three hours.

"Blackbirds win! Blackbirds win!" she heard the play-by-play announcer shout. She knew they would win. The team always seemed to honor her father's death with a win, no matter how close a game it was. Perhaps she was trying to make herself feel better, but she always convinced herself that the team won it for her and her father.

When her passenger seat was stuffed with two bags of groceries, she drove back to her condo. She carried the bags up the stairs, opened the door, and stepped inside. She surveyed the place: it was tidy, but needed just a little bit more cleaning. It was small and cozy, and there was enough room to entertain four people comfortably. She opened her sliding glass door and pulled the screen across it for ventilation. It was a beautiful late afternoon—butterflies were hovering above the butterfly bush that had been planted last spring in the gardens. Everything appeared fresh and lush. Earlier that morning, she had avoided thinking about Joe, except to remember that she was sitting with her father on the day he died right when Clarkson was a rookie and hit a homer. Francesca had watched her father's labored breathing. Minutes afterwards, his breathing had stopped.

Her father knew who Joe Clarkson was, but would he have liked him? Probably. It was difficult not to like Joe. Everyone loved him. He was a likeable guy. She always liked him.

As she dusted off some of her furniture after putting the groceries away, she thought about Jack and their strange exchange on the phone. She wondered if he would show up. Something had happened to Jack over the last two days, but she couldn't put her finger on it. Was he nervous about getting involved? She wondered if she should tell him she new about Sarah and the accident, but she didn't think the timing was right. They were just getting to know each other—and she thought things went very well on their date. And what of the kiss? Did he not find it as romantic as she did?

Her father's box of collectibles was on her bookshelf, and she ran the feather duster over it. They would look through it tonight. They would see the pictures and the notes and the ticket stubs. It was a key ingredient to the dinner party's success. She hoped Father John would not embarrass her by asking about Joe or anything silly in front of Jack. He wouldn't do that. Priests were supposed to be secretive regarding such matters.

After cleaning and vacuuming and fluffing up the pillows, Francesca made the salad. The roast was in the oven, and her side dishes were prepared. Francesca surveyed her kitchen. Her tools and gadgets were put away, and so she stole to the bathroom for a refreshing, hot shower. She let the water hit her face, her back, and run across her legs. She exhaled and let the shower massage her, turning the heat of the water up as high as she could stand it without scalding herself. Decompress, she told herself. No need for a hurried shower. This was the best kind: the kind of shower you let wash away all your fears and neuroses and worries. It felt therapeutic and energizing all at the same time. She dried off and stepped into a summertime dress and a pair of sandals.

Her favorite people were coming over for dinner, and she was excited to introduce them to Jack.

TWENTY-SEVEN

"Some of the best relationships begin when you hold a
baseball in your hand."
~*Joe Emerson, Blackbirds player, b. 1918-d. 1948*

Father John was the first to arrive. He was always early. "Prompt Father John," his fellow priests would call him. Prompt Father John talked to the religion classes today. Prompt Father John made his visit to the hospital. Prompt Father John got his income taxes done. That was they way they referred to him; they teased him constantly in such a loving and carefree manner, and he never seemed to mind.

He stood before Francesca with a bottle of good red wine, along with some cookies he picked up from the same bakery where Francesca got the cake, so she knew they would be delicious. He was wearing his casual priestly clothes with his collar. Francesca wondered if he ever grew tired of wearing the same wardrobe over and over.

"Well, I do get to wear different colored robes depending on the season," he said. "I've been told purple is my color."

"It's better than black, John, that's for sure."

"Oh, you're dropping the 'Father' tonight, eh?"

"Well, only because it's just the two of us. When Jack arrives, I'll bring the 'Father' back in. Just to impress him."

"Now, fill me in on Jack."

"His name is Jack Thompson, and he's a reporter. He's my, well, right now, he's my friend who I happened to kiss Thursday night."

"Not saving this for the confessional, I guess," Father John teased.

"Nope. Nothing to confess."

Father John looked at her suspiciously, raising one of his eyebrows. His light brown hair looked as if it had just been cut, and when he turned his face a certain angle, he looked so similar to his father, Ben, with his sharp features and high cheekbones. John's parents moved only last year to Florida, and he frequently visited them when he took his vacations.

"Keeping it clean, then, Francesca?" He laughed when he said it. She loved when he was funny. Moreover, he knew she was telling the truth. She wouldn't lie to him; she had no need to do so.

"And Mr. Clarkson?"

"Done," she said. "We'll only ever be friends. Which will be helpful to you."

"How's that?" he asked.

"Less time for you to spend on me in the confessional."

The doorbell rang, and Francesca's mother entered the foyer wearing a little blue sundress, sunglasses, and smelling of French perfume. She always wore French perfume. There was not a hair out of place, and Francesca could swear her mother looked better than ever.

"Just some mints and some gourmet coffee for dessert," she said.

"Very nice, Mom," Francesca said, kissing her on the cheek. Father John did the same, and the three of them went out onto Francesca's small balcony that was large enough to fit a table and four chairs along with one outdoor sofa with a side table. It was cozy, and Francesca had done a good job of stringing twinkle lights around the perimeter and adding some plants for ambiance.

She poured them each a glass of wine, and wondered when Jack might arrive. She hoped he wouldn't stand her up, especially since she was hosting the dinner. She hoped he would come, and that, whatever was troubling him, he might share it with her. After reading the stories about the accident, she had nothing but empathy for him and his situation. And yet, she didn't want to press him or ask him too directly about what he had said on the phone earlier. Why did he think it "wasn't a good idea" for him to come over? She had waited on the other end of the line for an answer, but none came. She wondered if it had something to do with his loyalty to Sarah. Some people had a hard time letting go. She should know. She was one of those people.

At seven-thirty, her doorbell rang, and she jumped up at the sound of it. She went running from the balcony to the front door, and opened it. Jack stood before her holding a bottle of wine, but wearing a very somber expression on his face.

"I'm sorry I'm late," he said, "and I'm equally sorry to bring bad news, but I guess it's better that it comes from me in person."

"What bad news?" she asked, concerned because he looked concerned.

"Joe Clarkson's dad died a couple of hours ago."

Francesca was left speechless and felt a pit form in her stomach for Joe. Those were words no child ever wanted to hear about his father.

Within minutes, she was dialing the telephone.

"David, it's Francesca," she said into the phone after finally reaching David. "Tell me what happened with Mr. Clarkson."

"Apparently, he had a heart attack today after mowing the lawn."

Francesca grew silent. Mr. Clarkson attended many of Joe's

games over the years. He was probably in his late fifties. A nice sweet man. And he was handsome like his son. She had met him twice.

"Have any arrangements been made?" she asked.

"None that I know of yet. Joe's boarding a plane for home. He'll miss the next few games."

"Will you let me know when you hear details about the arrangements?"

"Of course," David said. "I'll call you when I hear anything."

She hung up the phone and looked at her three guests, all of them trying hard not to eavesdrop on her conversation. She looked at Jack. "Thanks for telling me. No news yet. Joe's on his way home and will miss the next few games."

They were all somber, and Francesca didn't know how to continue the dinner party. Jack, not sure if he should stay, asked Francesca if she wanted to postpone the dinner.

"Not really. I'd rather not sit here tonight by myself. I'd rather have you three here. It may not be as jovial as I would have liked, but I have an adequate roast in the oven about to be done. Let me pour some wine."

Her mother followed her into the kitchen and whispered to her, "Would you rather us go, sweetheart? We don't have to stay."

"No," Francesca whispered back. "I want you to stay. Please. How strange that he died on the same date as Dad. Eerie, right?"

"A little," her mother said. She rubbed Francesca's back as she poured the wine, and then wrapped an apron around her waist. Then, changing the subject, she said, "Actually, Francesca, it smells better than adequate. I think this roast is going to be incredible. Did you fib and tell Jack you are not a cook?"

"Exactly. That way everything I make will seem amazing to him. Good game plan, right?"

"Clever," she said, smiling.

Jack and Father John were out on the balcony. There could have been an awkward silence hanging in the air, a little cloud of doom hovering over the room, but Father John didn't believe in awkward silences. He believed in putting people at ease and having them feel comfortable with those around them.

"I enjoy reading your articles in the paper," Father John said. "I try to have a way with words with my congregation, but often my homilies fall flat. I could probably use a few lessons in how to tell a captivating story."

"I'm sure your homilies are just fine," Jack said, chuckling.

"Francesca was telling me before you got here that both your dads played for the Starlings," Father John said.

"It's an odd coincidence," Jack said. "What's even stranger is that she knows all the stats from the year they played together. Apparently, at the age of eight, she had the team roster memorized along with each player's stats. And I thought I liked baseball."

"She adores it. Always has. Even when we were little—did she tell you we grew up together, even though I'm a little older?—she thought she was the baseball goddess. And her father loved the game as much as she did. The two of them could carry on about it for hours, and her sister Cissy wanted nothing to do with it. One Fourth of July, when we had our neighborhood picnic and annual game for the kids, she struck this boy out who was one of her best friends. He never spoke to her after that. It actually was pretty funny."

Jack took a sip of the wine, and placed it back down on the table.

Francesca called to them. Dinner was ready, she had said.

They walked back into the kitchen where the two ladies were setting out the food buffet style. The off-white tablecloth had flowers set in the middle, and the meal was spread across the table. The smell of home-cooked pork permeated the room, and the salad was tossed to perfection, with radishes curled on top as decoration. The vegetables were spouting steam. Jack couldn't remember the last time he was in someone's home for dinner. He would typically do one of three things on any given night: cook something along the lines of noodles for himself, grab dinner out, or eat at the ballpark. Even if this were—as Francesca called it—an "adequate" meal, it would be better than anything he would eat out of a can, in the microwave, or in the press box.

"Grab a plate and let's bring it to the balcony. It's really such a beautiful night," Francesca said.

They talked about the food, each one of them heaping a little bit of everything Francesca had made onto their plates, and settled into their seats on the balcony.

"Father John, would you like to give a little blessing?" her mother asked.

"I think I would," he said.

They all made the sign of the cross and bowed their heads.

"Tonight, Dear Father, we thank you for allowing all of us to gather at Francesca's house, and we do hope her cooking is better than adequate, because it sure smells that way. We ask you to bless Francesca's friend Joe as he mourns the loss of his father, and we welcome our new friend Jack into our lives. Please look after Archie Milli, Dear Father, on this tenth anniversary of his death, and Mr. Clarkson on this day of his death. May your love and wisdom always guide us, and may we never lose sense of what dear friends and deep love can do for us. We ask this in your name, Amen."

Jack looked up and across the table directly into Francesca's eyes. She swallowed hard and seemed to be fighting back tears.

Francesca looked up and across at Jack, who allowed the corners of his mouth to turn up just a little and gave her the tiniest nod of sympathy. In that one split second, she realized there was a world of understanding that passed between them without either one of them needing to speak a word.

Francesca's mother could see the resemblance as plain as day. Jack looked like Brad, and even used similar inflections in his voice when he was talking. His eyes were lighter, however, a more crystal shade of green. When she heard him laugh, it instantly brought her back to the days when Archie and Brad played ball, and she would spend time sitting in the ballpark during practices, watching them play and listening to their laughter echoing off the walls. She loved those days just before she and Archie married, when everything felt romantic and beautiful and light. Brad was his best friend during that short time on the Starlings, and June became her closest friend. Being around other players and their girlfriends and wives made her feel a part of things, and she enjoyed the camaraderie of the team and of Archie's peers as life seemed to move in slow motion.

When Archie and she decided to buy their first house, there were some things Archie wanted to do himself. His father had been a contractor for a bit, and he learned how to wield tools, measure properly, order the correct materials, and finagle his way through projects. But it was his brother who learned the business even better than Archie, as he worked for his father during the summers building additions and renovating existing structures. When Archie purchased the house, he and his brother set out to fix it up by altering parts of it, and embellishing others. After the accident that cost Archie his baseball career,

Francesca's mother became concerned for Archie. It had been his great love, and she knew it would break his heart that he could no longer play.

Francesca never knew that her father had suffered a bit of a breakdown afterwards. He was angry that the accident happened and took away his livelihood. He was frustrated that his hand would never heal and that he would never play ball ever again the way he did, with such promise and fortitude. When he was cut from the team, it was just an inevitability that could not be avoided. He struggled with his circumstances. Francesca's mother urged him to get help, but at the time, he wanted none, and spiraled into a depression. It took some time for him to find his way again. They had arguments, and the once quiet, humorous, sweet man Archie was went away for a while.

Part of the depression was blamed on the disconnection he felt from all his baseball friends who continued to play ball, and that was a hard pill for him to swallow. They didn't mean to forget about him, but they were busy, traveling with the team to locations across many states. He wasn't playing the game, and he lamented about his friendship with Brad and how they lost touch, and no matter how many times Francesca's mother tried to tell him to reach out and call him, he always made an excuse not to do it.

All those years when Francesca asked her mother why she didn't like baseball, her mother was lying. It wasn't because she didn't like the sport. She actually loved the sport. She just didn't like the hurt that resulted from it for Archie. Even though he got over it and fell in love with the Blackbirds years later when they moved to the city and he established himself in a new career, it was she who had a hard time readjusting and falling in love with baseball all over again.

But now, thanks to Francesca's career, one that she was passionate about, her mother found herself reconnecting with it.

She hoped, as well, that she could reconnect with Brad and

June.

Yes, she thought. She would like that very much.

"Come sit here, next to me, Jack," Francesca said, as her mother and Father John were chatting in the kitchen. Francesca pulled the box from the shelf and set it on the coffee table in front of her. They were looking though some of the photographs that Francesca organized in piles—team photos, individual photos, and group photos. Then, she showed him the other pile—the box scores she had carefully paper clipped. There were also press clippings, notes, and postcards neatly arranged. She wanted to be able to go through it all with Jack so she could share those memories with him.

"This is my dad here in the team photo, and your dad is right behind him," she said. "Can you believe that?"

Francesca's mother entered the room and said, "We were very close with your parents when they played together," she said. "We socialized all the time, and Archie really loved your dad."

"I need to tell them that I've met you. I'm sure they'd love to see you on their next trip down," Jack said.

"I would love that," Francesca's mother said. "You remind me a lot of your dad."

"Yes," he said. "I get that a lot."

They continued to rummage through the box, and Jack's face became animated as he read some of the headlines from the various newspaper clippings. Amidst the piles of nostalgia, Jack was almost at a loss for words.

"My dad wasn't a collector or a keeper," he finally said. "He didn't save too many things."

"Well, luckily for you, my dad was a collector and keeper of things, and I am going to make a copy of this photo for you. Here it is… the grand finale…a picture of our two dads together in their uniforms. I think this needs to be displayed in a museum."

Francesca had purposely held this one for last. Her dad and Bradley stood on the field, arms around each other, slightly leaning forward, their legs crossed, grinning at the camera. They looked like best friends.

Jack stared at the picture, and for the first time, he noticed how much he resembled his father. It was true. He did look like him. Hearing about Clarkson's father passing away earlier made him realize he didn't go home and visit his parents enough, and he certainly hadn't appreciated them for helping him get through Sarah's death. The amount of meals his mother had made for him, the nights they stayed overnight talking until dawn, or the way they allowed him to be silent or sad. He didn't know what he would have done without them.

Francesca's mother served dessert and coffee, placing one of Father John's cookies alongside the cake on each plate. They all ate, remarking on the superb quality of the cake and cookies, while Francesca confessed to purchasing the cherry cheesecake at the bakery.

"The meal was outstanding, Francesca. I've never had pork roast prepared like that before, and it was delicious," Jack said.

"So glad you liked it," she said, and she turned to wink at her mother without anyone else seeing.

"I really like him," Francesca's mother whispered in her ear as she kissed her daughter goodnight. Father John was shaking hands with Jack, then kissed Francesca, and the two left as Father John walked Francesca's mother to her car.

"I should get going too," Jack said.

"Really?" Francesca said. "It's still early."

"I know, but I'm sure you'll want to talk to Clarkson—Joe—and make sure he's okay."

"Yes, but not tonight. I'll call him tomorrow. I'm sure he'll want to be with his family. He's probably just arriving."

Jack hadn't budged from the door, despite Francesca's invitation to stay.

"I really should go," he said.

"Something's happened, hasn't it? Do you want to talk about it? It feels like something's changed since Thursday night."

Jack didn't want to seem ridiculous or sound like a child. Were he and Clarkson at the point where they might both be vying for her attention? He only went on one date with her; it couldn't be that serious already. It was ludicrous. Besides, the ballplayer with millions of dollars along with million-dollar looks would win. She was giving him the floor—to say what was on his mind—and he had a choice to make. He could both fib like a schoolboy and say "nothing," or he could be a man and say what was on his mind. He could tell her the truth.

"What is it?" she asked earnestly, observing him and wondering what he was thinking about not saying.

After a pause, he spoke: "Is it okay if I just come out and say it and you won't storm off and get mad?"

"Oh, Lord. What is it? I promise I won't be a baby about it like I was in the press box that time."

"I saw you kissing Clarkson in your office last night accidentally. I came to see if you were going to the bar. I don't want to be involved in a love triangle." He was starting to perspire. "There. I've had that thought all day, and now I've said it."

Francesca smiled, leaned against the door, and crossed her arms. "I like you, Jack. You're my kind of people."

"What does that mean?"

"Thank you for telling me your thoughts. Now that you've been honest, and showed up here for dinner tonight, keeping your promise even though you were thinking something in your head that's not entirely true, I'm going to do the same, only you won't want to believe it."

"What?"

"Clarkson—Joe—kissed me. I was not expecting that kiss. You must have seen us at just the right moment, because afterwards I pulled away. I told him I couldn't pursue the relationship any longer, and that I wanted us to remain friends and colleagues. I didn't go to the bar last night, and I didn't go home with Joe, either. I came home and went to bed, utterly exhausted. However, if I had known you were going to Cagny's, I might have come. It was just an unfortunate turn of events, I guess."

He felt like a fool. He had acted juvenile and insecure about something that wasn't as it appeared. He was embarrassed.

"I'm sorry," he said. "I may have been getting a little ahead of myself there."

"Not really," she said. "I've been looking forward to seeing you all day—all weekend, in fact. Besides our Thursday night date, tonight was the highlight of my week, actually."

"Me, too," he said. "And I love your mom and Father John."

"What's not to love, right?" she said.

"So is the invitation still open for me to stay for a bit?" he asked.

Francesca held the door open and motioned for him to come back inside.

Francesca reached over and put her hand on Jack's thigh while he recounted the story of Sarah and the accident, telling her all about that night, how devastating a loss it was for him, and how it has taken him years to heal. He placed his hand on top of hers.

"I can imagine how hard it must have been for you, but you must never blame yourself, Jack. Accidents happen, and sometimes they are totally out of our control," Francesca said.

"I know. It's a comforting thought, but it's much more challenging to live it afterward. I'm sure you feel somewhat the same way I do about losing your dad. I mean, you probably wished you could have changed the circumstances, but there was no way you could have. It's that feeling of being powerless when someone needs you that's tough to come to grips with, I think," Jack said.

They sat next to each other listening to Sting, embracing the music and the lull in conversation. Sometimes it was nice to just sit and not talk.

Perhaps they could have become romantic if they wanted to, but the idea of Clarkson's dad's death—and death in general—was too heavy. Francesca explained to Jack that she would probably fly out for the funeral if she could, and that she would want to be there for Joe and his family. Jack understood. Anyone who has dealt with losing someone you love could understand wanting to be there for someone you cared about. At one-thirty in the morning, Jack left to go home.

He stood at the doorway, facing her and holding her hands. He did not attempt to recreate the magic that had occurred between them on Thursday, because something compassionate and kind had been exchanged during the course of the evening. Francesca had talked openly about her relationship with her father, and Jack had spoken to a woman, besides his mother and sisters, about losing Sarah. It was extraordinarily therapeutic for the two of them, and a deeper connection formed as they sat and talked.

"Goodnight, Francesca," he said, reaching in to give her a sweet, short kiss on her lips, at the end of the night.

"Goodnight, Jack," she said, taking it a step further and hugging him tightly. They stood there in the threshold of her condo embracing for minutes. She didn't want to let go. There was something tremendously comforting and unusually tender about feeling Jack's warm hands wrapped around her body and the warmth of his cheek pressed against her own.

Twenty-Eight

"Love leaves a memory that no one else can steal, but sometimes it leaves a heartache that no one else can heal."
~ Unknown

The sun peeked through her curtains in the morning and awakened her a little earlier than normal. She reached for her phone and dialed.

Joe picked up his cell phone on the second ring.

"Hello?" he said.

"Hi there," she said. "You've been on my mind since I heard the news, and I just wanted to tell you that I'm so sorry about your dad."

"Thanks," he said.

"Are you okay?" she asked warmly and genuinely.

"I'm okay. My mom's not. She's a mess. It's tough to watch her suffer, you know?"

"I do," she said, and then Joe thought maybe that was an insensitive thing to say. He knew Francesca lost her father years ago, though he knew little of the details. She hadn't shared much about it, but she did understand loss, and hearing her voice was helpful.

"I'm just still in shock, even after thinking about it the entire flight home. It was very quick and sudden. He just wasn't feeling well, came inside, and the next thing my mother knew, he wasn't breathing. He went quickly."

"I'm so sorry, Joe," Francesca said again.

"The arrangements are being made, and I'll let David know as soon as I know anything."

"Okay," she said. "Is there anything I can do for you?"

"Your call means a lot to me, as you can probably imagine. Thank you," he said. "And maybe have your friend—was it Father John?—say a prayer for my mom."

"Yes, I will ask him to do that," Francesca said. "Take care of yourself, okay?"

"I'll try."

"Call me if you need to talk," she said.

"Will do," he said.

When David called her later that afternoon after learning the details of the funeral arrangements, Francesca asked Claire to book her flight to Texas. It meant she had to fly again, but she would put her fears aside because she had to: she had a friend who needed her and she needed to represent the front office. David had public relations duties to attend to as he was the primary contact for the media, and the team had a game, though they were on the road in Florida. Dan could hold down the fort in her absence.

She called her phone mail to retrieve her work messages, and there was one from Freddie.

"Hi Francesca. David told me you're headed to Joe's dad's funeral. I'm going to represent the team. Didn't know if we were on the same plane. Call me."

Francesca called Freddie, and they agreed to meet at the airport and sit together on the plane. Francesca was somewhat relieved; it always calmed her down when there was someone to fly with her. Freddie flew all the time. It was second nature for him.

She packed her bags, and reminded herself that she was doing the right thing, even though things were a little awkward with Joe. There was no doubt she needed to go, and she wanted to be there for him.

Francesca felt herself going over the details of the previous evening with Jack. Last night when she talked to him, she didn't mean to become so somber about her own father's death, but she felt he could understand it in ways that some others couldn't. His stories about Sarah were good for her to hear, and she could see Jack's pain. Although Sarah's death happened many years ago, it still was fresh to him. She wondered if she had waited for the right moment to become romantic. It was she, after all, who had kissed him in the rain on Thursday. Maybe he just wasn't ready to date. Lord knows she wasn't very good at relationships with men. They always seemed to end badly. The brief one she had with Joe was yet another case in point—fairy tale endings were not in her cards.

She closed her suitcase, tidied up her apartment, grabbed a bottle of water and her purse, and closed the door behind her. She was off to Texas to support Joe and mourn the loss of his father. The thought of it gave her a little chill. Death was so permanent, and the rest of your life you were left with questions you wished you didn't have, and they usually started with "What if" and "Did I do enough?"

She hoped Joe wasn't facing those questions today. First, there's an immeasurable loss that comes over you, typically followed by an unnerving sadness, followed by a touch of anger. In Francesca's case, her father was much too young. Over and over in her head she would ask why. Why so soon? Couldn't he have had a few more years here with us? And in Joe's case as well, his father was relatively young. He had just turned sixty.

The cab picked her up after only five minutes of waiting; she preferred not to leave her car at the airport car park and appreciated the door-to-door service. She put her luggage in the trunk, and within minutes, she was approaching the airport. Soon she would arrive in Texas.

There were many people at the funeral home to pay homage to a stand-up man like Gregory Clarkson. Members of his church, golfing buddies, relatives from near and far, and neighbors all gathered to pay their respects to a man they loved so dearly.

The casket was closed, and instead pictures sat atop of it and were placed all around the room of a man beloved by his community and networks of family and friends. People were hugging each other, sitting closely together, telling stories of Gregory, and trying their best to come to grips with a loss that was so sudden and disquieting.

Francesca entered the room and saw Joe sitting alone in the front row, staring straight ahead. She quickly looked around the room for Jessica, but did not see her. Flowers adorned the casket, as they were set on the floor, on the tables, and on stands on either side of it. Freddie was talking to a woman in the back of the room he remembered meeting at one point, and Joe's mother stood stoically, accepting condolences and hearing anecdotal tributes to her late husband by those who sought her out.

Francesca walked up the middle aisle and walked over to Joe. He looked as if he'd been crying. He turned to look at her.

"Hi," she said, sitting down next to him on the red cushioned chair. He looked down at his lap, embarrassed to have her see him that way. He wiped away a tear.

"Hi," he said, in a grateful tone.

She reached for his large hands, the same strong ones that held a bat and smacked a ball with force. The same ones that had been all over her body not too long ago. She held them in hers.

"There are no words I can say that can fully express how sorry I am for the loss of your father, but I am truly sorry. I'm very sorry."

She felt a lump grow in her throat, a reminder of the pain she once bore ten years prior when she buried her own father. Like Francesca, Joe had a good relationship with his dad, and she knew how much he was hurting and that he missed him already.

"Glad you're here," was all Joe said as he swallowed hard, and they both sat in silence, staring at the casket, she with both of her hands wrapped around his.

"You, my dear, are a good friend," Freddie said on the cab ride back to the hotel. He was looking sharp in his suit, and not a hair on his head was out of place. "Not only did you fly all the way here to pay your respects, but you were there for Joe when he needed you."

"I hope it helped a little. When my father died, I didn't want to talk to anyone but my friend who is a priest because I was so angry. He had to help me get over that loss."

"Well, your presence was very much appreciated tonight. I could tell."

"Where was Jessica?" Francesca asked innocently enough.

"I thought someone said she was there for the first half-hour then left. Apparently, she wasn't feeling well, but her whole family was there in support."

"I see," Francesca said. She wasn't worried about Jessica being there, but she was glad she wasn't. It gave her the freedom to be who she was—a friend to Joe now, back to how they were before—without having to pretend to be or do something she wasn't. Instead, she just was, and it all came quite naturally.

"Care to join me for an appetizer and drink at the bar?"

"I thought you'd never ask," Francesca said. "What time does our flight leave tomorrow?"

"Nine," he said.

They sat at the bar, and picked two chairs in the middle so they could see both televisions. There were two televised games, but not the Blackbirds. The team was in Florida, and the game hadn't started yet, but it was unlikely to be televised in Texas.

The bartender, dressed in a white shirt, vest, and black slacks, approached the two of them at the bar.

"Evening," he said. "What can I get you tonight?"

Freddie motioned to Francesca, as if to say, "Ladies first."

"A glass of Chardonnay," she said.

"And for you, sir?"

"A single malt Scotch, please," Freddie said, his almost radio-sounding voice rich and husky. Francesca looked at him and smiled.

"What?" he asked.

"I didn't know you had such refined taste."

He sat up straight and looked at her, a funny expression crossing his face, and then in a surprisingly good Groucho Marx accent, said, "My dear, there are quite a lot of things you may not know about an old guy like me, and probably some things you don't want to know about me." He was making a face, raising his eyebrows and tweaking an imaginary cigar when he said it.

He caught her so off guard, she started laughing. Her laughter enveloped the bar, and heads turned to see what was so funny, but all anyone saw was a distinguished looking guy making a pretty, young woman laugh.

"Ah, that felt good," she said. "After all that sadness tonight, it felt good to laugh. I didn't know you could do impressions like that." She was dabbing the tears with the bar napkin from the corner of her eyes, residual mascara leaving its mark.

"Never on demand, though. Only when it is unsuspected do I do them. I hate when people say, 'Do your impression of Steve Martin or Jimmy Carter.' You can't do it when requested, you know?"

She smiled at him. "Not really. I can't imitate anyone, but if I could, I might try to make a side living out of it. You know, help with life's expenses."

"Are you saying you need a side job?" he asked, looking worried.

"No, I'm not saying that, but a side job might be a good way to release tensions and energies, especially if it were more like a talent."

"You are talented. You run a whole department for a big league team. Not everyone can do that type of work."

"Thank you, Freddie," she said. Their drinks arrived, and they toasted each other.

"Plus, anyone can see how much you love your job."

She did love her job. She did it because she loved baseball— genuinely loved the sport and the camaraderie that goes along with it—and she made enough to make ends meet. As the years progressed, she did it for the love of people who loved the game. Her department helped build community, fostered goodwill, and in its small way, it made Bay City a better place. She was most proud of that aspect of her work.

Freddie was hungry, so he ordered a burger and fries and en- couraged Francesca to get something off the menu, insisting that he was paying and that she should indulge when she was being treated. She finally acquiesced and allowed him to buy her a small salad with a fully loaded baked potato on the side.

The square-shaped bar began to fill up, and before long, all the seats were taken. People were pointing at the televisions and shouting at a bad call. The bartender was trying to keep up with all the orders, and although it was hectic, he seemed to be handling the multi-tasking well. The waitresses serving the tables around the bar were hopping, taking and placing orders. As she looked around, she found it ironic that the hotel bar seemed more suited to women, with sparkling chandeliers, plants and flowers around the perimeter, and white twinkle lights wrapped around a faux porch area with a white trellis, than it was to men, despite that it was mostly men there watching sports.

At around nine, the bartender switched one television over to the ballgame; Texas was up 4-2 in the bottom of the fourth.

"Did Joe ever wish he could play for Texas?" she asked Freddie, who took the biggest bite of a burger she ever saw. He held up his forefinger, nonverbally telling her to 'wait a minute,' and he finished chewing.

"I don't know. He's never said anything," he said, speaking through the wad of food in his mouth.

"He could have been closer to his family, though, and his dad—and his mom—probably would have loved that."

"True enough," Freddie said, "but the sport doesn't really work that way. You know that. You go where you go, and sometimes the home team doesn't want you."

Her mobile phone went off at that exact moment, and she reached inside her purse to pull it out.

"Hello," she said, answering it.

"Hey," the voice on the other end of the line said. "You were on my mind, and I just wanted to see how it went today."

Her heart fluttered for a moment.

"It was good. I'm glad I came," she said honestly. "How are you?"

"Good," he said. "So you're holding up okay?"

"Yes. I'm actually sitting at the hotel bar with Freddie Montrose eating a salad while he inhales his burger that he doused with ketchup, mustard, pickles, tomatoes, onions, lettuce, olives, and mayonnaise. How many condiments do you like to put on your burger?"

"A dash of everything," he said, and then remained silent.

Francesca bit her tongue because it hit her, and threw her head back, laughing again.

"No!" she squealed. "Is that why some guys call you Dash?"

"I knew you'd find out at some point," he said.

"You're never going to live this down, Thompson," she said.

Freddie looked up from his plate when he heard her snort.

Twenty-Nine

*"The one thing you can't do in this game is become complacent. You have to
be smart; the smart players can figure things out, make them work.
Sometimes it means making adjustments,
and when you do it, and do it right, you reap the rewards."*
~ Duke Milton, Blackbirds Catcher

The cab pulled up to her mother's house. It was close to seven,
and she and Freddie decided to share one when they realized how close
Freddie lived to her mother. Therefore, since Francesca was staying the
night at her mother's, it made sense. Her mother must have been waiting for them, peering out of the curtains at the front window, because
she was halfway down the cobblestone walkway as soon as the cab
pulled up.

The driver opened the trunk to retrieve her luggage, and Francesca started to pay him, but Freddie was already out of the car insisting
on carrying her luggage and taking care of the driver.

It was a beautiful spring evening; the grass was remarkably
green from all the rain, and the flowers were blooming in all shades of
colors; pinks and lavenders and yellows bringing life to the green shrubs
around them.

"Hi!" her mother called, as she came down the front steps,
meeting Freddie and Francesca on the driveway. "How was your trip?"

"Sad. Mom, have you ever met Freddie Montrose?"

"I don't think so," her mother said.

"Freddie, this is my mom; Mom, this is Freddie."

"Does your mother have a formal name?" Freddie asked, poking fun at Francesca.

"Sorry—Freddie, this is my mother, Lillian."

"Nice to meet you, Lillian. Lovely name. You don't hear that one often enough."

"Thank you," her mother said, blushing. "And thanks for delivering Francesca safely."

"Are you kidding? I think she escorted me home. You've got a very independent, smart, lovely, and strong woman on your hands, Lillian. You've done right by her."

"Thank you, again," her mother said.

A plane flew overhead at that moment; the loud roar of it momentarily distracted Freddie. On occasion, the airport's flight path went right over Lillian's house; however, having lived near the airport for a very long time, neither Francesca, nor her mother, paid much attention to the planes anymore. It was part of their lives. You could get used to a lot after a while.

"You should bring your mother to an afternoon ballgame, Francesca, and then we could all go out to dinner," Freddie said.

Francesca raised an eyebrow to him.

"That sounds like a great idea," her mother piped in, enthusiastically.

The smell of Lillian's house was a reminder that Francesca was home. Some people were unaware of their home's particular scent, especially when they lived in it daily, but they were always reminded of its particular pleasant odor when they either went on a long trip or, as in Francesca's case, didn't live there anymore and returned back to it for visits. In fact, when she was younger and played with Evan, her neighbor, she was turned off by the smell of his home, and often avoided going inside of it. It smelled so peculiar, almost like a litter box, which would have been understandable, except they didn't have a cat. Additionally, Evan's mother was an unpleasant sort, shouting at her children from the front door, unfriendly and rude to those on her street, and always complaining about the contractors who seemed to be perpetually working on her home. She swore she'd never be that kind of wife or mother, even as a kid, and further swore that her house would always be an inviting place, like her mother's, where friends and family wanted to gather and spend time.

In Francesca's case as an adult, there was always a sense of nostalgia when she walked through the front door, so strong and overwhelming, it often felt like the years that passed were imaginary, that she was still a little girl in pig tails and cut off jean shorts looking for her dad to come outside and have a game of catch with her. Despite living on the outskirts of the city, they had a fairly large yard, and they would either toss the ball in the front or in the back as they waited for her mother to call them in for dinner. Her father never refused to go outside, even after a long day's work when he was tired. He would shed his shirt and tie and jump into his sweats. They would toss the ball and talk about their days, each one taking a turn to fill the other in on what had happened.

Francesca missed those moments. Since his death, she learned one thing for certain: you never get over the loss of a parent. The void, having been sweetly close to her dad, was one so wide and massive, that she wasn't sure that hole could ever be filled again.

She put her suitcase next to the front door and tossed her cardigan on top of it.

"I bet you're hungry," her mother said.

"Famished," Francesca replied.

"Now, don't kill me, but …"

She heard the shuffling in the kitchen. "S-U-R-P-R-I-S-E!" she heard.

"Oh, my God! Sam!" she said, flabbergasted.

"Bet you didn't expect to see me, did you?"

"No! Oh my gosh! When did you get here?"

"Just this morning. When you break up with your boyfriend, you want to come home right away and be with people you care about. I called your office yesterday, and your assistant told me you were at a funeral for a player's father. I had to know what was going on, so I called your mom pronto. Apparently, you've been keeping a lot of secrets, Miss Don't-Date-The-Players! Since when do you bend the rules?"

The two hugged. Lillian looked so pleased that she had been able to pull off the surprise. She called Francesca before she boarded the plane and asked her if she could stay the night to take her to a doctor's appointment. Francesca assessed now that it was all baloney. She set this up so Sam could surprise her.

"I have so much to tell you, Sam. You have no idea."

"And to think I considered us best friends."

Francesca felt awful, because that's what happens when you attend a funeral. Like a slap in the face, you realize all too well that there are no guarantees for how long you will be around. Her own father lost his life way too young, as did Sarah, and Gregory Clarkson. She realized she kept way too much inside of her—all her anguish, pain, frustration, ambition, love, hopes and dreams. It was there in her mother's kitchen that she recognized that she had closed herself off to people—to too many people—to too many people who mattered most to her, including her own sister, whom she didn't communicate with enough.

"Mom, I hope you have a bottle of wine, because I have a feeling we're going to be catching up for hours."

Sam looked at her friend and smiled. She put her arm around her shoulder and offered a stern warning: "These stories better be good. I just flew three thousand miles, and I demand to be entertained."

"I'll do my best," Francesca said.

Two bottles of wine later, having polished off most of it herself after unleashing years of stories, Francesca stretched her legs. They had been sitting outside on her mother's slate patio in candlelight dining al fresco at the pine table. Her mother hung white twinkle lights around the patio for ambiance. There were plates of antipasto, breads and cheeses, and a homemade tortellini soup that was Francesca's favorite. Additionally, Lillian baked a homemade chocolate cake, with powdered sugar sprinkled on top. As they ate, there were two things that were happening over and over. Lillian watched the girls, sometimes feeling like a third wheel, as Francesca would say, "I can't believe I never told you that," launching into descriptive details of the story, to which Sam would repeatedly say something like, "No way! You little hussy!" Lillian couldn't help but snicker and shake her head as she listened to the exchange between the two. It was more than entertaining.

"I still can't understand how or why you could refuse that gorgeous man," Sam said, after Francesca finished telling her relationship with Joe, and why she felt it was the right thing to let him go. "He's unbelievably hot! I mean, don't you remember how I used to drool over that poster I had in our dorm room?"

"Um, I think I remember, Sam," she said.

"Did you think he was attractive then?"

"I've always thought he was attractive," Francesca said.

"You didn't show it," Sam said. "But now that I think of it, you didn't show a lot."

Francesca raised another glass of the Pinot Noir to her lips, wondering if maybe she should actually stop drinking. She decided that would be her last sip, reminding herself she had to get to work in the morning.

"Francesca does keep a lot to herself," Lillian said, "but she did allow Father John and me to meet Jack."

"Who the hell is Jack?" Sam asked.

"Another attractive man she's about to tell you about," Lillian said somewhat mischievously.

"Good grief! I feel like I'm spilling my guts on 'Oprah.'"

"What better way to open up than among friends," Sam said. "Is he a ballplayer, too?"

"Nope," Francesca said. "Sports writer. Covers the Blackbirds."

"This is getting good," Sam said, diving into dessert. "Finally, Frannie comes clean."

It was Saturday afternoon and she found herself hustling as fast as she could to get there before time was up.

"Bless me Father, for I have sinned," she said out of breath as she huffed and puffed in the chair.

"What is it this week, Francesca."

"I haven't been a good friend."

The guilt had been killing her all week. She felt she had been selfish, that she hadn't let her mother, her sister, her friends, Joe or Jack in enough to understand the real Francesca. She hadn't given as much to them as they had given to her, including Father John.

"How so?" Father John asked. "This is fascinating."

"I just haven't been a good friend to anyone. I've been wrapped up in my own emotions, my own grief at times, and I've been unwilling to open up. I see that now. I'm sorry I haven't been a good friend to you, either, John."

"I think you're being too hard on yourself," he said. "Look around. People love you for who you are, and you are thoughtful and giving. I think what you're feeling is more about your own emotions—that you don't wear your heart on your sleeve. It's not always a bad thing; it can be good."

"Not if I'm closed off."

"True, so that part you can work on. But you're not selfish."

"Are you sure I'm not a little emotionally selfish?"

"Maybe a little," Father John said. "But we all are. Luckily, we have friends and family who can help us through challenging times and good times. So, let's focus on something positive in your life. How's Jack?"

"I don't know," she said. "I'm too closed off to find out."

"So fix it," Father John said.

BASEBALL & NICKNAMES

My sneakers were scuffed, my shorts were covered in splotches of red from the ice pop that had dripped all over them during the fourth inning, and I was a sticky mess. My dad soaked a napkin with his water so I could clean off my hands. I was sitting with my feet propped up on the back of the seat in front of me because no one was sitting there.

"Dad, I've been thinking about something," I said. "Cecelia has a shortened name, you know, 'Cissy', and she likes that."

"She seems to," my dad said.

"Well, you all call me Francesca, and sometimes Mommy calls me Frannie, but I don't really like the name Frannie. It sounds like an old lady name."

"Well, you were named after your grandmother. Sometimes her friends call her Frannie."

"Still, Dad, I don't like it."

My dad was amused by this conversation. He always seemed to love when I got philosophical about things or questioned why things were they way they were. We often had various discussions about life, which resulted in discourses and analogies related to baseball. But I had something on my mind that day, and I didn't intend to let up.

"Well, what suggestions do you have then?" he asked me.

"Can you think of another name to call me? I mean, Francesca's a nice name and all, but when I look in the mirror, I don't see a Francesca. It sounds prissy."

"Who do you see?" he asked.

"Me. I just see me."

"Well, does 'me' have a name?"

"I don't know."

"How about the name Frankie. I've heard girls called Frankie when their real name is Francesca. It's another nickname for it. And you seem to like hot dogs—ballpark Franks—a lot. And Frank Robinson was one of your favorite players. Might make sense."

"Really? Frankie? I like that so much better than Fran, Frannie, and Francesca. How do I change my name to that?"

"Well, let's see. I could call you Frankie from now on," my dad said.

"Really? That's so cool. I don't have to get a permission slip or a form or anything to do that, right?"

Dad chuckled. "Nope. No permission slip needed. Look at you! Just like that, you've got a new name. You're kind of like George Herman 'Babe' Ruth, Pee Wee Reese, and Marilyn Monroe."

"I know the ballplayers, but who is Marilyn Monroe?"

"You mean who was Marilyn Monroe. She was a great actress—very beautiful and funny—and she was married to Joe DiMaggio for a short time. Her real name was Norma Jean Mortenson."

"Well, at least I know who Joe D is, Dad," I said. My dad laughed. Looking back on the conversation, I know now it's because my father realized I knew the nicknames of ballplayers over the name of a world-famous, beautiful icon. I'm sure it made him wonder if we talked about baseball too much.

The sun started to dip in the sky, and I was pleased with myself. I just secured a new name. It had been eating away at me for weeks, and I finally addressed it. At my young age, Francesca sounded like a fancy girl with pigtails who liked to wear ruffles and patent-leather shoes.

"Archie!" someone called from across the aisle. My dad waved to him, and I watched the man get out of his seat and come over to where my dad and I were sitting. It was between innings, so people could move around a bit.

"Lou! So good to see you!" my dad said as he stood to shake Lou's hand.

"Good to see you, too," my dad's friend said. "It's been a while."

"Lou, this is my daughter...Fran...Frankie. Frankie, this is my friend Lou. We used to work together."

"Good to meet you," I said.

"You too, Frankie," Lou said.

To my father, I was Frankie from that day forward.

Thirty

"Women working in the front office in baseball? Sure, why not? We're here.
We're capable of doing this job as well as any man can. All it takes is brains.
I don't think with my boobs."
~ Isabelle Drake, Former Director of Community Relations for the
Blackbirds, in her upcoming magazine article,
"Women in Sports & The Power to Make It"

Every day was a balancing act when you worked in baseball. You had a job to do, and you had to do it the best you could. You had to please people, both internally and externally. As a woman in sports, you paid close attention to the way you treated others: if you were too stern or tough, you'd be labeled a bitch. If you were too soft, people said you needed to toughen up. You could do your job as well—if not better—than some of the men, but not having a set of balls prevented you from being an official a member of the baseball boys club. It's just how it was, which meant she had to do her job and do it well.

Francesca always knew that in order to be successful in her field, she had to stay focused, task-oriented, and approach her work with honesty, commitment, and enthusiasm. She was a taskmaster—she could handle her own responsibilities, and she could motivate others to get their work done, as well. She was always fair, innovative, and creative, designing programs for the club to pursue, whether they took place on the field or off the field.

A balancing act.

You had to attack your job with tenacity. Better to do too much than too little.

She remembered seeing an interview piece on a female editor of a magazine, who addressed what it was like to steer the ship, to be the top woman in the business. "We're here to work. If that makes me a bitch, than so be it," she had said. Those words resonated with Francesca.

She happened to feel the same way.

When people learned of the relationship she had with Joe, the gossip began. She could see people talking about her and acting uncomfortable around her. And while she wanted to address the gossips, instead, she followed the advice her father offered her. "When in doubt, don't let the tongue slip out," he would say jokingly. His advice on how to handle uncomfortable or tricky situations was not to speak unless it was absolutely necessary to voice an opinion or clear up facts at that moment. Of course, those words were spoken to her years before her professional career began, but she always remembered it.

David, who had been her colleague for over six years, and who was one of the best public relations directors in the league, admired her. They worked well together and collaborated on many club initiatives. "Just do your job. Hunker down with the work. Don't pay attention to the gossip and hearsay," he said on days when it would get to her and she would close the door to his office and pull up a chair. He was always a good listener and supported her. There were good people around her, and she pushed through it, keeping her nose to the grindstone and focusing on her tasks. Throwing yourself into your work during difficult times can help you get through it much better.

With her briefcase in her hand, her newspaper tucked under her arm, and her cup of Dunkin' Donuts coffee in the other hand, she walked to the front doors of the office. She was glad she wore her large sunglasses today. The sun was shining brightly; the team was in town for its next homestand and was scheduled to play an afternoon day game. Over the last month, good things had happened, and she felt better about herself and her life. Sam found an apartment about a mile away from Francesca, and Joe's bat was hot again after a cold spell, the result of Joe spending a little time with his family after his father's death, and then coming back to play. He was certainly missed in the lineup, and the team needed his bat to get hot again in order to win some games. Jack was on the road as well, covering the games, and they kept in contact while he was away.

As she routinely did every morning, she waved good morning to Eddie, the mailman who also served as a chauffeur and general help-er, and stepped onto the elevator. Light classical music—she thought it was Beethoven—played quietly in it now, but when game time came along, the station would tune into the play-by-play of Blackbirds radio.

David, who typically got in early, was returning from the kitch-en with his own cup of coffee when he saw her. He called to her.

"Hey, Francesca, I just wanted to let you know that Clarkson's in your office. I let him in. He wanted to see you."

"Oh," Francesca said, as she was caught a little off-guard. "Is he okay?"

"He wants to talk to you. I hope you don't mind. I had Eddie unlock your door for him."

"No problem," she said. "Thanks."

Without noticing it, her heart began to race—it was doing it on its own accord out of concern.

She took a deep breath and opened the door.

"Hi," she said, looking him in the eyes with a smile. "How are you?"

"I'm okay," he said, his voice sounding better than his mannerisms would indicate. "I just wanted to talk to you, and I thought it would be better to talk in person. I haven't been sleeping much this past month, so I'm sorry I'm here so early."

"Never too early to see you."

She didn't know if she should kiss him on the cheek, or stay as she was, standing in front of him with about a three-foot distance between them.

She put her purse and briefcase down, and instead of sitting behind her desk, she sat in one of the two guest chairs in front of her desk, urging him to take the other and sit down. He did. He postured himself the way he always did when he had something important to say: his elbows were firmly planted on his thighs, his hands clasped, leaning slightly forward, his head up meeting her gaze.

"So, I wanted to let you know something, and this time, I thought you should hear it from me instead of learning it from a source in the clubhouse."

"Okay," she said.

"Jessica and I decided we are going to marry," he said. "She was a great support to me and my family, and I've known her for most of my life. My father's death has put a lot of things into perspective for me, and we want to make this work, for her sake, the baby's sake, and my sake. I want to be involved as a parent the best I can—like my dad was." She noticed he did not say he loved her, but maybe he wouldn't use those intimate words with Francesca.

She eased back into her seat allowing his words to penetrate so that she could better dissect them. She wasn't expecting to hear what he came to say, but she wasn't totally shocked, either. Francesca heard her father's words again—*when in doubt, don't let your tongue...*

She waited a moment, looking at him and wondering, flashes

of thought barreling through her brain. Did he love Jessica? Did he feel obligated? Was he doing this out of guilt for the loss of his father? Would the marriage work? Could the two of them make it work?

And then she had another thought.

Who was she to judge?

He was her friend, and he was here telling her this because he wanted her to hear the news from his lips. Because maybe he wasn't selfish. Maybe he had thought this through; he was a smart guy. Maybe he cared for her in his own way and maybe she cared for him in her own way, but Francesca had known the truth long before he had spoken those words. *They could never have been.* It wouldn't have worked for them. His career, her career, travel, a baby with another woman. Francesca saw too many obstacles—all of it was too much.

She grabbed his hands, the same ones she held a little over a month ago in Texas, and then, carefully, thoughtfully, she said the words aloud that were waiting to be spoken on the tip of her tongue.

"I'm so happy for you," she said. "Truly, I am."

The end of romantic love. How does it start and how does it finish? Is love a tangible thing you can see and touch, or an intangible idea, a romantic notion so full of grandiose ideals and expectations, that it is often elusive? And moreover, how is romantic love to be sustained in this world of growing divorce rates and separations, of limited commitment and often an unwillingness to work it out?

Francesca was no psychologist, nor was she an expert on love in any regard, but she believed love was constantly evolving. That it was always in motion, always changing, altering, growing, dwindling, but ultimately, a successful love always allowed two people to come back to each another, despite the peaks and valleys, those changes that happen to each person in a relationship, even if the changes are not happening simultaneously.

She always admired her parents and their love, the way they supported and cared for one another. She put stock in love because her parents put stock in love, and because she saw first-hand what it meant to truly care for someone, even when one of them only had months to live. Her mother was a strong woman, far stronger than Francesca gave her credit for, and she admired her ability to be a rock for her father when he was suffering. When he was dying.

Watching her father's physical form deteriorate, and watching both her mother and father suffer through it, was enough to scare anyone away from falling too deeply for anyone. Francesca was starting to realize that over the years she had protected herself from any kind of serious relationship, steering clear of anything that could involve a long-lasting broken heart.

And yet, here she was, alone in her office, and she and Joe had put a grown-up end to their relationship. The tumultuous fling that brought her back to life, that allowed her to feel again, was done. Despite its end, she was not feeling melancholy about it; in fact, she felt quite the opposite. She was grateful for it. She realized, through her whirlwind romance with him, that she had a pulse. She had intricate, boundless feelings; she had the capacity to love, and the overwhelming desire to trust in it.

For years, she had walled herself up, a prisoner of her own mind, partitioning off her heart, her emotions, and walking through life focused only on work...work...work...and protecting herself from feeling hurt...hurt...hurt.

Shit, she thought. She had a life to live.

And it was about to start.

Now.

Thirty-One

"Of course there's always a certain romanticism to baseball. You can't help but become emotional about it, like you do with anything you love. The stories of yore are a marvelous collection of fact and fiction, where truth melds with fantasy to produce hope and optimism each time a new game begins. It's difficult not to become swept up in each and every spectacular moment."
~ Jack Thompson, writer, from his upcoming book,
"Curves That Make You Swoon:
Great Pitchers of The Game of Baseball."

Damian Gaynor worried about his friend Jack Thompson. Each day, Jack would be in the clubhouse getting quotes, talking to players, jotting down notes in his little reporter's notebook. He spent countless hours on the field pre-game, and then Damian would see him leave the ballpark late at night, after having turned in his story on deadline.

He couldn't help but respect the guy. The way he threw himself into his work was admirable, and sometimes, just watching Jack attack his work with such enthusiasm and professionalism inspired Damian to want to be a better ballplayer. The power of good work habits was contagious.

Additionally, Damian couldn't help but feel a sort of responsibility to Jack. Having taken care of him a little in Chicago, helping him get through the loss of his fiancée, Damian had an affinity for him that he had for no other reporter. On occasion, they dined together, and they even got in a game of golf here and there. Jack was a good guy, and he deserved to be happy.

That's why Damian couldn't keep his mouth shut. He felt a sense of friendship toward him; he wanted to help him in any way he could. He would say something today. Part of him knew he shouldn't nose in, but he felt it was the honorable thing to do, and Damian regarded himself as someone who wanted to help in times of need.

He would feel it out.

Yeah. That's what he would do. He would get a sense whether or not what his gut was telling him was correct.

"Dan—are we ready to head to the field?" Francesca called across the hall and into Dan's office. The crew was setting up to shoot the public service announcement, and she didn't want to be late.

It took her a full year to organize and arrange the new program, directing its every move. She wanted to tap into kids and get them reading, so she instituted the Blackbirds Book Club. If Oprah could do it and make it successful nationally, she hoped she could too on a local level. In conjunction with the city, *The Chronicle*, both the city and county middle schools, and education leaders, the Blackbirds were about to launch a summer reading program for kids by encouraging them to read and earn points that they could cash in at the Blackbirds store and/or receive tickets to a game at Blackbirds Park.

"Coming," Dan shouted back. He was printing the script for the PSA.

Francesca threw herself into the new initiative, and she was very proud of what it could be. Now was the time to make it happen. The spot would air during Blackbirds games on TV, on the radio, and be featured on a billboard in the heart of the city. It was all coming together.

When they reached the field, the Blackbirds video crew was setting up for the shoot. They decided to place a stool on the field for the player to sit and showcase the beautiful outfield as the backdrop. Damian Gaynor showed up right on time wearing his uniform.

"Good morning, Damian. Thanks for doing this for us. We knew you were the perfect person to launch this initiative."

"Happy to do it," Damian said. "You're looking well."

"Thank you," she said. "As are you." She had the script in hand, and was about to talk him through it, when he started a conversation.

"By any chance, are you dating anyone?" Damian asked her, out of the blue. She looked at him, and was puzzled. "Strange question, right?" he asked before she answered.

"A little strange. I don't typically discuss my personal life at work."

"I get that. But I might know someone who may be perfect for you if you're not attached to anyone at the moment."

"Damian Gaynor. Are you a ballplayer and a matchmaker?"

"For you, I'm happy to serve as both, in addition to being a spokesperson for your new program," he said.

"You've got all kinds of charm going on this morning, don't you?"

"Maybe. But I want you to think about getting to know a friend of mine. Do you know the reporter Jack Thompson? He might be your kind of guy," he said.

She smiled and lightly punched Damian in the arm.

"You know, he just might be," she said.

It only took twenty-five minutes to shoot the PSA. Damian read his lines, it was shot from three different angles, and the sun shining on the striking green, outfield grass lit up the scene. As they were breaking down and Damian was chatting with the crew, Francesca looked at her watch. It was only ten forty-five in the morning. A lot already happened that morning, and a novel idea came to her.

She packed her things in the bag, which Dan took from her hands to carry back upstairs. She thanked the video crew, and they told her they should have something pieced together in a few days. The spots were scheduled to start running soon on the Blackbirds network. She could feel herself becoming excited by the prospect of this entire program working out.

"I'll see you later," she called over to Damian. "Thanks for getting out of bed this morning to do this. We'll see you later this afternoon for the game."

Damian walked over and once again thanked her. "Don't forget what I said, you hear?"

She pointed to the temple on her head with her index finger and tapped. "I've got it right here," she said with a wink.

And then he walked over to her and pointed his finger to the left side of her chest. "Let me know when you've got it in here," he said.

As they walked up the ramp to the offices, Francesca turned to Dan. Her eyes were wide and she wore an expression on her face that Dan hadn't ever really seen before.

"I need to leave the office for a while, but I'll be back around three before batting practice. Do you think you could hold down the fort until then?"

"Sure, of course. Anything I need to know?"

She smiled at him. "I've got to run an errand, but I need you to ask David for an address now. Think you can do that for me and call me with it?"

"Have I ever let you down?"

"No," she said, giving him a big hug. "Not ever."

THE BIG HURT

It was a week or two before he died. The days were monotonous, as they felt never-ending and sad. I began to lose track of time and place. Reading to my father became part of our existence together. I would read to him for hours, sometimes from a book, and sometimes from the sports page of the newspaper.

"We could use a DH like Frank Thomas," I said, after reading a piece about his latest hot streak.

"Ah, yes," he said wearily. "The Big Hurt would be an excellent addition to our lineup."

The sound of his tired voice made me feel sad. A deep melancholy came over me, the kind that felt twisted and mangled and knotted inside. I felt weak, but I had to be strong.

"Sometimes I wonder what I will leave to you, Frankie," he said that evening as he awakened to find me in the chair next to him. I was relieving my mother who needed a solid night's sleep in her own bed.

It was so frustrating to watch the deterioration of his body when his mind was still completely intact. Sharp, witty, sweet, and funny, he looked as he always did, but his insides were not cooperating. I prayed that he would climb out of the bed, full of energy, and want to toss the baseball around with me in the yard. His rich, dark hair and his perpetual olive skin—almost flawless—made me wonder if he could bounce back and kick the disease in its ass. But it was not meant to be.

"You have taught me so much, Dad. There are too many things to say now, but I'll always remember them."

"You're a good daughter," he said.

"And you're the best Dad," I said, as I leaned into him, raised his hand, and kissed it.

For a moment we sat in silence.

"Whatever you do in life, do it for love," he said. "Life without love can be empty. I have so much love around me. It's what sustains me."

It's what's killing me, I thought. If I didn't love him so much, this wouldn't hurt, and I wouldn't be in agony, trying to be strong, but wanting to fall apart.

"Even though I won't be with you, Frankie, I'll always be with you," he said. "And someday, it won't hurt so much."

I started to cry real tears. And then, I was sobbing.

He patted my hair, and I looked up and found him crying as well, a single tear streaming down his still youthful face.

At that moment, I was frightened of the future. I wondered what it would be like to face it without him, protecting me, holding my hand, and helping me get through it.

My heart hurt, big and strong, as pain shot through my body—the pain pounding, pulsating incessantly as I choked back tears and wanted to scream at the top of my lungs—Why? Why? Why?

Thirty-Two

"If you don't have passion for the game, if you don't have heart,
then this game isn't for you. Only those
who love it deserve to be here."
~ Zeke Watson, Blackbirds Hall of Famer

Francesca was driving her car with her sunglasses on, windows rolled down, and music playing. She left the ballpark, only telling Dan where she was going. She was driving as fast as she could. In search of moral support, she dialed Sam's number and she picked up right away.

"I've been dead for years," Francesca said.

"That's not necessarily true. You're alive, and I'm talking to you. Hello to you, too."

"No, dummy. Emotionally. Emotionally, I've been dead for years."

"We all know that," Sam said. "That's a given."

"Oh, my God!" Francesca said. "You're no help!"

"But I'm honest. You have been emotionally challenged for years, but guess what? I've seen a change in you. You are coming into your own. You're the comeback kid. Your little fling with Baseball Boy has brought you back to life. You saw its possibilities, and you like it. Is that the pep talk you were looking for?"

"Better."

Francesca stopped at the light and took a peek at the directions.

She needed to make a left hand turn somewhere. Yes, right here. She flicked on her signal.

"Okay," Sam continued. "If I can be serious and frank with you, I think the death of your father had an impact on you that was far greater than anyone could imagine. You loved him, you lost him, and it hurt a lot. I know that was the root of the problem, but Frannie, it's been years. He would want you to be happy. He wouldn't want you mourning him until you grow into old age. He would have wanted you to find happiness."

"I found it professionally," she said.

"Yes," Sam said, "but not personally. It's time you tried to find it on your own now."

"That's what I wanted to hear."

"You're welcome," Sam said.

"Thank you. I'll call you later. I'm about to take a leap of faith."

"Baseball Boy or Newspaper Boy?"

"Jack," she said.

Jack knew the number when he saw it appear on his screen. When Damian Gaynor got involved, you knew something mattered to him. He had saved Jack once from himself, and now, he was calling to gently push him in a new direction. But what Damian failed to realize was that it was already set in motion.

"I like this girl," Damian said at the tail end of his speech over the phone. He was telling Jack all about the "the woman he should pursue" and that he thought they might be "perfect together." Like his father at the pulpit, Damian could be persuasive and animated. And he didn't stop talking for twelve consecutive minutes. Jack didn't have the heart to interrupt him.

He listened to him and his soliloquy as he sat on his balcony, his feet up on the table, as he watched some of the morning boats move in and out of the harbor. He loved the way the sun glistened on the water and the sound of the gulls flying around them.

When Damian was done talking, Jack grabbed his wallet, and within minutes of hanging up with him, he found himself in a florist shop holding a fluffy bunch of white hydrangeas paired with deep red roses, as he handpicked each one. He remembered Francesca and her mother talking about gardening on the night they had dinner together, and Lillian expressing how she couldn't wait for her seven hydrangea bushes to flower.

"Hydrangeas and roses are my absolute favorite flowers," Francesca said, and Jack made a mental note of it.

He hadn't picked out flowers for a woman since Sarah. There was something invigorating about actually wanting to do something like this.

A woman who loved baseball. He marveled at how she could rattle off those stats—and he would place a bet that she knew all the team stats as well. She was intelligent, kind, witty, and he found her absolutely striking; from the photographs he saw of her father, she inherited many of his physical features, including the dark hair and olive skin.

As the woman wrapped up the flowers with tissue paper and a shear ribbon, he could envision taking Francesca to Italy. His mother was Italian, though his father was not, and he always wanted to go and see the country, drink the wine, and taste the food. He had never left the United States, and for that, he felt like a naive, non-worldly person. But his sports writing jobs had been so involved and required so much commitment, that there was little time for travel for pleasure. But there always seemed to be plenty of time to travel for work. He always seemed to be working. He was tired of working all the time.

He paid the woman, and thanked her for making the flowers a work of art. He bolted out the door and back down the street to his condominium. He loved the convenience of living in the city and that he could walk to most locations, and the most important ones at that: the grocery store, the liquor store, the dry cleaners, restaurants and bars, and now, the florist. He had to go home and shower and get ready to go to the ballpark.

It was a game day, after all.

Francesca knocked on the door four times, and there was no answer. She didn't want to call and ruin the surprise, but she thought maybe now she would have to dial his number. Jack didn't tell her that he lived in the hip, vibrant part of the city, the hot spot where folks in their late twenties and early thirties were living; his fourth floor condo overlooked the water, and it was a great view.

With her cell phone in hand, still standing at the door, she decided to knock one last time.

"You looking for someone, Baseball Girl?"

She turned to face him. Only her father—and once her mother—ever called her that.

"Maybe," she said, with a twinkle in her eye. "Does a guy named Dash live here?"

"Only if a beautiful, smart, stat-spewing woman is looking for him."

"Good," she said. "Because I want to take him out to lunch."

From behind his back, he produced the bouquet of hydrangeas and roses.

"You saved me the long, embarrassing walk to your office carrying this assortment of flowers for you. Everyone would think I've gotten all soft and mushy."

"Well," she said, moving closer to him and reaching to accept the flowers, "I think you have."

He brushed the hair away from her face, and leaned in to kiss her.

"Yes," he said. "I think I have."

Thirty-Three

"Why do I work in baseball? Because I love it. Because I love to hear the crack of the bat, to feel the sunshine on my face as I watch a game, to watch my favorite players do their job and do it well. I enjoy combining my love for the sport with my ability to do good things out in the community, create new programs, and make our fans happy. It makes it all worthwhile. Plus, quite frankly, it reminds me of my dad."
~ Francesca Milli, addressing a ninth grade class at
Johnson High School Career Day

There was a strong, consistent warm breeze blowing that October morning, as the sun rose brightly offering yet another glorious day. Francesca popped out of bed and opened her front door to grab that morning's edition of *The Chronicle*. The headline read the following: "Clarkson's Bat Bolsters Team," and then the subhead: "Blackbirds Ready For Game One." By Jack Thompson.

She wanted to get there early today. The team made it to post-season play, something they hadn't done in years, and she wanted to immerse herself in the elation, stroll the park, see the decorative bunting again, and take a moment to relish all of the magic.

The game wasn't scheduled to begin until eight o'clock that night, but the gates would open as early as five to let fans come in and revel in the excitement. Plus, the networks were going to cover it, so she wanted a few moments of peace to breathe it all in for herself. For years she gave everything she had to the ballclub, a place she loved so much, and she couldn't wait for the culmination of her hard work—along with all the hard work of her peers—to be showcased during the playoffs.

She showered and wore her best black dress and her most comfortable heels. She even curled her hair for the occasion. In her stylish shrug, she grabbed her best purse, her briefcase, the gift, and out the door she went humming to herself.

Everyone she cared about—minus her sister who would be watching from home—would be there tonight for both the game itself and the post-game party, regardless of whether the team would win or lose: her mother, who was looking forward to seeing Freddie again after a recent double-date with Jack and Francesca; Sam and her new guy, Jeff, the financial planner; Father John, who would not be wearing his collar, but instead a Blackbirds Jersey that Francesca purchased especially for him reading "Father John" on the back; and, of course, Jack. They were all coming to the game, and they would all attend the party as well. She was permitted to have four guests—her mother, Sam, Jeff, and Father John. Jack and Freddie, as members of the media and team, respectively, received invitations from the club; however, Jack was able to obtain two extra tickets, and was able to invite his parents to both the game and the post-game party. Francesca experienced nervous butterflies knowing she would be meeting his folks for the first time, and Lillian would be reintroduced to them for the first time in thirty years. She had no doubt the night would be one to remember.

In fact, the excitement of the playoffs and her personal life caused her to feel slightly euphoric and unbalanced, as if she were drunk on life, similar to Ebenezer Scrooge's giddy behavior when he receives a second chance at life, running about and shouting with glee on Christmas morning. It was funny how that feeling made you want to jump out of your skin and embrace the world with delight.

It almost seemed unfathomable that she could experience that type of bliss, and she pinched herself, a reminder of the madness of it all. It was quite remarkable how every once in a while, the stars do align, and the way that you see yourself parallels the way others see you. And the ones dearest to Francesca knew and understood that she finally allowed her protective shell to be cracked.

She parked the car in the employee lot along with the other seven early birds who were there at that hour, including David, who was probably already writing the night's press notes. It was quiet, and the ballpark was dressed in red, white and blue bunting, as it gracefully fluttered in the wind. Francesca had to use her key to get in the doors, and Eddie, positioned at his morning post, wished her a pleasant day.

"Mind if I leave my briefcase and purse in the mailroom, Eddie? I don't want to go to my office just yet."

"No problem at all, Missy," he said. He always called her that, and she loved it.

"Oh, and this gift is for Joe and Jessica Clarkson's baby. Can I leave it here, too?"

"Sure, put it right here," Eddie said. "I hope he wasn't disappointed he had a baby girl. I was hoping there'd be another slugger in the family."

"I don't think he's disappointed at all," Francesca said. "In fact, I think he's quite smitten with her."

She went out the back door and onto the promenade where she could see the ballpark. Like a grand dame on her most majestic day, the ballpark shined as it never had before. It was a beacon of hope for the city; it was a chance to feel some Bay City pride and bring home a championship trophy.

She found the seats that were similarly situated as the ones that she sat in at Old Blackbirds Park, and walked down to them. Her father never had the chance to fall in love with this ballpark. She was alone in the seating bowl, but she could hear the grounds crew revving up their mowers, getting ready to manicure the field for the big show.

"Well, we made it, Dad. But you probably already know that. We have a chance to win and to win big," she said aloud to the seat that was her father's. "And I'm happy, Dad. And mom's happy; and Cissy, Cam and the kids are happy. We all turned out okay, despite the fact that we had to say goodbye to you too soon. And you'd like Jack. He reminds me of you. In so many ways, he reminds me of you."

The head groundskeeper appeared, looking up at the sparse, but floating clouds that graced the morning sky, some bright white, some with a hint of grey, and then continued his inspection of the field. He carefully examined areas of the outfield first, moving over toward the infield, making sure it looked good for its appearance on television that night. It was a gorgeous ballpark, reminiscent of those from the glory days, from the era when everyone wore a suit and tie to a game, and little girls held their dads' hands as they ate Cracker Jacks and watched some of the game's most notable icons play on the fields.

Blackbirds Park felt iconic today, and Francesca felt blessed to have been a part of it all for so many years.

She checked the time and realized she'd better get to her desk. There were things she had to do before the game began.

"Wish us luck, Dad. We love you, and we miss you."

Just as she stood to leave, a single drop of rain fell from one, lone solitary cloud and landed on her hand.

EPILOGUE
A GAME OF CATCH

I picked up the scrapbook that sat on the shelf of my nightstand, where it always had been. It was the one that used to be so difficult for me to open, but today, I was ready.

Just the two of us were in the house; my three-year old daughter was running through the sprinkler with her dad in the back yard.

I started to go through it, explaining who he was, how he touched so many other people's lives, how he had so much kindness in his heart.

My son was seven and full of questions.

"Is that him in his baseball uniform?" my son asked.

"Yes, it is," I answered. "He had all different uniforms. See?"

He turned a few pages, looking at the man who posed in home and away uniforms. The photos were black and white, but we could see that one jersey was darker than the other, and the socks in one looked much lighter.

"Wow. That's an old uniform."

"Well, that was a long time ago. That was when your grandfather played in the minor leagues for the Starlings. And look, there's Pop-Pop right there behind him," I said. As I'd become older, it looked even more aged to me now.

"How long did he play in the minor leagues?"

"Only one year. There was an accident and he hurt his hand so badly, he could never play ball again. But Pop-Pop played for a while. And so did Daddy for a short while before he became a writer."

"It makes me sad that Grandpa only played for a little bit," he said.

"Well, it might seem that way, but actually, Grandpa had a very

good life until he died. A lot of people loved him and he loved a lot of people. And he loved baseball, too. Just like you do. The Blackbirds were his favorite team."

"Did you ever get to play catch with him even though his hand didn't work right?"

"Oh, yes. We had many games of catch. All the time."

I flipped to the photo I knew he would like. It was the one on the baseball field from the annual Fourth of July barbecue. I had a big grin on my face.

He studied it.

"Do you know who that is?" I asked, pointing to the little girl standing next to the tall, handsome man with chiseled features, dark skin, broad shoulders, and brown hair. In the photo, he was years younger than I was now.

"That's you!" he said excitedly. "Your hair looks like a boy."

"Sure does," I said. "And I can throw the ball like a boy, too."

"How? You're a girl."

"Grandpa taught me. He and Grandma taught me so many things, but since he's not with us any longer, I put this together so we can remember him through the pictures and stories I wrote about him. You're lucky. Do you know why?"

"Why?" he asked.

"Because you look a lot like him, and you are named after him."

Archie looked at the photos that graced the pages, looking intently at his grandfather, at my father's face.

"I wish I could have known him," Archie said. "He looks like he would have been a nice grandpa."

"He was nice. As nice as you."

"I bet Grandma misses him," he said.

"She sure does. We all do."

"I bet he could hit the ball as good as Uncle Joe did when he played," he said.

"You're probably right about that. Grandpa was good, but not that good, and Uncle Joe's going into the Blackbirds Hall of Fame this weekend, which is why we're celebrating with him later."

He gave me a mushy hug, and I almost knocked the ball cap from his head. I straightened it out, and reached for his glove that had been placed beside him on the floor. That one little gesture of endearment, the resemblance to my father in his eyes, the album, dusty from being locked up—they all caused my eyes to fill with tears. My son looked worried for a moment.

"So, can we go have a game of catch now?" he asked, moving the hair away from my face and grabbing my hand to lighten the mood.

"We can have a game of catch anytime you want," I said.

ACKNOWLEDGEMENTS

Thank you to the following people for reading *Baseball Girl*
before it was in its final form, for offering advice,
and for providing quality, insightful feedback.
Your comments were invaluable to me.

I am grateful and touched by the efforts of the following people:
Jennifer Bumgarner, Chrysti Cantilli, Brooke Fowler,
Colleen Healy, Mariana Huberman, Elizabeth Johnson,
Diana Mark, Amy Nelson, Amy Parker, Chip Rouse,
Charles Steinberg, Anthony Verni, Mark Verni, Julie Wagner.

And especially to my mother, Leni Parrillo,
who read it again and again.

Author's Note

While comparisons may be drawn to my professional experiences working in baseball for thirteen years, this book is a work of fiction. Using the world of baseball as a backdrop, *Baseball Girl* incorporates two love stories within it: a romantic love triangle and a deep love for a father.

Those of us who have an affinity for the game of baseball understand its magic. America's pastime continues to be cherished and revered. Spending time with those you love while watching baseball is a treat; it creates memories and long-lasting friendships, something I can personally attest to having worked professionally in the sport. I wanted to pay homage to the game, but also tell a story rooted in love.

It was my friend, Julie, who encouraged me to write a novel about baseball when I was lamenting about another project I was writing and became stuck in a rut.

"I don't know why you don't write a story about baseball," she mused.

Thankfully, I listened.

Honestly, it was fun to write these characters. I wasn't interested in writing a bad guy or drawing an evil antagonist for Francesca. Both Joe and Jack are good men, and they both care about Frankie. Sometimes in life when we make a choice in love, it's not between good and evil, but rather what we believe may suit us in the long run. Sometimes you have to let go of something—even if you love it (or him or her)—if you believe it's not right for you.

That said, I'd like to thank you for making the choice to read this novel. It means the world to me.

Go Blackbirds!

~ Stephanie/March 2015

Book Club/Discussion Questions

1. Have you ever lost someone very close to you? If so, what emotions did you feel?

2. Why do you think Francesca had such a difficult time moving on from the death of her father? Do you think she ever fully recovered from that loss?

3. What insights into Francesca's and Archie's lives did you get from the flashbacks? Which of Francesca's stories stood out to you most?

4. Why did Francesca's mother dislike baseball? Was it what you expected to learn about her?

5. Why do you think Francesca is so guarded? Why doesn't she believe she can tell Sam all her stories? What is she afraid of?

6. When loved ones pass away, we tend to treasure and keep things that "belonged" to them to help us remember them. What did Francesca keep? What did Lillian (Francesca's mother) keep? What do you keep or treasure that belonged to someone who has passed on?

7. Do you think Joe Clarkson truly loved Francesca? Do you think it could have worked between them?

8. Freddie plays an important role in Francesca's life. What role does he fill?

9. What role does Father John play in Francesca's life? What role does Sam play in her life?

10. How did Francesca change after learning about Sarah's death?

11. Has there ever been something that's kept you from loving someone else? What was it?

12. The attraction between Jack and Francesca takes time to build. What did they ultimately see in each other?

13. What lessons has baseball taught the characters, even the supporting characters like Freddie, Dan, Damian, and Lillian?

14. Which do you think is more difficult when one begins to question a relationship: letting go or hanging on?

CPSIA information can be obtained at www.ICGtesting.com
Printed in the USA
LVOW11s0117080515

437628LV00006B/310/P